# The Bell, Unrung

by Kimberly Evans

Copyright© 2015 by Kimberly Evans

All rights reserved under International and Pan-American Conventions. No part of this book may be used or reproduced in any manner whatsoever without written permission from the publisher except in the case of brief quotations.1

This book is a work of fiction. This edition was produced by amateurs and machines. Any irregularities are likely to be unintentional.

ISBN-13:978-1519141163

ISBN-10:1519141165

## CHAPTER ONE
### The Letter, Undelivered

May 12, 1933

Dear Millie,

Happy Birthday to my Dearest Niece!

I can't believe you are already ten years old. How time flies! Three years is too long to stay away. Be sure to tell your mama to send you back East for a visit. I could come down to the train station in Springfield and pick you up. I don't have much, but I could send her some money for your ticket.

This is the first planting season since your grandfather passed last winter and I fear I made an awful mess of it with the plow. My rows were not as straight as his, instead meandering this way and that, like notes on sheet music for a lively tune. Old Chester misses the way you brushed him and the apples that you gave him as treats. He was patient with me and would have happily marched straight, back and forth. I mucked it up with my clumsy management of the harness and the reins. What a sight I was by the end of that day; hay in my hair, dirt on my face, and a tear in the hem of my dress. You know I gave him two apples for his work that day!

Still, it's always a joy to see the first sprigs of green coming from the rich, if poorly plowed, fields.

Blossom had a female calf this season, so we'll have another milk cow at last. It's a great blessing to have meat from the males, but I can sell the milk all year long for seven cents a gallon. Actually, folks around here don't have much cash since the bank closed, but they will trade for honey or wool and we get on just fine.

Last fall I traded with Mr. Perkins down on Wilbraham Road for a wide-armed rocker made of golden maple. Papa always thought that such fine things were impractical for simple folks like us, but I'll tell you Millie, sitting in that beautiful chair in the evening with my knitting or my mending makes the hours fly by.

It's been a warm spring and everything is going faster than usual. The birds had already got all the strawberries before I got to check them, but I mixed the sour rhubarb with the last of our apples from the root cellar and made a jelly with a nice tart bite. I'll be sure to save you some for when I see you again.

Some new barn cats have taken up residence with Blossom and the goat (that goat is so mean we never did give her a name). In particular, there is one cat family I think you would like. There is a glossy black mama with perfectly symmetrical white socks on each foot. She has one baby who is all black, not a drop of white, with bright yellow eyes. Her other kitten is fluffy and she has a tail striped like a raccoon! The mama is a little skittish, but still the kittens scramble all over each other to greet me, hopeful that I'll offer them some milk or an egg.

So dear niece, life here is much the same as it ever was; I wake with the roosters and sleep when the stars come out. I do my work, try and aid my fellow man, and pray. I pray for you, Millie, and dream of the day when the good Lord delivers you back home.

All my love,
Aunt Eleanor

## CHAPTER TWO
### William, 1918

William was wounded on an ordinary Tuesday, in an ordinary July, in a desolate, ruined place. It was an unmarked spot amidst hundreds of miles of identical trenches. There was nothing extraordinary about it, no songs would be written about the incident, no strategic ground was gained, and no vital intelligence obtained to ensure victory. It was a pointless and inconsequential moment. And yet it changed everything for William.

He could clearly remember the sixty-three days on the front leading up to the day he was wounded. He knew it was sixty-three because he counted, marked each day clearly on the edge of a spent German artillery shell with his bayonet. He had waited all of those days in a trench in the mud. The trenches stretched for miles but William only saw his section. He was in France but he could have been anywhere. Mud was mud.

His unit operated on a rotation system. He moved every two weeks. They started in the middle at the relief line. Here, they held supplies for the front line: ammunition, food, that sort of thing. Periodically they would bring supplies up to the front as needed. Mostly soldiers in the relief line just waited. They occupied themselves with cards or music. And waited. The first week he had arrived there was a lot of activity. The line had taken a direct artillery hit the week before, and the entire unit worked rebuilding a stretch of trench, but beyond that first week there was no big project. It was a holding pattern; tension was built here and nothing else.

In the front lines the stakes were much higher. Some days the shelling and machine gun noise was almost continuous. Life in the trenches, literally deep pits in the mud, was what William imagined when he thought of hell. There was water in the trenches that had collected every time it rained. His feet had been wet every minute of those sixty-three days. There was no way to describe the smell. Rats, rot, shit, blood, sweat, gunpowder, and fear. All this combined with boredom and frequent moments of terror.

Once in a while he had been sent out of the trench for a couple of hours to patrol or reset the barbed wire in no man's land, between their front line and the Germans. Out in the devastated countryside nobody talked, no one. The lack of speech made the scene even more horrific. Words are humanizing. Up top, it was all the silence of sweaty anxiety. Gunfire near and far punctuated the work. The time flew in a way, but other times it dragged. A machine gun blast could sometimes feel like it had happened so fast it was like a strike of lightning, a brief flash, fractions of a second, then utter destruction to clean up after. The blink of an eye, boom.

Sometimes things went in slow motion. Corporal Lazlo stood forty feet away bending down to pick up a section of rotted out wood. He was smiling for some reason. Lazlo was a short guy, a hairy guy, the son of Greek immigrants. He had curly hair, a shave that never looked smooth, bushy eyebrows, and hairy arms. All the men teased him, and wondered what his mother looked like. He showed them a picture of his beautiful wife and everyone pitied her and teased him about how she ended up with such an ape. Maybe that's what he was thinking about when the bullet hit him; his beautiful wife and their little baby back at home.

Corporal Lazlo was standing there, smiling, and in slow motion he was knocked back. The way William saw it that day was in slow motion. An invisible hand pushed the corporal. The motion was as if you had dropped a coffee bean into a tall clear glass of honey. The viscosity of time in that muddy field slowed the bullet, so he could almost see it pressing on the corporal's chest, then piercing his shirt, then piercing his skin, passing purposefully through muscle, then bone, then heart. The corporal drifted down like a feather dropped from someplace very high. Eventually he settled in the soft mud and the blossom of red slowly spread across his chest. His breath left him last, a slow whoosh of life leaving the body like an afterthought.

William didn't remember the day he was wounded. He didn't remember leaving the trench, leaving his unit, or leaving France. He just woke up one day; he didn't know what day it was, in a white room full of strangers. The bed next to him was occupied by a man whose entire head was encased in gauze. He said man, but he couldn't be sure. Where the feet and lower legs would be there was nothing. His legs just ended at the base of his thighs: no knees, no ankles, no feet. The bed next to him was occupied by a semi human stump. His hands were just a shade darker than the white sheets and they clenched and unclenched in no particular rhythm. He made a sound, not really a human sound, no words, nothing distinct. He made a moan, kind of a hum. This sound would be William's constant companion while he remained in this ward; the arrhythmic song of someone who had forgotten the words and the tune forever. Eventually the pitch and the volume of the moan increased until it was a scream, piercing and urgent.

A nurse entered the ward. She walked directly toward the

scream, but she didn't rush. She walked with determination, stopping at a cart near the center of the room and withdrew a syringe and a small bottle. She spoke soothingly as she administered the medication. William could tell the moment it kicked in, all sound stopped and it would be hours before the humming resumed.

"You look alert today," the nurse said to William as she came to his bedside. She smiled as she took his pulse and looked at his chart. "I see they've lowered your pain medication. Welcome back. How are you doing with that?"

She might have been talking about someone else. He hadn't been anyone or felt anything for a while. He didn't know how long. He had been in the trench and now he was in a clean white room with metal beds. He struggled to sit up a little bit higher. The nurse stepped forward to help him. There were twenty beds, all draped in white sheets, each one was occupied with pieces of soldiers. People without legs or arms. Everyone here had something wrapped around their head and William had a sudden, awful feeling. The floor fell apart and the future crumbled. His equilibrium failed. Gravity failed. He knew in that instant that parts of him would be missing too. He fought against the pull of the morphine that had soothed and smoothed his recent days, months, or years and opened his mind to the reality of his body. He was missing an eye and half of his left hand. He had a horrible burning pain in his gut and a hot itchy patch on his left thigh.

"I need some more of that pain medication," he said and waited as she depressed the plunger and sent him back to oblivion.

He spent some time in another ward to heal up the damage the shell had caused as it ripped through his intestines. He had lost a kidney and his torso and leg had been sliced up by flying debris and shrapnel. He saw his hand when the doctor removed the bandages to repack it.

"Could have been worse. You're lucky," the doctor said. William had lost his pinky finger, ring finger, most of his middle finger, and much of his palm. "You still have your thumb and index finger, so you should be able to grip some."

When the doctor said this, the soldier in the next bed wiggled his arm which had no hand at all, his right arm ended in the stump just below the elbow. "Sure," William said without conviction. "I'm lucky."

He lay in the hospital bed and laughed at the man he had become. Part of a man. Damaged almost before he had began. He was nineteen years old.

#

The journey from his home in Colorado could be recalled in sharp crisp memories: the train car filled with eager apprehensive recruits, the scratchy newness of his uniform, and the first glimpse of the bustling harbor in Newark. He had never seen the ocean before and the flat gray plane of the sea was the first thing about his enlistment to scare him. At an instinctive level he knew that this crossing signified the end of his boyhood. The water spread in front of him and he stared out across it for a silent fifteen minutes without moving.

He remembered clearly the men gathered in the mess hall and the ensuing clatter of utensils on metal trays. The men formed a homogeneous entity in olive green, stripped of individuality by their common Uncle. The twenty dollars he lost playing poker with a scrawny kid from Pittsburgh still irked him. On William's eastbound trip spirits were high as they faced the great unknown. They were heroes of the western world ready to save democracy.

On his westward journey, from muddy hell to home, he knew that hero was an overused word, an optimistic fabrication of people who slept in clean, soft beds. He knew that the medal pinned to his chest was dipped in blood, some of it his own. He thought briefly of throwing it in the water but the distance to the aft deck seemed endless. He ended up spending the entirety of the crossing below decks. He sought comfort in the cocoon of his bunk and the unending hum of the engines, but solace never came.

Disembarking in the States could have been a joyous event and for some it was. A redhead in a short black coat squealed with delight and raced up to fling her arms around a soldier William had seen only in passing. Eye contact was a rarity among the returning soldiers. The war was not yet over. This was not a ship of victors. This was a vessel of remnants and remainders, the used bits of a grander strategy.

The little red head launched herself at her boyfriend or husband joyously, raucously, and he caught her by rote. He had forgotten that a woman could be soft and welcoming and warm. Slowly his arms came up, wrapped around her and squeezed like she was his only life raft. No one was waiting for William. He shuffled down the ramp with other men, all of them blinking in the sunlight.

In expectation of their arrival, the dock was decorated with banners and colorful streamers. A band played an upbeat set of songs. Patriotism poured from brass instruments and clanging drums. It all seemed excessive, even painful for men who only saw the world in shades of gray and red. Bandaged, battered, broken, all the smiles of welcome were forced. William didn't even try. He made his way quickly to the transports.

When he returned from the Great War, his hometown of Golden, Colorado threw him a parade. In his mind it was a somber affair, all perceptions were colored by combat--the mud, the noise, the stench. He couldn't imagine that anyone in attendance really wanted to be there, least of all the guest of honor. A handful of veterans from previous wars marched stiffly by. Their uniforms fit poorly as the garments had hung in closets gathering dust while their owners had expanded or shrunk with age. A few ancient warriors were pushed along in creaky, high back wheelchairs. As they passed him they all saluted, but not with muster precision. William received their soft, civilian acknowledgment and responded in kind; the military crispness was gone from him as well. He noticed that all the survivors had the same look of weary apprehension.

The organizers had brought out an antique fire pump pulled by a matched pair of glossy brown horses. It had a loud, unpleasant, brass bell that clanged up and down the street. They had gathered a group of a dozen teen-aged girls carrying the US flag, the state flag of Colorado, the county, and a handful of others he didn't recognize. Given the velocity of the wind today, each flag required two girls to keep it earth bound. Maybe on a calm day the girls sang or cart-wheeled as part of their promenade. Today it took all their effort just to maintain order but the girls still smiled pleasantly and waved the best they could as they passed.

Beyond the flag bearers a team of eight Clydesdales plodded along. Their harness bells jangled in an attempt at gaiety. The mighty horses were followed by a single shiny convertible. A politician, the lieutenant governor perhaps, perched on the back seat and beamed over the crowd. As he approached the Hart family his expression brightened and he waved a bare hand which he immediately returned into his pocket. The temperature had plummeted in the past half hour and the dull, pale sky to the east foretold more snow before too long. They were all glad, though none would admit it, when the new city fire truck signaled the end of the festivities with several brief shrill blasts of the siren.

He had been back home in Colorado for less than a month and already has jaw hurt from the constant clenching and forced smile.

His mother stood to his immediate right, clinging to his arm in loving support, pointing to members of the high school marching band as they passed, as if he had never seen a trombone before. It was a cold day in February and she wore her best fur coat and trim leather gloves. Tears ran down her face, presumably from the wind. His mother carried on valiantly, pretending that her beautiful baby boy hadn't been mangled by battle. She persisted despite William's resistance to comfort.

He was disturbed by her optimism because it was false at its core, like an egg past its prime. On the surface, things were back to normal, fresh and full of well nourished potential, whole, but he imagined she too could smell the sulphur even before the shell was cracked. The most painful part was Margaret Hart's insistence that his time away hadn't changed anything, when in fact that was the only truth he knew. It was the only conversation he could possibly have. He clenched his jaw because otherwise all he could do was scream and shout obscenities and his mother didn't deserve that.

"Look honey," she said gently. "The children made you a card!" The mayor approached them to present the hand-made offering with full governmental pomp. William extracted his right hand from his mother's grasp to receive the official handshake.

"Welcome home, son," Mayor Simpson said. He briefly smiled and made eye contact, then lowered his head. He didn't look away from the colored paper he held in one hand and the ceremonial handshake between them. William's damaged left hand stayed firmly in his pocket. The mayor retreated as quickly as possible.

William's father, Peter J Hart, employed about three quarters of the people in attendance at the parade. The remaining spectators were their wives and children. The Harts owned the lumber mill and logging rights and had recently acquired controlling interest in a mining operation. It never hurt to show respect to the boss's family.

William's father stood as far from him as possible while still maintaining the appearance of the family unit. The Harts stood in a straight line along Main St near city hall; his father at one end, followed by his brother Robert and his family, his brother Tom and his new bride, their mother, and William at the end, his injuries politely hidden from his father's view by distance.

Peter Hart was not overly tall, but seemed more so because of his impeccable posture. He didn't sag or slump even at rest. His suits repelled, as if by edict, any evidence he had ever visited the mines or the mill, though he personally led weekly routine inspections. William had once seen a speck of sawdust on the cuff of his father's pant leg. Only once, briefly, before it was swept away with a huff of disgust. His father seemed impervious even to the wind as they stood along the main street. His hair remained precisely in place as the rest of the spectators were buffeted relentlessly by the elements. His mother's eyes continued to water. To his far right, William's father checked his gold pocket watch. Perhaps the shuffling veterans had slowed the procession by a minute or two. The watch was snapped shut with a click audible even from fifteen feet away. Serious people were punctual.

William's older brothers were a matched pair with just over a year between them. They had inherited their maternal grandfather's height, each of them over six feet and their father's coloring, dark hair and eyes their mother described as 'indigo'. Robert's waistline had expanded as his family did. His wife, Patricia, was an excellent cook.

Tom remained trim and fashionable as his wife preferred the library to the kitchen.

William had been a surprise baby, born twelve years after his brothers. When he came along his mother was frantic for something to cuddle and there was forever a distinction between the boys and the baby. The likeness between the three Hart siblings was often remarked upon, good looking boys. William was the tallest of the trio at an even six feet tall. His time in the army and a final growth spurt had transformed him from a bean pole of a kid to a full-grown man. His slouching posture was a recent habit, but his mother stifled her expected nagging at him to stand straight.

William had planned to join them in the family business of mines and mills when he came home from the army. Given his aptitude with machines, he was to be trained to manage the operations portion of the business as their grandfather had. He had planned to have a grand adventure, see the world, then come home, be successful, marry a nice girl, and live happily ever after. He had also planned to keep both eyes and all of his fingers.

Robert held a little curly haired toddler tight at his side to protect her from the wind. His wife, Patricia, held a swaddled infant against the pregnant bulge of her belly. Their older children were not in attendance. Tom's wife, Gwen, was a pretty blond who never spoke except to answer a direct question. Tom said she was quite funny in private but never offered any examples. Now, of course, she was just one more person who wouldn't make eye contact.

William had caught Robert's three year-old daughter spying at him over her father's shoulder. She had taken one look at him and burst into tears. William felt like his little niece Katie was the most honest person in his family. At least she was truthful about how disgusting he looked. At least she had the guts to cry and screech and turn away. Robert had shushed her and apologized, but he couldn't force himself to look at William's damaged face either.

The wind dispersed the crowd quickly as the parade ended. The grand finale reminded William of something muddy and desperate, the fireworks were worse. The well wishes of the town overwhelmed him. The Harts maintained their position in front of the bank. They lingered, unsure of continuing obligations. His father checked his watch, and then straightened his already perfect jacket.

"We have a 2 o' clock appointment," he said as he kissed his wife on the cheek. Robert kissed his wife as well, while Tom straightened his jacket.

"I'm sure William is tired," Margaret Hart chirped as she patted her son's arm. "It's been a big day."

His father nodded, pocketed his watch, and turned on his heel, Robert and Tom falling into step behind. "We'll see you later at the office, then," he said over his shoulder. William imagined his father's jaw hurt too.

#

The following Monday William sat in an office at his father's mill. The desk was squat and broad; the dark wood was practical rather than elegant. It didn't gleam under layers of wax and polish, it was a desk made for unadorned commerce. The chair had good contours, so that one could comfortably sit as long as was necessary. To the left were three identical filing cabinets, empty except for two dozen unused folders and a pile of blank sales receipts imprinted with the company logo. The wastebasket beneath the desk was square and brand new. A leather blotter was centered on the desktop. A matching cup next to it held four sharpened pencils. The center drawer contained a small tray of paper clips.

The aroma of dusty disuse permeated the office. On the door the name of the previous occupant, a man he had never met, had been scraped off but not yet replaced with his own. In the office to his left, his brother Tom tallied columns of debits and credits, while down the hall a secretary tapped a steady staccato on her typewriter. From across the hall, his brother Robert had left in a flurry early this morning, loaded down with sample cases and his heavy over coat.

"It will take you a while to get up to speed," Tom said, distracted, polite. He dropped a thick pile of technical manuals on the desk. "Just take your time," Tom said to William, his wounded, damaged, superfluous brother. "Don't worry about anything." Tom laid his hand on William's shoulder. He squeezed, and then left, shutting the glass topped door behind him.

Below, the factory floor buzzed with the noise and activity of the whirring massive saw blades. Raw, rough logs thudded into one end of the production line. Debarked, edged, trimmed, sliced, and planed the lumber emerged in smooth uniformity. Men shouted indistinctly -- warnings, direction, humor. Upstairs in his clean office, with its big desk, chair, cabinets, he tried to read but the words were indecipherable. His orphaned eye refused to cooperate and his head pounded. William tried to follow his brothers' directions and not worry. It made for a long day.

The scent of sweet sawdust mixed in his drowsy mind with the smell of mud. It wasn't a hallucination per se, he was fully aware of reality around him. The clock on the wall ticked steadily to remind him of his failure at assignment or contribution. His desk continued to hold no actual work for him to do. When he sat still too long he couldn't help but remember what he'd seen and done.

#

His forty-fifth night on the front had been a dark one. It was the new moon and even the distant stars were reluctant to shed any light. The thick blanket of clouds helped gather the sound down low and he could hear any peep of noise at various distances as if it were right next to him. He was assigned to act as a sentry while the others in his unit did some repairs closer to the German line. He could hear his unit to his left, prying apart a barricade and replacing the rotten wooden slats with fresh. To his right, he suddenly heard the soft squish of boots in mud. His heart pounded and he strained to see any shape in the unrelenting darkness. Another squish caught his attention, this time closer, maybe ten feet away, walking toward the repair team. William stood, stock-still, in the inky night. One more squish and the German soldier, a man about his age, emerged from the darkness. Even though William had been expecting him, the moment of the German's actual arrival came as a shock. William almost spoke, almost cried out, almost apologized for what he was about to do, but he kept cool. He thrust his bayonet into the invader's throat. The other young man couldn't make a sound as he fell; he just bubbled a bit as his body hit the ground at William's feet and sank into the mud.

William stared at the man, the boy, for a long time until his breathing slowed. He wiped his bayonet on the soldier's shirt and returned to his post. It was still dark, still quiet but William felt the night had grown much, much colder.

#

Somewhere far away the whistle blew signifying the change of shifts. William sat in the same place he had been all day. No name was on the door. No one had come to call. The technical manuals on his desk were unread. He filed the empty folder in the cabinet; all the forms were still blank.

Tom poked his head in. "Why don't you go ahead and head home," his brother said. "Don't want to push too hard your first day back." His hand was once again on William's shoulder with an affectionate squeeze but no eye contact.

As William was leaving, the sawmill roared back to life with the next shift--men, machines, progress, profit. He understood the concepts, but not his place within them. He worried idly that perhaps he had no place at all.

Over dinner at his mother's table, his father laid out the master plan for William's future. William couldn't hear it. Or rather he heard it, the tone was familiar and he understood the basic vocabulary, but it made no sense. He caught every third word, but couldn't follow the meaning: configuration, disbursement, dilution. His father's voice became a buzz; his mother's voice was the cawing of a territorial blue jay. The words in William's head came through as "mud," "barbed wire," and "boots." Under the table his knee, his left knee, began to shake, to tremble beyond his ability to control. He was surprised that no one pointed it out and asked him to explain himself. To William the motion was all-encompassing, unavoidable, inevitable. No one seemed to notice.

The plates and silverware clattered as he rose abruptly. "I need to stretch my legs."

The snow that had threatened that morning had blown in softly, covering the landscape with muffling, silvery snow. The moon rose low in the sky, not yet full, but somehow watery and swollen. He had thought to walk and let the cool of the night air soothe the heat building in his lungs. His throat was tight as if fighting tears, but he knew he had nothing to cry about. He was, as everyone pointed out, lucky.

Three hours passed before he thought to head back. The moon off the snow made everything blue and shadowy. The silence wasn't complete. Automobiles strained up the long hill toward the mill and the drone of machinery came from somewhere in the valley. Trees-- lodge pole pine, Engelmann spruce, Douglas fir--broke the wind and made the air seem warmer, though when he entered the house a habitual glance in the hall mirror showed his nose and cheeks to be pink and chapped. He continued quickly along, his face was still monstrous.

"William?" His mother called, her voice pitched high with concern from the front room. "I was getting worried."

"Sorry," he grumbled. He was suddenly, desperately fatigued.

"You didn't even bring your gloves!" She said as she hurried over and clasped his hands, both hands, between hers to warm them.

He glanced down at his left hand, half a hand. He had lost some feeling in it, but as the heat from the house sank in it tingled, almost painful. It was furiously red and looked almost alien, like the claw of a crawdad. He pictured a glove made for five fingers on a hand with only two. Would he stitch up the empty sockets or let them dangle vacant?

"I'm sorry to have worried you, mom. It's a pretty night and time got away from me." He kissed her on the cheek and went upstairs to his room.

He doubted he would sleep, but dutifully lay on his narrow boyhood bed watching shadows on the wall and hoping he wouldn't dream.

#

A portrait of William stood in the den. In it he was a young boy, maybe three or four. Still in short trousers. The boy stood in the center and stared out with cherubic intensity at the viewer. In the distance stood their father with a shotgun, the two older boys, and a Springer spaniel poised to give chase. At William's side was an identical spaniel with a limp duck in its mouth. The painter was second rate and the proportions all were a little off and the figures all seemed too angular. William's face was too close to the viewer and had an expression that would have appeared threatening if the subject hadn't been portrayed as such an angelic, feminine figure. The eyes were glossy, the cheeks were pink and plump in a nod to Botticelli.

Needless to say, William was teased mercilessly by both his brothers and any of his friends who happened into the den. William tried to avoid that realm, but rumors had spread about the portrait and visitors tried to sneak in to get a glimpse of it themselves.

The family had never owned dogs like were in the portrait. They had once had a Labrador retriever who died when he was ten and was never replaced. To his knowledge his father had never hunted for gentlemanly pleasure. They all knew how to handle firearms, simply because they lived in Colorado and predators and nuisance vermin were always a possibility. The painting was entirely a fabrication showing just enough resemblance to the Hart boys to subject them to ridicule. His mother loved it and sat in the den in the afternoons as she did her reading and correspondence. When he needed to address his parents about some trouble he had gotten into at school, the conversation always took place under that terrible portrait.

William stood at his mother's writing desk and drew out a single sheet of her cream colored stationary. The ink was blue, the pen nib scratched along the smooth surface of the paper. "Dear Father," he began, followed by platitudes that made him sick. "Dear Mother," he wrote but no more. The date at the top of the page caught a teardrop, solitary. He wiped it quickly away with the pad of his thumb. It still smudged, but minimally.

He didn't have the words to describe the painful restlessness that grew in his belly spreading out to his legs, his arms, and on to the missing parts of him. It pounded in his head all the time. He couldn't read, couldn't think, couldn't get control of it. The simplest tasks were beyond him. All he could do was walk, and lift, and carry. What words could he write to his parents to apologize for disappointing them? He would not be taking his place in his father's business. He would not be providing his mother with grandchildren.

What he wrote was, "Good-bye," and little else. He packed a few things and left for the train station. He would catch the first train heading east, but beyond that he had no specific plan.

## CHAPTER THREE
## Millie in the City, 1933

"Millie Cage!" Mrs. Crenshaw had a voice that seemed too big for her small frame. It made Millie jump, sending her chalk clattering to the wooden floor in the crowded classroom. "Are you reading again?"

Millie had her math book standing up along the front edge of her desk, creating what she hoped was a barricade to protect the book of Sherlock Holmes stories she had on the desk surface. Apparently the plan had not worked as well as she had hoped. "Yes ma'am," she said in a quiet, but unwavering, voice. "But I already finished my work." She held up her tablet to demonstrate rows of long division neatly executed.

Mrs. Crenshaw nodded curtly. "You can help your neighbor, then."

Millie's neighbor was Mary Sue Simmons, a girl so quiet her voice was like the wind across the lake, a haunting echo on a still day. Mary Sue looked after her younger brothers and took in washing from the families on her street, so she was always half-asleep at school. She had been falling behind in her studies and Millie guessed that she would soon drop out entirely, even though they were only in the fourth grade. Many others had gone, even in the few months that Millie had been at this school. Millie put her book away and she focused her attention on helping Mary Sue with her quotients.

Mary Sue shifted nervously in her seat. Millie knew she was uncomfortable being the center of attention. The shy girl tugged at a tear in her shirt, trying to cover the gap by pulling the edges closer together. Millie's clothes were newer, pale blue shirts and dark blue skirts. The nuns at the orphanage made sure that all the children were neatly dressed and well fed. Mary Sue lived with her mother and four siblings. Her oldest brother and her father had left to look for work.

Millie laid the math book down flat open to the appropriate page. "Let's see how far you got," she said. Mary Sue yawned and pointed to a problem at the bottom of the page. The girls were working quietly when Mrs. Crenshaw made her way back around the room.

Where Oklahoma was flat and dusty and lonely, Chicago was tall and dirty and crowded. Neither place had a drop of green or a blade of grass to spare. Near the school there was a strip of land, of scraggly, threadbare turf just wider than she was tall. Sometimes Millie pretended that the buildings were pushed apart by this grass, that the living plants were strong enough to move concrete. The space was only bright right around noon when the sun shone down straight from high above. The rest of the time her patch of grass was in deep shadows and always cool. When she first came to the Chicago it was the tail end of winter and it never got sunny enough to melt anything. The dirty, wet ice shrank only by spoonfuls each day until at last it was finally dissolved.

Outside in the school yard, Millie sat on a wooden bench inside the schoolyard fence while the other girls played hopscotch or jumped rope. At other schools she had attended the girls drew their hopscotch squares with a stick in the dirt, but here in Chicago the whole yard was paved like a sidewalk and they drew the pattern with chalk smuggled out from the classroom. She preferred to play barefoot, with her toes in the cool dust. Here the asphalt hurt her feet and hopping with shoes on wasn't as much fun. Some days she played with the other kids, but today all the activity across the street drew her attention.

Mary Sue came over and plopped down next to Millie, passing her a metal cup half-filled with water. "I'm sorry my father didn't wait for these jobs," Mary Sue said dejectedly. "They're finally hiring at the machine shop."

Across the street a line of men, three deep, filled the sidewalk all the way down the block and around the corner. Uniformed police officers stood in the street to control the crowd and to keep them from blocking traffic if they were to expand or to become unruly. It didn't seem to be necessary.

A kicked ball escaped the confines of the schoolyard and rolled into the shin of a somber man on the other side of Wright Avenue. He picked it up like it was precious, like he had just remembered what a ball was for, and carried it over to the children. He lobbed it cautiously over the tall metal fence without a word, then retreated to his place in the line. His hair was neatly combed and his gray jacket fit him loosely, like he had borrowed it from someone else. "Thank you," Sammy Mitchell called as he went back to his game. The greeting was unacknowledged.

Some conversations murmured quietly, but for the most part the men stood straight and silent, eyes facing forward, waiting for someone to open the doors so the line could progress. Half of them had been here since Millie came to school at 8:30 and the crowd had continued to grow throughout the day.

Sister Mary Frances told her that a thousand men had come to apply for four positions at a plant across town.

"I'm sure your dad would've been hired if he was here. He's a hard worker," Millie said to Mary Sue. She didn't think it was bad to lie to the sad little girl if it gave her hope that her father would come back soon.

Millie didn't wish for a reunion with her own father.

#

Millie's mother died in Seminole, Oklahoma the week before Valentine's Day. Millie made a picture at school to help cheer her mother up. She used the biggest piece of paper she could find and carefully cut the edges into a lacey fringe. Inside the cut border she drew and colored every kind of flower she knew. She couldn't remember the names of every single one of the blossoms that her Aunt Eleanor had shown her in the garden, but she knew that each one had a name, a story and some even had a song: sweet peas, morning glory, lily of the valley.

*Bright coral bells upon a slender stalk*
*I see them every morning on my garden walk.*
*Oh, don't you wish that we could hear them ring?*
*That will only happen when the fairies sing!*

Millie sang as she colored and snipped. Millie guessed that her mother would remember this too since she and Eleanor were sisters and they had grown up together. Her mother needed to remember pretty things.

The week before she died, Millie's mother, Caroline, looked as dry and dusty as the Oklahoma landscape around them. The land here was flat and brown. The buildings near their apartment house sprang up from fields of nothing like a mistake, like someone couldn't think of anything better to do here so they built a city. The buildings were tall and angular; they huddled close together for a few blocks then the town quickly fell away to a sprawling vacancy. It was the bleakest place they had ever lived. Millie thought that if she could get her mother to think of these flowers, and her family, and their farm, Caroline would feel better and they could just move along.

Millie didn't think that sadness could kill a person but her father said it happened all the time. He said that some people just weren't tough enough or smart enough to get around the hard times. He looked at her mother when he said this, but her mother didn't pay any attention. She just stared out the window at nothing.

"Papa, don't you think we should take her home? I think she would feel better if she was back at the farm."

"You mean Hemford?" he asked as if it were absurd to even suggest it. His laugh was big and hearty and he tousled Millie's hair like he cared about her. Her mother didn't care about anything at all. "We've got bigger plans ahead of us. How'd you like to see a real city?"

Every little girl thought her mother was the most beautiful woman in the world, but in Millie's case it was actually true. Everybody said it. Millie had seen men make fools of themselves, fumbling or stammering when her mother, Caroline Abbot Cage, smiled in their direction. Millie's mother looked just like Helen of Troy, a person so beautiful people fought a war over her.

Caroline Abbott Cage had hair as golden as the noonday sun. It fell in soft waves around her face. Her skin was smooth like a china doll with pink cheeks and ruby lips. Millie's mother always smelled faintly of lilacs, even in the winter when no flowers bloomed. Anyone who was lucky enough to get a kiss on the cheek would know that her breath was as sweet as fresh new mown grass in an alpine meadow. Her teeth were small, white, and symmetrical. When Caroline moved she glided across the room as if she danced to some music no one else could hear. Her shoes tapped daintily on the floor when she wanted, but if she preferred to be ignored, an uncommon occurrence, her feet didn't seem to touch the ground at all.

Millie's mother knew the power she had over people. "Don't squander your beauty," she said as she straightened Millie's hair or clothes. "God gave little boys lots of advantages, but only one to little girls."

Millie didn't think it was completely true. She was smart and kind. Millie was a good reader, good at math and art. She knew how to follow directions and when it was okay to break the rules a little.

Millie got the impression that Caroline treated her beauty like an obligation, something she owed to Millie's father or to the world in general as the price to breathe air or eat food or have nice clothes. Millie's mother acted like it was a burden to be pretty and charming, like she hated it and yet it was taught to Millie, her daughter, without question.

Millie thought it was probably Caroline's worries about that beauty, the weight of expectation that made her need those little bottles of medicine she drank every night. Millie's mother didn't have a cough or sick stomach, but she said her bones ached and her eyes hurt from seeing so much brown, the hills, the fields, the sky. Millie looked at the little bottle on the bedside table while her mother slept and her father was out. "Laudanum" she read and tried to sound it out, but the word made no sense. It was something she had never heard before. Big words like "chrysanthemum" or "Philadelphia" were things or places she understood. On the bottle it also warned that it was "poison" but her mother drank it anyway.

"It's medicine, honey" her mother said. "Bring it over here."

Caroline's voice was still sweet as ever, the tone still cheerful and bright even as it got softer and slower. Over time the phrase "Bring me my medicine," was like an elegant whisper, a puff of a breeze just strong enough to blow the white fluffy seeds off a dandelion.

When Millie asked her father about it he got quietly angry, like she had called him an ugly name. Then he smiled, cheerful and shiny again like a polished bell, pretty but too loud. She didn't ask again.

"Some people fall short," her father said. "Not us. Right?"

That night his wife died, Millie's mother, Richard Cage kissed Millie good bye, sweet as always, on the tip of her nose. He smelled of spicy cologne and his cheeks were smooth from a recent shave. She wiped a dab of shaving foam from his cheek. "Miss Kellerman is right down the hall if you need anything," her father said as he closed the door behind him.

He often asked their neighbor, Miss Kellerman, to look in on her, which meant that Millie had plenty of time to read. Miss Kellerman entertained regularly, mostly nervous men who didn't say hello when they passed Millie in the hallway.

Miss Kellerman was good at a lot of things; she braided Millie's hair with a ribbon sometimes and painted her nails with shiny, smelly red polish. She let Millie walk around in her high heels, something Millie's mother never let her do. Miss Kellerman had a big wooden radio that she played all the time. Millie liked to go over there in the afternoon to read her book. Miss Kellerman's radio and the sound of her jewelry jingling in the tray as she chose which pieces to put on soothed Millie. They didn't talk much, but it was nice to be somewhere with someone else's activities. Millie's own apartment was always too quiet.

Millie didn't actually see her mother die. Her father had said goodbye around 5:30, after a dinner of franks and beans that Millie heated up in a dented pot. Caroline came to the table but she didn't speak and she spared two smiles, one for Millie and one for Millie's father. Maybe these were the only two smiles she had left.

Millie took this as an encouraging sign, but as soon as her father left Caroline went back into the bedroom and shut the light. Millie sat on the floor out in the hallway near Miss Kellerman's door so she could hear the radio while she read.

After a little while the door opened and a nervous gentleman left in a hurry, his coat flapping behind him as he rushed down the stairs. Miss Kellerman emerged next, looking tired and in need of a hairbrush. She said, "You need to get to bed, Millie, it's late."

Back in Millie's own apartment it was extra quiet. The lights were still on, just as they had been when she left. The dinner dishes were still on the table, right where they were when her mother smiled at them, as if they were waiting for the continuation of a lively conversation that never happened. Millie gathered up the dishes and washed them. She wished they had a radio like Miss Kellerman. The sound of everything was too loud; the tinkle of silverware, the drip of the faucet that never stopped.

Millie opened the door to her mother's room as quiet as she could, but it still gave a squeak loud enough to fill the whole apartment. Her mother's room was dark and the blinds were closed. The light from the living room intruded behind Millie, shining on her mother's soft face. Millie got closer and leaned down to give a kiss goodnight. A dribble of drool ran down her mother's cheek. Up close Millie could see the difference between someone alive and someone dead; it was as if every drop of color had left Caroline's skin. Millie knew that if she touched her mother, lifted one of her beautiful hands to hold it, it would be limp, like it had no bones.

Millie didn't have much firsthand experience with death. Her Aunt Eleanor did, and she had told Millie about how her mother, Millie's grandmother, had died a long time ago and her little brother, Millie's Uncle Johnny had passed when he was a boy. Eleanor said the whole town came over and said prayers and read from scripture. Millie didn't have a bible but she thought her mother would like stories about Robin Hood just fine. Millie's father had always told her panic never helped anything so she stayed calm. She read out loud and she prayed until she couldn't. Millie fell asleep in a chair next to her mother's bed.

Millie didn't think that Miss Kellerman was the best person to tell about her mother's death, She was a grown up, but she had delicate sensibilities. Last month when they found Mittens, the cat from downstairs, dead outside the front door, Miss Kellerman screamed loudly and jumped back, then cried and carried on. Mittens had been in a terrible fight or something and had a jagged, bloody gash on his belly. The blood had matted, and there was dirt and grit all over him, but Millie still felt like Miss Kellerman had overreacted. Millie didn't know what she would do about a dead person. Her dead mother.

Mr. Armstrong, the landlord, was gruff and loud and Millie felt small as a baby rabbit when she talked to him. He smelled sour, like old laundry, and even though he gave her candy sometimes, she didn't like it when he came around. Her father didn't like him either and would always lead them the other way if he and Millie saw Mr. Armstrong outside the building doing something. She knew her father would be upset if she asked the landlord to come in and help her. She decided to just wait until her father got back and let him figure out the best thing to do.

That quiet night in her mother's room, Millie took out the postcard with a picture just like her grandfather's farm on it. She thought that the farm was the most special and beautiful place on earth. And the postcard was special because it reminded her of that and when she used to live there sometimes. The white house in the picture wasn't as big as the real place and the wall out front was higher in real life. The image showed their house, and their cows, the gardens and the apple trees. She hadn't been there for a long time, since she was little, but she imagined it was exactly the same. She couldn't wait to go back. On the reverse it said, "Dear Millie; you always have a place here. Love Eleanor." The writing was faded from handling. This card was her most prized possession and she carried it everywhere with her, in a pocket usually. One time she even carried it folded up in her shoe. The night her mother died she slept with it tucked under her pajama top to protect her against nightmares. It didn't work. That night she was plagued by dreams of her mother fading bit by bit like smoke. She woke with the scent of sulfur in her nose and her father's aftershave.

"Wake up, Millie," he shook her shoulders. His voice was calm, but with a growing twitch of panic in his movements. "We have to go."

There was never any time to be sleepy in her father's world. She was always expected to be wide awake and ready for action. All she wanted to do was lie down with the blanket over her head. Millie scrambled up and tried to hug him, tried to share her sadness about her mother's pale body in the bed. He was already off toward Millie's room, already moving to her closet, pulling out her suitcase and stuffing it with her clothes. "I'm heartbroken about Mama," Millie said. Her cheeks were wet from tears as she trailed behind her father. She saw that his suitcase was already packed and by the door. "What are we going to do?" Millie asked as she entered the room.

Her father was already dressed in a neatly pressed suit and shiny shoes. Millie was still in her pajamas. He knelt in front of her and grabbed her arms so hard it hurt a little. "You mother is with the angels now. They'll take care of her. But right now I need to take care of us, so hurry up and get dressed and we'll be on the next train out of here. All right?"

He said this last part like it was a question, but it really wasn't. Richard Cage would be on that train with or without her.

Millie knew that her father didn't always do the right thing. Sometimes he lied, sometimes he left a place without paying his bill, sometimes he cheated. Millie thought her father should have known better, but maybe he just didn't. Maybe he didn't know that when a family member died, you were supposed to tell somebody, supposed to mourn them and pay your respects, and it was all right to cry. That's what Eleanor had told her.

"Papa, we can't just leave her here." She reached over to him, to pat his hand, or try to hug him again. He went into the living room without noticing her attempt at comfort. She heard him take down the can where her mother kept the grocery money.

"Millie, just get dressed," he called from the living room closet. Hangers clanged and squeaked as he moved them along, removing suit jackets as he went. When Millie entered she saw that he had left her mother's clothes behind.

"Papa, we have to tell." She followed her father's trail and ran her hand across her mother's pretty dresses. She could still smell the lingering perfume.

"What you have to do is get dressed, Millie!" Her father stopped smiling. He could no longer even pretend to be calm and confident. He raced frantically around the apartment picking up their few personal things from throughout the furnished rental and shoved them into his satchel. He gathered up the tiny bottles from around the bed-stand, dumped them in a pillow case, and he threw it out the window to the alley below. She heard the tinkle of glass as it hit the ground.

Millie returned to her room to put her clothes on. She selected a dress her mother purchased before she got sick. She patted the postcard in her pocket for guidance and courage. Her father paced anxiously near the front door.

Millie said another prayer over her mother, a short sentence she hardly got to finish before her father came behind her and herded her out of the silent apartment. As he turned to lock the door forever, Millie slipped past him down the hall.

"I just have to say good-bye to Miss Kellerman" she said over her shoulder.

She wondered how different things would be if she were bigger, a grown up.

She and her father were on the 2:30 train. Millie didn't remember much about the train ride to Chicago. She slept some through it, read a little; mostly she just looked out at the landscape as it flew past. The view from the train was always the same anywhere they went. Out the window they would see the backs of things, empty places with no reason to stop. Maybe this is what her mother had watched out the window all those days; just another place they didn't need to be.

Her father did the same thing he always did, getting ready, practicing his name, and hers, over and over in a low drone whisper until it came out just right and sounded natural. Her father was a person who had to practice sounding honest.

The train that morning didn't soothe her like it normally did, the gentle sway of a maternal rocking. This time she felt every bolt in the rails, every wooden tie, every time they slowed but no relief from the journey came. When she slept, Millie expected her dreams would have frightened even a much bigger person. Her mother was dead and nobody seemed to care.

When they arrived in Chicago, Millie was ready to see something. From miles of brown fields and dirty gray snow the city sprang up like a surprise, a great unexpected temple of smoke stacks and tall, straight buildings. Millie imagined it was like seeing Oz for the first time, although the bumpy train ride was hardly the yellow brick road and she had made no friends along the way.

Her father loved the big city. He became more animated as the miles progressed--muttering, memorizing all the way, rearranging and organizing the contents of his wallet, straightening himself up.

When they disembarked, Millie barely got a glimpse of the grand train station, just a brief view of the busy city streets. It was overwhelming and noisy and had a bad smell. It was February and here the streets were covered with dirty slush. Millie felt in her pocket for her postcard. In the picture it was always summer, the trees always bore fruit, the cows always had plenty of grass to eat.

She felt increasingly sick to her stomach as her father, Richard Cage, grifter, flim-flam man, con artist, pulled her along behind him as they crossed the city. He had a destination in mind but he didn't tell her. In fact he walked so quickly, just far enough ahead, just fast enough that she couldn't catch her breath to speak and he wasn't near enough to hear anything if she did. He carried Millie's suitcase under his arm, but had left his own in a locker at the train station.

The Order of St. Anselm's Home for Girls was housed in an

imposing brick structure, with evenly spaced windows and a big front door right in the middle. It had a little grass all round it, even in a closely packed neighborhood, like its neighbors were scared of it and gave the building some space out of respect. Inside the people were friendly but drab, plump nuns in matching black uniforms, full skirts and hair covered by stiff black cloth.

Sister Mary Theresa came over and held Millie's hand while her father filled out some paper work. Sister Mary Theresa seemed nice, her hands were soft and she smelled of peppermint and a little bit like moth balls. The other sisters stood on the opposite side of the room in a cluster.

Her father turned to them, crying tears that were only partially real and said, "Take good care of my angel."

The sisters fluttered and nodded assent and showed sympathy, compassion for her father's plight. They said they were sorry about her mother even though they never met Caroline or June or whatever other names her mother used. Richard leaned down in front of her, hugged her close and whispered in her ear, "I'll be back in a month, kiddo." He winked but nobody saw it; Millie's eyes were already closed.

Millie didn't speak much for a week. She wondered what she could say about her mother. Would anyone believe her if she did say something? Would they be able to picture how beautiful Caroline was? And how that beauty had faded away to nothing over time? Would they believe her father had left his family behind like a thumbtack he pulled off his shoe?

#

Mrs. Crenshaw came out and rang the big brass bell to call the children back inside for afternoon classes. Sometimes she let one of the students do it, but today she did it herself, swinging it back and forth in front of her so the big clapper struck the inside with enough force to make the metal sing. The other children were now lined up along the inside of the fence, watching as the mounted police came up the middle of the street near the school. The men in the job line all turned in unison toward the sound of hoof beats. There were four horses, each with a tall straight-backed rider in full dress uniform.

The mounted officer nearest the school pulled a bullhorn from his belt and made an announcement.

"The positions have been filled." His voice boomed, perhaps it would have even without amplification. He had big red fingers like sausages and a thick brown mustache. He had a doughy face, with fat jowls and bushy sideburns. From his position on the horse he looked like a giant compared to the children peeping through the fence on one side of the street and the ordinary men on the other. "Please disperse. No work here today."

The men in the line, who had been patiently silent all day, released a collective breath. It was the sound a tire might make on its way to being flat. Not a POP all at once, this was the sound of a slow leak, the sound of a thousand pinpricks. It was the sound of surrender.

#

Millie lived at the orphanage with the nuns and seventy-five other girls, but she went to public school a few streets away. You could instantly distinguish the orphanage girls; they all wore identical outfits of light blue shirts, navy blue skirts and navy jackets when the weather was cool. They had it better than a lot of their classmates, many of whom were dressed practically in rags, clothes too big or too small, passed along by brothers and sisters. In the higher grades there were fewer children in each class as they had to leave and work to help with the family. Some children, all ages, didn't go to school at all, Millie saw them as she and the other girls walked to school. They always looked hungry and sad.

The walk between school and the orphanage usually took about ten minutes to make. When spring arrived it was a nice stroll. The girls took their time at it, stretching out the journey to twenty-five minutes or half an hour of relative freedom. When they got back there would be chores, then homework, dinner, and prayers before bed. Now that it was staying light until later, the walls of the orphanage seemed to close in. They squandered the time outside joyously by taking different routes and exploring a bit more of the city each day.

One street had fancy hotels all in a row. Each one had a smiling doorman out front in different color of gleaming livery, long bright coats with shiny buttons, each head topped with a sharp brimmed hat. On the corner the doorman of the Imperial Hotel always tipped his hat until they had all passed.

The street where the hotels were had gardens with bright flowers along the walks and there was no garbage on the sidewalks. All the benches were freshly painted and the fountains burbled with optimism. As they passed by, music spilled out every time the doors opened and once in a while they would catch a glimpse of a tuxedoed musician carrying an oddly shaped case for a trombone or a tuba. One time they had even seen two men in work clothes pushing a full sized harp. These people always went down an alley toward the entrance at the back, near the kitchens. Men in stark white aprons and jackets lounged near the door of the kitchen as they wiped their brows from the heat and smoked cigarettes or played cards on their breaks.

One Friday Millie saw a long shiny car pull up under the hotel awnings. The doorman ran up to the car and opened the back door for a lady in a long fur coat and a velvet cloche hat. The doorman trotted up ahead of her and opened the hotel door and she walked through without hesitation and without speaking to him. Two bellman came out and with her driver loaded six, seven, eight pieces of matching luggage onto a rolling brass cart. The two bellmen struggled to get this cart moving toward the door. The strain of the weight of her bags showed on their faces.

The street was quiet during the day but Millie liked to think about how it must be during the evening. Sometimes she heard the musicians practicing and people humming the tunes in the street. She could practically see the women in their twirly skirts being lifted high in the air. She envisioned a riot of colors swirling and hopping until they were exhausted. They would stumble out of the club as it closed and into their shiny cars. She could almost hear them laughing.

A few streets over, the mood was less gay but still lively. This was the main business district at one time, but now many of the businesses had to close. On the street many enterprising people tried to capitalize on the traffic around the remaining commerce. Men sold apples, shined shoes, and hawked newspapers on every corner.

Down another quiet, tree-lined street were the homes of the affluent. Buildings with steep pitched roofs dipped over on either side of the street. Houses here didn't have big lawns, they instead had stately shaped topiary bushes behind low stone walls. In front of Millie's favorite house was a sweeping marble staircase with twenty steps. She ran up them one day on a dare as the other kids clapped and cheered. The broad steps had gently curved metal railings that reached out in a welcoming embrace, inviting visitors to approach the massive red double doors at the top.

The polished brass door knockers were in the shape of lion's heads. They were higher than the top of Millie's head. She stood there on the top landing, which had a brass compass medallion set right into the stone. She stood on East and wondered what would happen if she lifted the scalloped crescent and knocked. She stood on her tiptoes and caressed the lion's face. It was so big that her hand barely covered his nose. The metal was warm in the afternoon sun.

"Come on down, Millie," the other girls called in a nervous stage whisper from the sidewalk.

What if she were invited to a party here? She would wear a yellow dress, bright summer yellow like the sunflowers on her grandfather's farm. She wouldn't even have to knock, the door would open and they would welcome her. There would be music and dancing and a whole room full of sweets. There would be lemon meringue pie on white porcelain plates with a silver stripe, a tower of cupcakes with pink icing and cherries, fat, round chocolates, and ice cream in a big crystal bowl. She could eat until her stomach hurt and no one would scold her.

"Millie!" the girls cried from the sidewalk. "Someone's going to come."

The truth was, it was unlikely that anyone would come. From her vantage point on the steps, Millie saw through the windows that the interior was empty. The contents had been sold to satisfy the tax man or the banks. She turned and looked at the house across the street. Down the street a yard man was out front trimming a tall conical bush. Directly across the street one house had its windows boarded up and the house next door had a "For Sale" sign out front. Another had a sign in the window that read "Rooms For Rent." From a distance the street was still straight and beautiful. Up close it was apparent that the neighborhood had begun to decay.

Millie raised her hands in triumph like she had just run a

marathon. She took a deep bow and trotted down the steps to be greeted with accolades at how brave she was. They all saw that the people here were mostly no longer rich. They knew something big had changed in the city but no one wanted to say it. They knew when they were standing on the street they were walking through a ghost town.

As the girls approached the orphanage the streets were noisier and more active. They recognized some of the kids from their classes at school. Here the buildings were apartment houses tightly compressed. Every inch of the neighborhood was filled with families. Behind every house were lines filled with laundry and children playing in the yard. The people who had work and could afford to keep their apartments had taken in cousins, aunts and uncles, and grandparents.. Sometimes a dozen people would be packed into an apartment that comfortably fit five. Still, the street in general was a happy one. In the evenings everybody who had a fiddle, guitar, or harmonica would come out on the stoop and play. Now that it was spring, they could leave the windows open and after lights out, the older girls at the orphanage would sit at the window or on the fire escape and listen to the music until very very late.

Millie's room was on the street side and she found the drone of the traffic soothing. She stayed in the white walled room with ten metal framed beds. Each narrow bed had a little wooden trunk at the foot for each girl to keep her belongings. A few of the girls had something that they had brought with them, a rag doll or framed photograph. Millie's trunk was filled with books from the public library. She was a fast reader and she always had to get a lot of books so she wouldn't run out until the Sisters brought her back to the library in two weeks time. If Millie had her way, she would go to the library every week.

Right now she was reading a book called "Winnie the Pooh."

It was kind of a babyish book but she liked it anyway. She liked how it was about characters who were friends no matter what, even Rabbit though he was sometimes fussy, and Eeyore even though he was always sad, and Piglet even when he was scared. They were friends who helped each other, no matter what, and stuck together even though none of them were perfect.

It was Millie's terrible secret that she had intentionally spilled grape juice on the library copy so she could keep it. When Sister Katherine walked her into the library to tell the librarian about the accident and show that the book was ruined, Millie hung her head and looked sad, just like her father had taught her. She had her fingers crossed behind her back.

"I'm so sorry," she said, biting her lip to make her eyes water. "It was an accident," she lied. That night at prayers she begged wordlessly for absolution and knew that God would forgive her if she promised never to do anything bad like that again. The pages were purple and wrinkled, but she still read it over and over.

#

The sisters packed up a sack lunch for each of the girls to take to school. This usually consisted of a sandwich wrapped in wax paper and an apple. Once in a while Sister Mary Patrice would make oatmeal cookies with raisins. The girls always walked the same way to school and left their meandering for the afternoon, down Armitrage Street then left on North Fremont and then through the alley behind the big white church where the hard times men slept. Hard times men – that's what the girls called the men who stood in the churchyard in the mornings next to the statue of our Lady of Fatima.

Hard times guys were different from bums or tramps. Bums were people who stayed in one place and expected other people to give them something without doing anything in return. Tramps were like bums, but they moved around. Millie knew that there was nothing good that came for free. She had seen firsthand that nothing but trouble came from getting something without working for it. For some folks this is okay, they didn't mind always looking over their shoulders, leaving town in the middle of the night, or running from the cops. What people didn't realize was that working for something and doing the right thing was usually easier than messing up. Every action had consequences, the idea was to try to make the best of things.

Bums were usually people who had given up and turned to the bottle to get through the day. She knew alcohol was illegal, but that didn't stop people from drinking. Now they just drank in secret; some of the liquor was crazy expensive but folks didn't care. They either had more money or they took money out of the mouths of their children. Some of the alcohol was poisoned as no one was watching over the process and the people who made the hooch at home and in the back woods added things that weren't safe. She heard of people going blind or even dying from drinking it, but they still let alcohol lure them away from their own good sense. There were some people who would pay any price to be numb.

Hard times guys will work when work is available. These are men who'd had jobs, careers, and lives built around them. When their jobs disappeared some men fell apart and became bums and ran away rather than face a new truth. They ran either by killing themselves, or taking to the streets, or lost themselves in a bottle. The vast majority of them just became hard times guys and did what they needed to do in order to survive. Some were proud at first and clung to the vision of their old lives. They tried to be choosy and only do work for which they had been trained and at a rate of pay close to what they were used to making. Eventually for most there came a day of realization, when the bills came due and the babies were hungry, and the hard times guys did whatever they needed to do. They stood in lines, they worked in pits, or they traveled far to look for any scrap of opportunity.

Many of the children at the orphanage were hard times kids. It was rare that both parents were dead. The more common scenario was that the parents were unable to provide for them. Too many mouths to feed and the parents couldn't scrape up enough to get food or clothes and had lost their homes and couldn't even provide the necessities. The bare minimum to sustain life was beyond their reach for some. In such circumstances an orphanage seemed a kindness.

Millie had seen these kids dropped off; they usually didn't cry or cling, their mothers did, but the kids were already too tired. Their faces were dirty and blank, sometimes their clothes were ragged and torn. These kids usually looked like a pile of used rags walking around. Once they were clean and well and had some food in their bellies they would play around like a normal five-year-old. They always had a little fear in them though. If supper was ten minutes late it would cause a panic in the dormitories. Some would cry, some would pace like wild dogs. Eventually the food would come and they ate it so fast if you blinked you would miss it and they ate with their faces close to the plates, spoons moving so fast it was like a blur. On those nights everyone took seconds, no matter what was on the menu.

All the kids, including Millie, knew what it was like to do without. This fact more than any other shaped them. The nuns could speak of charity and of helping your fellow man, but it wasn't really necessary. The orphanage residents knew at a deep level, perhaps more than anyone else, what it meant to be lacking and longing. It made a few mean and stingy, but for the majority it had the opposite effect.

These children were generous in the extreme.

So when they walked past the hard times men, standing in line for soup or the chance at a job, the girls shared what they had. In the afternoon whatever they had left from lunch, an apple, carrot, some crackers, they gave it. The man perked up when they saw the line of girls in matching outfits, light blue shirts, dark skirts. Perhaps they thought of their own families far away, perhaps they were eager for some food, perhaps just happy to see something pure and bright in a harsh world.

The girls shared what they had willingly, without a thought, just smiled and skipped away, most not realizing that they had given not just a cracker, but hope for someone to hang on for another day and hope that things would get better soon.

There was a routine in Millie's life here at the orphanage. They got up at the same time, morning prayers, breakfast, school, chores, homework, prayers, bed. Sometimes on the weekend they had a field trip. One time they all took the subway to the aquarium where there were veritable oceans of sea creatures, fresh and saltwater fish, seals and penguins. They had been to the art museum. Sometimes people came to the home to teach them crafts or sewing or painting. Millie supposed she was lucky to be in Chicago when her father had surrendered her. Back in Oklahoma, where they had been, there was nothing to help them when people hit hard times. They were on their own out in the rural counties. She had seen children living in a car on the side of the road. She had seen kids sleeping in a cardboard box. She knew she was luckier than most, but she was still lonely even with the other children around.

Sometimes in the night, Millie lay awake and stared at the ceiling. It was too dark to read but she liked that it was quiet with only the traffic for company. Occasionally one of the younger girls would have a nightmare and Millie could hear her cross the room, whisper a bit, and then the creek of bedsprings as she crawled into bed with a sister or a friend. Sometimes in the morning half the beds would be empty and the other beds would holds two or three occupants. There was no criticism, usually no mention at all, in the morning. Everybody had moments when it was too much to be alone.

Some of the kids had dreams that their parents would be coming back for them. Millie did nothing to dissuade these thoughts. Some of the kids got letters regularly from their fathers who were searching for work. Millie's mama was dead and her papa was no good, so she didn't hope for a reunion of that kind. What she did have was a memory of a place she used to go, where people loved her and the grass was green.

She kept her special postcard under her pillow when she slept and in her pocket when she was up, same as always. It showed a farmhouse with trees on one side and a hand stacked stone wall on the other. A barn stood in the rear, and long rows of vegetables covered most of the drawing. It was like a picture in a book, but Millie knew it was real. She knew there was a cow and some chickens. She knew those trees were maples and that in the coldest months of the early spring there would be a cauldron bubbling to make maple syrup from their sap.

When the Sisters spoke of heaven, this was the place Millie pictured. Some people thought Heaven was perfect but Millie knew that it couldn't be. Heaven was full of sinners who have repented and been forgiven. Heaven had to be a place where anyone who tried their best, was kind, and asked for help could be blessed.

On Fridays the nuns always sent the children to school with

lunch consisting of sardine and mayonnaise sandwiches. Nobody liked this; each child, all seventy-five of them dreaded Fridays for this reason. They knew that they would be hungry all afternoon and they counted the hours until dinner. On the way to school on Friday mornings each child carried their lunch sack, not putting it in their satchel for the possibility of a contaminating odor. They walked as quickly as possible and took the most direct route to school so that they would pass the white church in the least amount of time. The hard times guys were always ready for them and the seventy-five little girls, all wearing matching outfits, quickly and efficiently rid themselves of the offensive food.

There were more jokes than tears on Friday mornings and a certain festivity to the transaction. Each knew the other was doing a great service as the children were saved from having to eat the distasteful sandwich and the men were saved from another day with an empty belly.

#

Millie often walked down the street alongside the other kids with her nose in a book. With a big book this was nearly impossible. The act of balancing it as she walked distracted her too much from the story. Books like The Hardy Boys mysteries worked well as they were printed in smaller, more manageable volumes. In the morning, since they always took the same route, she could make the whole trip without looking up from her reading. She relied on the rest of the students to move across the busy intersections on the way and without completely facing forward she could angle her head to attain a fleeting glance at the shoes of the girl in front of her.

She almost didn't care what she read; fiction, history, biography, poetry were all the same in her esteem. She was a sponge, absorbent and empty waiting to be filled with ideas. Even a bad book taught her something, even if it it were just a lesson in comparing typeface and binding.

On her way to school that day she had her head down as usual, her mind a million miles away with Scheherazade and the Forty Thieves in that foreign landscape of sand dunes, camels, candles reflecting off the ceiling, and piles of gleaming gold. She could feel the heat and smell the rich aromas of spiced meat and sandalwood. When they passed the hard times guys she handed off her carrot sticks absently, without thought, just stuck out her hand to deliver food she wouldn't eat. One of her teeth was loose and the crunchy carrots hurt a little bit.

A hand on her left grabbed at her, instead of just taking the bag as it was offered. This moment stopped her in her tracks, causing the girl behind her who was talking to her friend and not paying attention either, to bump hard into Millie causing them both to stumble.

He still didn't let go.

Millie sat on the ground, knees scraped from her fall. She tried again to extract herself from this stranger's grip, as she gathered her book and dusted it off.

"Let me help you," he said, his hands still grabbing her arm. She looked at him then, square in the face. He was thin with his cheeks sucked in and his mouth drawn tightly together, like he was trying to smile but couldn't remember how. His face was unshaven and his hair stood off the top of his head like he had been pulling at it in frustration. He was tall and his forearms were devoid of any muscle. His hands were cracked and calloused. He looked like a figure of the desert, like he had been rooted by time until all sweetness and softness he ever had were dried up and blown away.

He ran his pale gaze up and down her like he was searching for something or remembering something, but whatever he sought or thought was something he didn't like. He smiled and she saw his teeth. They were brown, broken and black, rotten just like she knew his soul would be if she could see that.

This exchange took only seconds and then the other hard times guys busted in. They stood like a barricade between the tall pale man and the little girls.

"Back off, Scarecrow!" Joe was a big guy. He used to work at the meat packing plant and his arms were like two fat hams. Joe had kissed Jenny Rogers on the hand when she gave him a piece of pecan pie.

The scrawny man raised both his hands as if in surrender and backed away. "Okay. Okay. I was just talking to her," he said. But he wasn't, he hadn't said a word with his mouth. With his eyes the conversation was one-sided; he had told her that he would never repent.

The scene was almost forgotten, but the girls walked quickly and quietly the rest of the way. Now that spring had come to the city people were more forgetful and full of hope for a minute. They forgot how their feet hurt from cold in the winter, or the smell of surplus corncobs burning in the stove because nobody could afford coal. They forgot that the summer in the city was as hot as a furnace and everything would smell of old beer and urine and mud. Here in May, they thought of baby things being born and pretty pots of purple flowers in the window box. People imagined, for one month, that nothing bad could happen.

## CHAPTER FOUR
## The Incident

On one Wednesday afternoon, Millie stayed after school for a long time. She had to clap the erasers, and wash the black boards in the primary school classrooms, and re-stack the math books before she went home that evening. Her smart mouth had gotten in the way of her good sense, again, as she had exclaimed, loudly, that President Teddy Roosevelt was the best because he had created the national parks system. The point she made wasn't the problem, the teacher had taken exception with her speaking out of turn.

It wasn't dark yet when she left the schoolyard, but it was drizzly. It was overcast and grey and there had not been a moment of sunshine at all. Perhaps this explained her enthusiasm for the great outdoors and President Roosevelt. Millie hoped that some poetry might cheer her mood.

She turned the corner to the white church and walked down past the churchyard behind it as she had done a thousand times before. She spoke loudly, sometimes stomping her foot in the rhythm. "Trees" by Joyce Kilmer.

> *I think that I shall never see*
> *A poem lovely as a tree.*
> *A tree whose hungry mouth is prest*

*Against the earth's sweet flowing breast;*
*A tree that looks at God all day,*
*And lifts her leafy arms to pray;*
*A tree that may in Summer wear*
*A nest of robins in her hair;*
*Upon whose bosom snow has lain;*
*Who intimately lives with rain.*
*Poems are made by fools like me,*
*But only God can make a tree.*

Millie liked to read. She liked poetry. But "Trees" by Joyce Kilmer was just plain dumb and she resented being forced to memorize it. First, it didn't make sense. The leaves were like arms and then they had birds nests in them. The rhymes of "Trees"were babyish and the content was boring. Millie went back and started at the beginning so she could get the it over with. "I think that I will never see..." The sound of her words and her voice made her walk home less lonely. The drops continued to fall at a hesitant pace, undetermined whether to stop or soak.

She didn't see the man they called Scarecrow until she practically bumped into him. He reached out with his skeletal arms and grabbed her by the shoulders. He grinned, in a tight and uneven smile, as if this were just a mistake, a bump, something worthy of a brief apology, a 'pardon me,' and everyone could just go on their separate ways. The way he looked at her, like he was examining a jellyfish, made her feel small and he was so tall that this distressing pale stare came from a great distance. The difference in their sizes made them seem like two different species, or the very least like two very different breeds of dog, like a toy poodle versus a Great Dane.

He opened his mouth and she could see his black and brown

teeth. His breath smelled like the trash behind the butcher shop on a sunny day. Meat and blood and death spilled from between his thin cracked lips. When he spoke it was like a rusty gate.

"What's the rush, Princess?" he asked, drawing out the S so that it was almost like a whistle or a moan. "Sit with me a while and let me get a look at you."

She didn't want him to look at her. His eyes were like those of the dead fish. She didn't want to smell his terrible stink or to have his dirty hands on her shoulders, but he wasn't letting go.

\#

William Hart found Chicago to be a disappointment this time through. When he had been here eight years ago, fall 1925, the city buzzed with energy. That year he worked with a band of Lithuanian tile layers as a journeyman apprentice. He had no intention of becoming a master tiler, he just liked the weight of the materials: boxes of square ceramic tiles, buckets of grout, 50-pound sacks of Portland cement. It was good work, steady and blissfully lacking in polite conversation. His co-workers at first attempted communication enough to extend an invitation for a beer after work but stopped after the third refusal. He spent that winter working on upper floors of unfinished buildings, surrounded by dust and non-English speaking colleagues. He felt like an animal, a draft horse, a pack mule. He didn't share ideas, or think, or feel much of anything beyond the urgency of elevating his heavy load up countless flights of stairs.

If he were just a dumb animal it was easier to ignore his ruined face and troubled mind. If he fell into bed exhausted at the end of the day it was possible, sometimes, that he could sleep the untroubled sleep of the drunkard or the fool.

Chicago this time, spring 1933, had no opportunities for

oblivion. There was no work to be had. Drought-plagued farmers had flocked here from the dusty devastation of the plains and the Negroes had trekked here from the heartbroken South. Immigrants still crossed the ocean in waves dreaming of a land of peace and freedom. Some who hit the road were kids, chasing opportunity and adventure only to be disappointed again and again and again, and finally ending up in the city with countless other defeated searchers.

The Depression had affected William in an unexpected way. Since he had come back from the war he needed to work, hard physical labor amidst strangers or machines, some kind of situation that precluded all thoughts, conversation, or interaction. He had found this system after he left home. Back then his family had tried to help him by giving him an office with his name on the door. What he really needed was to be in the guts of the factory. He needed to feed tall lengths of pine into the whirring, tremendous sawmill where they were sliced into countless uniform boards. The noise, heat, dust, fatigue of the place would help him sleep, far removed from his sixty-three days in the mud that had changed him so dreadfully.

Now that times were hard, in order to do a job, he had to stand in line for hours and often with no results. He would do a job for free sometimes when his head got too heavy with thoughts and he needed some relief from himself. The problem with this is that other men in the lines were looking for work to feed their children. Every box he lifted, truck he drove, every nail he hammered, or crate he packed took a nickel out of somebody else's pocket these days.

Despite the sheer number of people within her boundaries, maybe because of it, Chicago cultivated an atmosphere of camaraderie. When thirty guys slept on the floor of a bunk house, none of them with work, money, or prospects, each was humbled. Each knew he was no better than anyone else, no luckier. William sometimes slept in the bunkhouse, sometimes huddled out by a campfire near the rail yards. He had tried renting a room in a boarding house, but as the lack of work had already made him irritable and edgy, the landlady's and other tenants warm smiles and general compassion chafed like sandpaper.

Most nights in the bunkhouse each man retreated into his own thoughts or memories. Once in a while William's face alone was not enough to discourage conversation, on nights like this William had to leave to get alone. Tonight it had driven him to the little grounds keeper's shed at the back of the church.

Most of the hard times guys were decent people just trying to get along, to make a little money to send home to the kids. A few of the men were more trouble than they were worth. Some people took the nation's tragedy as an excuse to run off, hit the road, and find adventure. This demographic bothered him especially because it struck a little to close to home. As they talked over stubby cigarettes and illicit hooch about freedom and evading the stifling bonds of responsibility, he thought ruefully of his own parents' reaction to finding his bed empty with just a note of good-bye. His own youthful disrespect for his mother's feelings hurt him more than he cared to consider.

One man in particular was more likely to drive him to solitude than any other. The guy was called Scarecrow, partially a nod to his angular and poorly assembled physique, Scarecrow seemed to be all knees and elbows, and partly because he was terrifying to listen to. He talked all the time, and about ugly things; rape, theft, assault, mutilation of animals. He liked to tell a story about an old man in Philadelphia he had set fire to, then sat and ate a sandwich as the man tried to escape the flames. Scarecrow told that story frequently, each time with more details and loud cackling laughter. Scarecrow's arrival usually cleared a room. A few of the guys had taken to replicating the 'caw' of a blackbird to warn others to stay away when he came around.

On this particular night William had been banished to this shed behind the church by private demons rather than conversation. He realized it had been forty-five days since he had even come close to breaking a sweat on a job. William's need for work, for labor to blissful exhaustion seemed unattainable here. William hadn't quite discovered a workable solution. He felt he may be going mad with idleness. He'd taken to walking at night for hours at a time, miles. Some nights when sleep evaded him and nightmares came, he ran until he thought his heart would explode. Running to nowhere, with no purpose, only gave him more time to think, the very thing he was trying to avoid. No, he needed real work and he needed it immediately. He was finally waking up to the fact that it wasn't going happen in Chicago. Tonight, outside the caretaker's shed on the the cemetery he smoked a cigarette just to give him something to do with his hands. Frustrated even with that simple action, he stubbed out the butt against his shoe and watched as the last flicker of ember faded away.

He was eager to leave Chicago but had no clear destination to expedite his departure. The Depression was spread so wide that one place was really no better than the next. The inertia of this statement had him by the balls and he felt increasingly helpless to control the pursuit of memory hot on his heels. He had never trusted banks, a fact that he was glad of after so many had failed. He kept his money rolled up in his sock. He also had some buried in coffee cans in an old graveyard in Chattanooga, Tennessee. He picked one of the town's founding fathers, the man who had owned the banks, and every September he had planted a pot of chrysanthemums and a can of money on the dead man's grave. In the past couple of years work had been hard to come by, so he had to make a trip down there periodically to dig some of it up. It was somewhere, but the thought did nothing to spur him into action. Maybe next week.

Tonight the half empty moon hung in the sky, its edges softened by a light haze of rain. He thought briefly of getting a hotel room, a woman, and a bottle but remembered that he no longer drank, or slept, and a random woman who had to close her eyes to be with him held little appeal. He lit another cigarette, took one drag, and immediately snubbed it out. The pile of crumpled butts at his feet continued to grow. He really was losing his mind.

Across the cemetery a blur of movement caught his attention. Someone small but fast was determinedly making their way to the north exit. The figure looked back at intervals, as if being pursued. William stood up and saw Scarecrow quickly gaining ground on his prey.

Was it wrong that his damaged hand began to twitch in anticipation of a confrontation? Probably. William didn't care. If some of his restless energy could be dispelled by a simple fistfight, he'd take it. Anything to change the direction his mind raced. The fact that Scarecrow was a terrible person just made the idea all the more appealing. His boots on the wet grass made no sound. Scarecrow wouldn't know what hit him. William smiled for the first time in weeks.

"Stop! No!" the voice came out, tiny and terrified, a child. William didn't make his presence known. The little girl screamed for all she was worth, but it made no difference. She didn't stand a chance against someone who had no soul. William picked up the pace, abandoning stealth in favor of speed.

He heard Scarecrow's gasp as she bit him, heard the smack of her head as she hit the ground, heard the squish of the mud as Scarecrow dragged his victim somewhere more private away from any possible prying eyes.

The first punch he delivered to Scarecrow's face felt better than anything William had ever done. Blood spurted from the bastard's broken nose. William shook out his fist, spit on the man, and went to see if the kid was all right.

"I probably deserved that," Scarecrow wheezed through his pain. "We could share her, you know. I'm not greedy. We could all have a real good time."

Did William know what he was doing when he turned Scarecrow's face into paste? Possibly. Probably. But he didn't care. It still felt better than anything and he continued to pummel long after a reasonable man would have stopped.

#

"Mister, you should stop," Millie said, finally finding her voice again. He didn't. William kept pounding, spraying the pulp of what used to be a person. She took a few steps forward, trying her best not to look down at the mess. She laid her hand upon his shoulder and she spoke again. "You have to stop."

William Hart turned to her so quickly it made her jump. His gaze was vacant and unfocused, staring at something in the far far distance. He shook his head, shaking it like he was trying to chase flies away from his hair.

He looked at Millie then. He looked to the man on the ground and jumped up quick, like he was surprised at what was there. Then he backed up just a little and sat down against one of the headstones and he sobbed.

Millie had seen grown men cry before; her father, of course, when he was play acting. One time she saw one of the men from Oklahoma, he cried slow tears that streaked his dirty face when the movers came and took everything away. She had never heard anything like this though. It was like the sky had fallen apart.

Millie's head still hurt but she was starting to think better. The man was covered with blood and guts, it would be dark soon, and the rain continued in a steady saturation. She realized the cold had been affecting her. Her teeth chattered and so did his.

"We can't stay here," Millie said quietly, calmly, like he was a skittish horse. He didn't hear her behind the rain and his sobs. Millie stood there and looked at him, unsure what to do. He was about her father's age with brown hair now pressed down over his forehead with wet. Half his face was a terrible scar. Where his eye would be, he had only a wrinkled chunk of flesh. The scar looked pink and angry and pulled the skin together tightly, making his eyebrow and mouth a little crooked. He was probably a handsome man before he got hurt. But now he looked like a monster. The truth was, Millie had met a true monster this evening and William had saved her. She trusted him without completely understanding why.

"Mister," she approached him with no fear. She brushed her hand in his hair. "Come on, it's raining. And we can't stay here." She gestured with her head at the body on the ground.

The scarred man, her angel, seemed to see the good sense in her statement. They were both completely soaked.

"You go on home," William said. His voice was deep and smooth and quiet. He started to walk away from her into the heart of the cemetery.

The orphanage was just past the white church. She could be there in ten minutes, back where there were clean dry clothes and a hot meal. Millie could picture it, how the nuns and the police would fuss, and frown, and ask a million questions.   Sometimes killing wasn't wrong, it usually was, but sometimes people just did what they had to. She wasn't sure anyone else would understand that. Millie had felt Scarecrow's hands on her, his breath. William stepped in and did the right thing. Nobody else in her whole life had done anything that big for her; she owed him.

Millie decided right there that there was no way she could abandon him. In a strange way, they were now connected. She started to run after him, leaving her damp book of poetry lying in a puddle of blood that was rapidly being washed away by the rain.

#

"Hey Mister." Millie ran up toward him, pulling him back into the present. William didn't slow, just walked steadily on. He thought how no one would miss Scarecrow. But wondered if the brutality he had just demonstrated meant that he had lost more of his soul than he had imagined. More perhaps than a man could afford to lose.

"Mister!" Millie ran to keep up with him and he could hear the way her breath raggedly caught in her chest. She would be done soon; she would fall back, eventually sit down among the headstones and maybe cry. Then she would go back to her people. They would find Scarecrow, maybe the church ladies would even throw him a better funeral than he deserved.

What did William deserve?

He slowed his exit imperceptibly. What did he deserve for taking a man, a piece of shit man for sure, but still a man, and rendering him to his base elements? What did William deserve for acting as judge and jury and eliminating the possibilities for growth and change? Maybe Scarecrow's future included redemption and changing his ways. William thought maybe he should go back and wait for the police to arrive. The brutality of his crime might indicate that society at large would be safer if he were behind bars.

He let Millie catch up to him. He turned to face her, to face the consequences of his actions.

William was not expecting her to fling herself at him and wrap her arms around his waist.

"Get off," he said as he extended his left hand to help pry her off. She looked at his hand, what was left of it, and she turned her face up to his. When he looked at her he saw feverish impassioned devotion. She took his damaged hand, laid her forehead against it then touched it with her lips in a chaste kiss.

"Go home," he said again and hauled her to her feet harshly and abruptly. "It's raining," he said as he softened his tone.

"You saved me," was all she said and she patted his hand soothingly and mumbled under her breath, eyes facing toward the ground. As he listened to her closer, he realized she was reciting the Twenty-third Psalm.

"You need to go home," he said. The rain refused to let up. It rained sheets over both of them. The blood washed down his clothing leaving them a macabre pink color.

Millie stood her ground. She stood straight and tall, with her fists clenched at her sides. "We have to get some dry clothes and somewhere to sleep."

She took his hand, his half hand, and took the lead and brought him across the cemetery, away from the orphanage.

She was walking away from her life, the life she knew. He didn't know why she did it and he didn't have the energy to question it. The adrenaline crash was coming and he needed to sit down for a while. He let the little girl guide him.

## CHAPTER FIVE
### Unlikely Fugitives

Millie guided William through a series of back streets and alleys he wasn't familiar with. He wouldn't have known these neighborhoods, even if he had been paying attention, which he wasn't. This was the kind of neighborhood he had grown up with, stately houses for people who were interested in making a good impression. William hadn't belonged in a place like this for fifteen years and he couldn't imagine what the girl thought that they were doing here.

The unlikely pair took a turn down a common alley that the big townhouses shared. It was now nearly completely dark and William could barely make out a set of stairs leading down a sheltered hallway to a basement level entry door.

"Break it," Millie said as if this were just an everyday occurrence in her world. She took his hesitation as confusion at her meaning. She tapped one of the small panes of glass above the door handle with her finger. "It'll be okay. We need to get dry. Just break it. No one lives here." She gave him a soothing nod, pulled his hand from his pocket, and pressed it to the window. "Go on, break it," she said.

"I'm too small."

He was shivering and cold. The house was dark, as were others on the street. The nearest light he saw was way down the block.

She nodded encouragingly.

He grabbed a stone the size of his fist from the road. He rapped this with a short sharp tap against the glass sending the fragments tinkling down to the floor behind the locked door. He pulled the sleeve of his jacket over his hand, reached in through the hole, flipped the deadbolt, and quickly shuffled her in before him. The dimly lit interior proved to be a laundry room beyond a mud room. Along one exterior wall was a huge soapstone sink and buckets for washing up. The interior ceiling was covered with long rows of clothes lines and at one end was a cotton sack filled with towels. The interior wall had a table for folding and an ironing board. In the cabinet at the far end of the room was a bag of clothes intended to be recycled as rags and folded at the bottom shelf were old clean blankets, such as one might use to line a dog bed.

It was a room full of remnants, things left behind in rush to be anywhere else. It was abandoned, as so many places, and people, had been. The room smelled of must and regret.

Millie didn't think about the past. Neither should he, as hypothermia threatened them both. Millie had found a couple of teeshirts in one of the bags of rags. She extended one to him. "Where should I change?" she asked. "I don't have my pajamas, but I think it will be okay for tonight, right? My clothes are soaked."

William stared mutely at the dingy cotton garment she offered him. His own shirt was caked with blood. His knuckles were bruised and swollen. "I guess it doesn't matter," he said. He was grasping to find anything that did matter. His shirt was caked with blood and brains and mud, his knuckles bruised.

She was tired, verging on cranky and clearly annoyed by his imprecise answer, "Fine." She tossed the shirt at him. "I'll change in the hallway, you change in here. Then I'll wash your shirt and you can hang it up. Then we can sleep. OK?"

He didn't answer, just stood there staring at the blood on his sleeves.

"I don't hear any changing!" Millie called from beyond the doorway. He began to unbutton as instructed. It was a rote motion executed without thought. He set the garment covered with pieces of Scarecrow into the big sink. Removing it had restored some of his senses; he turned the tap and let the clean water do its work.

"Good job!" Millie said soothingly as she stood on an overturned crate in front of the basin and scrubbed William's shirt. The water ran pink with blood as she worked.

Millie fell asleep as soon as she settled on the pallet of blankets they'd made on the floor. William had no such luck. He could just get up and walk away, sneak away. He knew the freight schedule pretty well, it would be easy to just go somewhere, anywhere, maybe West. They might be hiring still for that big dam. He'd been unwillingly idle in Chicago for too many months, and his savings were getting pretty low. It was either go back down to Tennessee to retrieve his cash or get some honest work if that were possible. He'd never been west of Colorado and he'd heard the Pacific was dramatically blue.

Leaving would be the best course of action, the best way out of this terrible mess. As he thought of what was left of Scarecrow washing down the hill in the cemetery, he wasn't sorry he'd done it. Now he just needed to get the image out of his head. If he could do that he would be all right. And if not all right, at least he would be somewhere else. As soon as he left, Millie would go back to wherever she came from. It would be better if the leaving started now.

She whimpered in her sleep, small sounds like a kitten. She

began to thrash and kick, desperately pawing and clawing and reliving her need for escape.

"Stop," she cried out and she tore at him frantically.

"Hey kid, wake up." He touched her shoulder which made her fight harder. "Millie!"he yelled to snap her out of it.

With her next frantic kick and punch he wrapped both arms around her and held her close. She calmed then and nestled into his side. He covered her with a blanket, he covered them both. He lay there with her head against him and listened to her breathing eventually become slow and even. His chest was wet from her tears.

Millie woke two more times that night. Each episode started quiet, ended with her thrashing and kicking and crying, and she could only be soothed by a full body embrace and the measure of time. For the first time in years, William had no nightmares of his own; he had spent all his efforts on banishing hers.

Around six a.m. he awoke to find Millie carefully examining the scar where his eye used to be. He pulled back quickly. Nobody ever looked at the injury; it made people uncomfortable. Hell, he didn't even like to look at it in the mirror. He had all the time, of course, the first few months. It had been an angry cherry red, swollen to the size of his fist. It was a Frankenstein creation of flaps of skin folded over and sewn together. The thread was long gone by the time he was well enough to look in the mirror, but he could still trace their path on his flash. It took some time for his remaining eye to get used to being a widower and for months he had walked into the corners of furniture and walls.

"It's ugly right?" He had the urge to fill the quiet of his thoughts.

She shook her head and smiled. "It shows how brave you are.

That must've hurt?"

"Yeah," he said. "It did. Still does sometimes."

"Can I touch it?"

Nobody had touched it since he walked out of the hospital sixteen years ago. His mother had purchased him a fancy, black satin eye patch when he first came home. It was the kind of thing a villain with a top hat would wear in an afternoon vaudeville. He thought, *Is this what my own mother thinks of me now?* Of course the patch did nothing to cover the part of the scar that ran down most of his cheek and gave him a crooked smile. It didn't cover the part of the scar that bisected his eyebrow and ran up to his hairline. The eyepatch his mother had bought him was a costume for an actor in a play but William was a real life monster.

"Can I?" Millie asked as she sat next to his head, perched on bare knees under a torn shirt from the rag bag in a stranger's home. "I promise I'll be gentle."

She waited for his permission to proceed. She touched tentatively at first but soon began a careful exploration from top to bottom.

"It's soft," she announced, her voice filled with wonder. "I thought it would be hard like a seashell."

And then, her curiosity was satisfied and she moved on to another topic.

"I had a dream last night," she said. William had experienced her dreams first hand; he had a tiny scratch on his right arm from where she had clawed at him. Millie had a different agenda in mind. "I know where we need to go!" Millie's eyes shone with enthusiasm and she pulled a folded postcard from the pile of her nearly dry possessions. She had refused to lie down until each of her trinkets was laid out on the table to dry overnight.

The postcard was an etching of a farmhouse. It was a pleasant, boring place with trees, cows, and chickens. There was a barn in the back with some apple trees and a low stone wall along the road.

Millie smiled at him and seemed to expect comments. "That's a real nice picture," he said as he handed it back to her. "Real pretty."

"That's where we need to go!" she said with continued excitement.

This was why he didn't pal around with kids. Living in a fantasy world and playacting were never his strong suits, not even one he was a kid himself. He preferred sports with rules, playing fields, and boundaries. He did okay with athletes, but with what everyone else he was in the dark.

Her smile dimmed a bit when he didn't match her enthusiasm for the adventure. She looked at the postcard and started to shine again. "It's real, you know. I've been there." She pointed to the thin border around the edge, about worn out from being handled. 'Hemford, Massachusetts' it said in faint letters. "My granddad is a little cranky, but my aunt, Eleanor, is very nice and they have some cows we can milk, and there's cider, and we can pop corn, and my bed is so cozy!" She hugged herself and mimed the word cozy.

He knew from her clothes that she had it better than most. He had seen this kind of uniform on some of the kids in this part of the city and knew she lived at the orphanage that the German nuns ran. She had carried two apples in her bag and hadn't been made stingy yet for hunger. She had offered him one for his dinner last night.

The city had gotten hard over the past couple years. After the crash, it just seemed to dry up all around, desiccated. William had arrived here a few months ago, drawn by the memory of the vibrant place it used to be. There were still pockets of prosperity, always were. Some people were never touched by anything; they skated at the edges of any crisis. Every year though, more of these people would be sucked down into the black hole of the depression. More families would go bust, more kids would be relinquished, and Millie's orphanage would get a lot more crowded.

"This family you have there...?" He hesitated and hated to say it. "Do they want you? I mean, can they take you in?"

Some people couldn't, it was a simple fact, but probably beyond the ken of the child. And some people simply didn't want another mouth to feed. These days all life was about survival. There is only so far a budget could stretch before something broke. Some people had all they could do to feed the kids they already had without taking on another.

Millie had a moment of hesitation and William was sorry to put that notion in her head. He had no choice. It was a hard thing not to be wanted, to be in a world but without a place. He had abdicated his place and he knew that it was relief his family felt when they saw his empty bed. It was better to face the facts of the situation at the front end.

"I have a letter. It's from a long time ago, before we moved." She presented it like an ancient and delicate artifact. It was a sheet of paper, folded in quarters and tattered on the edge of the folds.

"You carry this with you everywhere?" he asked as he carefully spread the paper on his knee.

"My Papa told me you keep what you really need close, you never know when you're going to have to leave."

"All right," he said but it made him wonder at this little girl's transient upbringing, but he would think about that one some other time.

*December 20, 1929*

*Dear Millie,*

*I hope this letter finds my dearest niece well. I miss you desperately, especially around Christmas. I remember the year you were here with me for the holiday. The tree we had that year was much nicer than the one we've got now. This year's specimen is a bit on the scrawny side. The ornaments you and I made cover every inch of it and I still had to set up a dozen on the bookshelf. I thought they would be lonely if I left any in the box so I brought them all down to enjoy the celebration. I put the lace angel on top and your favorite star near the window to guide your way back home.*

*Your friend Jessup helped to string popcorn and cranberries. Really, I did the stringing and he sat on the floor and begged me to toss him kernels to catch. He's grown to be a good dog, even though he was such a foolish and mischievous puppy. He keeps me company in the evenings, but his conversation is quite limited as he's only interested in chasing rabbits and taking naps. Last month alone he kept the fox out of the hen house four times, so he earns his keep.*

*We had an early snow this fall. The big maple near the north pasture still had all its leaves, they were quite drab this year, and the snow was heavy and flat. Unfortunately that old tree couldn't take the weight. It woke your grandfather and I with a great crash in the middle of the night. We both flew down the stairs in our night clothes. We threw on our boots and coats and ran outside to see what had happened. The moon was near full that night, big and white, and the snow was bright and reflected it back so the yard was shining like day in the middle of the night. Up on the hill we could see it perfectly, the big tree that had been there forever was split right in two with most of it lying on the ground and the rest just a crooked finger pointing up at the sky.*

*When we looked at it in the daylight we saw that the inside was all rotted out. Imagine, a big tree like that, that looked so strong, was really nothing but a shell. Your mother and I used to climb all over that tree like monkeys when we were girls. I cut off the swing that used to hang there; we'll have to find another place to put it when you come back to the farm.*

*Your grandfather misses you, he won't say so of course, but I catch him, from time to time, looking at your photo and the picture of the lamb that you drew for him. He says he doesn't care for sentimental things, but keeps that drawing right on his dresser.*

*Merry Christmas. I love you Millie and I pray that God keeps you safe until He brings you back to me.*

*Love, Aunt Eleanor*

He folded the letter as carefully as he unfolded it. It was important to treat valuable things with respect. Millie had read the letter over his shoulder. Now she sat and smiled like the Buddha, content and wise. "See?"

William was at a crossroads. That's not true, William felt as though he were in an endless field of corn. He imagined a place with no landmarks, nothing to suggest which direction he should go. He was alone, no clouds, no crows, nothing in sight at all but tall stalks whistling in the wind. The corn silk tassels had turned brown. The crop was ripe. The harvester would be here any day.

William had brutally killed a man, but Millie was the only witness, and she, for reasons he still didn't understand, didn't care. If anybody had happened to peek out a window, his identity would have been shielded by rain and dark. When he emerged from the basement safe harbor, he was just as anonymous and unworthy of attention as he had ever been.

Millie, however, was surely on everyone's watchlist. When a ten-year-old girl goes missing and she lived a few blocks from where a dead body was found in the middle of the cemetery, the whole city takes notice. She stood out like a sore thumb with that orphanage uniform.

"You should go back. Just go back and tell the truth," William said. William wanted the kid to have a good life. He liked her, she was funny and brave and kind. She deserved to be just a little kid and go to school, play with her friends, grow up safe.

She screwed up her face and curled her hands into fists again. "I'm not going back. If you don't take me I'll go by myself. I'm pretty sure I could figure it out."

William shuddered to think of her out in the world by herself. He didn't doubt she would try it. If not this year, the next, or the year after. That tattered postcard represented something for her. It was a place, but more than that it was an idea that there was somewhere she would be welcome and made safe.

If it didn't work out, the nuns would be thrilled to take her back. Christ, they'd probably put in it the paper and call it a miracle. Either way, back to the orphanage or on to the farm, it would be a miracle if they found that farm, if the family was still there.

He realized this morning that he had lost most of his money in the cemetery. He imagined that somebody felt very lucky this morning. He hoped it was a guy with a family to feed. If he hadn't lost that money he could have just bought them a couple of tickets. Now he had to find another way.

He was thinking of them in the plural now: we, us. He was

committed to the idea of making a thousand mile trip with a ten-year-old runaway. He should have been questioning his sanity, instead all he felt was relief. He was awake and he wouldn't reach for numbness again.

"There's a train leaving at eleven," he said. "Gather your things."

#

The Chicago rail yards were an intricate spider web of steel, noise, and smoke. It should have been chaotic with hoards of arrivals and departures day and night but to William, there was a divine sort of order and symmetry. Though the trains came and went-- screeching, shaking, grinding-- the massive locomotives seemed to almost touch, to kiss. Despite their sheer size the trains were docile and domesticated. They wound their way through the yard in perfect, solemn solidarity. Here the trains knew and obeyed their assigned tracks and schedules like well-behaved behemoths.

William had found reprieve in this regularity through the nights that followed days of futile job searching. He had taken to haunting the yard like a hulking ghost. He had thought repeatedly of hopping a train, but lack of a clear destination deterred him. Hard times were everywhere, inescapable. The futility of his situation strangled his sleep and threatened to dismantle his tenuous hold on sanity. The rail yards helped.

Now charged with the care of a stubborn ten-year-old, the yards seemed rife with danger. He overcame his aversion to human touch and took Millie's hand as they picked their way across the humming tracks, balancing on ties and navigating the unstable piles of gravel distributed by countless trains. Millie had entered the yards full of adventurous optimism but slowed until each step was imbued with caution and trepidation. William knew older, more streetwise men who would have turned back at this point. Millie was propelled along, despite her fear, by the unrelenting drive to get home to her family. William, after so many years adrift, couldn't help but admire the little girl's singularity of purpose. He tightened his grip on her small hand and pointed out the path of stable footing.

He located a likely box car on the appropriate track and, after a moment of uncertainly, spanned her waist with his hands and hoisted her into the car, before climbing up himself. He slid the door closed to the last inch where he could peer out until the locomotive began to pull away.

"Hello," Millie said in a quiet clear voice.

William spun around, first to Millie, and then to the figures huddled in the shadows at the far end of the car. Trouble could come from a territorial burst. People would fight to keep what little they had. Or it could come from the greed of desperation, from people who got along off the misfortune of others. He was alert, prepared to fight if needed. Millie looked tiny sitting in the corner. He rose to his full height.

"We don't have anything, mister," came the tremulous voice in the dark. The speaker was young, fourteen maybe, just a kid. His companions, three of them all together, were equally diminutive and cowed. "We're just trying to get to Albany."

His eyes adjusted to the dim light. The kids looked exhausted and malnourished. Their eyes were huge and sad in their gaunt faces. They were cornered; William blocked the only exit. He moved from the door and sat next to Millie. "Don't worry, kid," he said. "We're just traveling too."

From a distance away, the engine roared into life and they felt the first hint of a hum as the cars began to vibrate. A thud and a mighty shudder measured the progress as each car was engaged like beads on a string. As the engine moved, each car was dragged, pulled, taken as the sound came closer and louder until the odd band of travelers in their dark and dusty rail car sat up on edge in dreadful anticipation.

Each car closer and closer joined in the eastward crawl. Finally the progression reached them. That their car should join this line, though inevitable, though they heard it coming, and that it was the desired course of events, it was still a shock. There was no way, not for even experienced riders like their young companions, to prepare for the noise and the shock of movement. They were all jerked back with a jarring metallic clang that shook their bones and teeth. They pulled forth with tremendous force that sent Millie toppling sideways. William righted her and pressed her against his side for safekeeping. If she were frightened she didn't say a word, just sat still against him. He could feel the tension in her but she didn't complain.

They wound around one last hard right as they exited the rail yard, then straightened out and continued. The ride was far from smooth. The rattle on the steel rails crept up through the floor of the car. The hard metal held the chill in the early part of the day, then heated up as the afternoon drew on, leaving all of them pulling off coats and shirts. Nothing was cushioned or softened. They felt every bump, heard every creak, squeal, or squeak.

Changing trains in Albany brought no relief. The boys had jumped off as they pulled to a slow, relentless halt. They immediately scattered with no goodbye. William leapt with Millie in his arms before the train had stopped completely. He oriented himself quickly and deciphered which train would take them to Massachusetts. The night was dark. A heavy blanket of damp chill smothered all sounds. He didn't see any people. On the last leg of their journey they were alone; the box car was empty but none more pleasant.

#

When they slowed on the approach to Springfield just after dawn, William gave her a gentle shake. "We're almost here."

They climbed down the ladder connected to the side and slipped away across six tracks and climbed under a fence on the other side without being noticed. It was early but there were still people out and about. This city started to wake up around them as they walked. Shopkeepers opened big glass doors with bright painted trim. They could hear the tinkle of the door chimes up and down the street. One man outside the bakery nodded and went back to sweeping the sidewalk.

This cheered him. He was worried since they left the train that Millie's status as a missing person would draw unwanted attention to the fugitives, but they seemed to just blend in.

He stopped in his tracks and they went back. They hadn't eaten in quite a while. He decided this would be as good a use as any for his last couple of dollars. The bell on the door jangled behind them as it shut. The air in here was warm and the smell of yeast and cinnamon greeted them like a long lost friend. Millie stood captivated but didn't approach the counter. She performed a silent calculation that involved the fingers on both hands.

Her outfit was crumpled, wrinkled, and stained from their journey, but she made efforts to arrange herself. The jutting hair was beyond her abilities, but Millie valiantly restrained it with a bright blue barrette she pulled from her bag. She finished with a general, rejuvenating smoothing. She looked pretty good for a kid who had slept on a train.

She gestured that he should bend down to hear a whisper. "I only have a little money, but I think it should be enough to get us something."

"You have money? From where?" William asked and crouched down so he was at her level.

She scoffed at him. "Here and there." Her voice got even quieter; she was insulted at his questioning her self-reliance. "Collected and saved. My mother taught me that it was a woman's responsibility to have at least pocket change on her at all times in case things went wrong. Things have definitely gone wrong, William. We're almost there, and I'm hungry."

She shook her head to chastise him, "Stealing is wrong." William was about to respond and jingle the change in his pockets when a woman came through a curtain at the back.

"That's exactly right, my girl," she laughed. The shopkeeper's hair had once been red but it had now faded to a jaundiced gray that she wore pulled back into a braid wrapped around her head. Her dress had once been a brilliant color blue with little white flowers on it, now a shade close to her hair color. She wore a long simple white apron and sturdy black oxfords with white socks. Her face was creased with deep wrinkles, the skin on her neck hung loose, and she had a big mole on her chin. She had never been a great beauty but when she smiled it was impossible not to respond in kind. She looked like an apple head doll his mother had made around Christmas.

The woman stood behind the counter and directed all her attention on Millie, ignoring William completely, which suited him fine. "What would you like?" Her voice had just a hint of a Scandinavian accent from her youth.

Millie burst out, "Everything!" she said, turning pink from

embarrassment. She produced a little hand-made pouch, from which she drew a small handful of coins and lined them up in a row on the counter. The metal clicked on the glass top of the case as she set each one precisely down. "This is all I have. How much will this buy us?" Millie's fortune was seventeen cents.

"This will buy you a good amount. Where do we start?" The woman pulled a white paper sack, a large one, and opened it with a snap.

Millie pointed to a big round loaf of hearty whole-grain bread with seeds. It was big enough to feed them both.

"Really?" the old woman asked. She lifted her head and met William's gaze across the room. She nodded as she dropped a big loaf into the bag. "What else?"

The back bakery wall had a long glass case with many shelves. Most were empty now, but he imagined at one point they were filled with mounds of colorful sweet creations. In hard times people spent their money on practical things-- baguettes, peasant loaves, dinner rolls. Today they offered very little variation from the basics. The petits fours, decadent iced cookies, and dark chocolate brownies would have to wait for a brighter year.

"Do I have enough for another one of those big ones with the seeds?" She turned to William, "We might need more for later, right?"

"We might," he said. The woman popped a second loaf in the bag.

On top of the counter, under a glass dome, were six perfect cupcakes. They perched in fluted paper cups, had fluffy pink frosting, and each was topped with a little purple daisy made of piped frosting. It was the kind of thing that he suspected most kids would go for first. In a time of hardship such sweet delights were rare.

The woman behind the counter snapped open a smaller bag. "What else?"

"I should probably save some money. Just in case." Millie eyed those cupcakes, but held her resolve as she gathered her remaining coins and hid her pouch once again. "Thank you very much," she said. "You have a nice day." She looked everywhere but at the temptation of the cupcakes.

The old woman snapped open a smaller bag. She held Millie's gaze as she lifted the glass confectionery dome. Millie's smile was so big it rivaled the moon. The lady plopped the pink treat in the bag and folded the top down.

"You come back here anytime," the woman said. "You come back real soon." They thanked the woman and left. They ate their bounty on a bench outside the big brick public library. As soon as it opened they went inside to look at a map. Millie had been much younger and her recollections of Hemford's location were too vague for proper navigation, they revolved on phrases like near the river and up the hill. William was sure she would remember the surroundings once they got closer, but the last few miles of the journey would need some concrete guidance to be successful.

He borrowed a pencil and paper and traced their route: Wilbraham Road to Stony Hill Road to Main Street to North Road. It appeared to be fairly straightforward and only twelve miles away.

He had twelve miles to determine whether he had made a colossal mistake. It was one thing to deliver an adorable ten-year-old to the loving arms of her family but there were a thousand ways for this scenario to go wrong. Could he find them? Would they welcome her? Would they turn on him for helping her get out of Chicago? What if this Eleanor and the grandfather chased William out of town with a pitchfork?

Millie chattered as they walked about all the things they would eat and see and do when they arrived at the farm. William found some comfort in her optimism. The urban center of Springfield was densely packed, as all cities are, but Springfield didn't seem to fare as bad as other regions. There weren't so many boarded-up shops on Main Street, and he didn't see any bread lines though maybe the city kept them tucked somewhere out of sight. Springfield was a small city and the dense urban canyons quickly fell away to neighborhoods, villages, then hamlets, then farms, then fields. The neighborhoods closest to downtown were made of sprawling federal style houses with wide and deep green lawns. The streets branching off the main road curved graciously back into the glades of maples, poplars, and occasional flash of the paper birch. There were mere glimpses of these houses through the leaves of the dense trees. The houses along the side streets were like stately old matrons who wore their brick façades and gleaming white coats well. They were beautiful and elegant and rooted in tradition. The houses were surrounded by sweeping manicured lawns and bedecked with coordinated flowerbeds. There were very few people visible and the walls retained the secrets of the dwellers within.

Further along the houses were less grand and more tightly packed, humble homes of clerks, mailmen, and teachers. Children played in yards, clothes hung on lines. Here symptoms of the depression were more evident in the peeling paint and sagging porches coexisting with the neatly mowed lawns. The folks here still had pride even if they didn't have money.

In the driveway of a tiny white bungalow with faded green trim, a stout man in a light weight gray flannel suit was kicking the tire of a black Model A. He walked to the passenger door gave it a hard smack then walked all the way around it, pausing to spit viciously, to stand in front of the open hood. He reached in, fiddled with some wires, then returned to the driver's seat to try it one more time. The engine whirred and chugged but the ignition didn't catch and the motion closed with an extended shudder and finally a clunk. He pounded the steering wheel with his meaty fists.

"Need a hand?" William asked quietly. The man had not heard them approach. The expected reaction of shock and revulsion at seeing William's scars quickly faded as relief flooded his face.

The man was a few years older than William, his hair had receded past the center of his head. The Friar's fringe that remained was neatly trimmed, and the smell of bay rum aftershave radiated off him in a five-foot radius. A polished brown case rested on the front passenger seat and the car had been recently washed.

"What I need is a miracle," he said, laughing, as he exited the car. "I never did have any skill for cars beyond pointing the wheel and pushing the pedals. Any help would be much appreciated."

The wife came out onto the front porch. She had a tight, constrained look, like someone who had seen her share of trouble. When a stranger arrives, her first reaction was fear. "Who's this?" she shouted across the small yard and wiped her hands nervously on a blue cloth towel. A boy, four or five years old, appeared inside the screen door and she shooed him back inside. "Who's that man, Jasper?"

Jasper called back, still grateful they had stopped. "This fellow's going to help me make it to that job interview."

Her face opened like a rose, unfurling all doubt. She was pretty when she smiled. She wore a yellow dress that hung off her shoulders, like she had lost weight since she'd bought it.

William said, "My girl is thirsty. A glass of water would be much appreciated and a place where she can sit while I take a look at this." Millie was dead on her feet and she shuffled around the vehicle to give a halfhearted wave.

"Good heavens, Jasper. You didn't tell me there was a little one. Come here, you. I'll heat some more soup. Timmy was just about to sit down and have some." The wife took Millie gently by the hand and shepherded her into the cool dark of the bungalow.

William leaned in to the main engine compartment. He tugged on a few wires, poked the carburetor butterfly valve, and checked the air filter. He bent to the red toolbox Jasper had retrieved from the garage. It looked to be several years old but barely used.

Jasper shrugged, "I'm not much good with cars."

"Me either," William said, which made them both chuckle. He selected a socket wrench from the box and went about removing a spark plug. He examined it, cleaned the tip and replaced it, then duplicated the process with the others. He went to the driver's seat and fired up the ignition. It sputtered and coughed a few times but it soon settled into a familiar idle.

The wife and the kids rushed out onto the porch. It was as if they'd never seen an automobile repaired before. William supposed after a few years of bad luck people begin to wonder if anything would go right again.

Jasper pumped his hand seriously. "Where are we headed?"

"Hemford," Millie said authoritatively. William picked up the tools and shut the hood.

"Not too far. Right on the way," Jasper said. He kissed his wife, ruffled the boy's hair and straightened his suit.

When William looked back Millie was already asleep in the backseat. The landscape was pretty here, rolling, but no real mountains like in Colorado. The landscape was raised by soft swelling hills with occasional rocky outcroppings. Water was plentiful and everything was green.

Jasper had been out of work for about six months. His employer, a manufacturer of musical instruments, had been able to last past the initial crash of 1929, but a subsequent year of declining sales forced them under. Jasper was the regional sales manager and finding a job in management had been an elusive goal. If he didn't get this position, he and Barbara would be forced to move in with her parents, something that nobody was looking forward to.

William found he learned a lot about people just by sitting quietly. Most people took his silence as a tacit encouragement to continue. With a decent guy like Jasper, William didn't mind listening. His endless flurry of words suited them both. He hoped things would go smoothly for each of them this day.

The road from Springfield was recently paved, wide with even grading and curves that allowed speed to be built. The road between the train station and Jasper's house were wide enough for two cars to pass with plenty of room. As they got closer to Hemford the ride had become increasingly bumpy, sidewalks disappeared, and fields ran right up the edge of the road. Arriving in the town proper the road evened out again and the main street was paved but the side streets were mainly hard packed dirt or gravel. At the far end of town the tarmac continued but the farms and trees quickly closed ranks around it. In a fast car the town of Hemford would go by in the blink of an eye.

A town square looped off the main thoroughfare. It was an expanse of closely trimmed grass, with a small uninspiring monument in the center, a single bench, and a few lonely little trees. Around the edge of the square were a church with a tall steeple, a brick town hall, a few stores and a handful of houses.

Jasper shook William's hand and hugged Millie as he dropped them at the intersection near the center of town. Millie was practically vibrating with excitement. William felt a growing knot in the pit of his stomach. Time changes people. What they loved yesterday may be old news tomorrow and hard times accelerated the process of forgetting.

William saw a few people out on the street but no one paid them any notice until Jasper pulled away, then the big man and the little girl garnered their attention. People who had walked singly now clustered in twos or threes to discuss the newcomers.

"Where to, boss?" he asked Millie as he put his damaged hand on her shoulder, good hand free in case it was needed.

"North Road is steep and winding," she said as they reach their final turn off. "You'll be tired by the time we get to the top." The nap in Jasper's car had revived her. She ran up ahead of him at various points to see what was coming ahead and then ran back to report.

"Red raspberries!" she exclaimed as she reached up to pop one in his mouth before running ahead again. The berry was still hard in spots, it would probably be sweeter in a week or so, but Millie's enthusiasm was contagious. William thought back to the time he had spent surrounded by hard gray concrete, where nothing really grew but fancy flowers on a rich man's terrace.

At the top of the hill the road flattened and started to head back down. There on his right was a farmhouse with trees, a barn, and a low stone wall along the road. Millie stood in the center of the road with her hands crossed over her mouth.

The images in Millie's postcard were condensed and compressed, the pictorial representation of someplace vast shrunk down to fit four-by-six inch card. It was like a map portraying the whole of the Atlantic Ocean with a twelve inch swath of blue. Where the picture showed two apple trees the hill easily held a hundred. One fat hog was really three in an enclosure that could have held nearly two dozen. To the left of the house fifty yards had been cleared of trees and brush, but only a tiny fraction had been plowed and planted. From his place on the road he could see how the weeds encroached.

Though he knew next to nothing about farming, the business lessons of his childhood dinner table couldn't be silenced. He added up the projected revenue as he looked around the Abbott spread. He calculated the apples, the market crops, and the livestock and throughout his assessment he heard his father's voice bemoaning the cardinal sin of "underutilized capacity." The place was as silent and empty as Millie's picture. It was a beautiful day at the height of the growing season and the farm was deserted.

The house itself had faded significantly since Millie's etching had been produced. It was still an elegant, sturdy house made of strong straight planes forming a solid rectangle. The front porch that interrupted the clean lines was clearly an afterthought after the initial construction. From the side view an irregular conglomeration of extra rooms had been added on over time, but the heart of the house remained--solid, linear, symmetrical, no nonsense. The two-story structure had once been painted an austere white, now weathered to a distressed gray. The deep green shutters and trim peeled more on the sunny side of the building than the shaded. The big hickory out front had a massive limb hanging over the porch steps, suspended only by a wayward vine. The stone wall had tumbled down in a few places and grass sprang up amidst the stones that delineated the curving front walk.

Despite a few years of neglect the house at the top of North

Road still retained an air of dignity. From a seat on that front porch, one could look down on the whole valley stretching below. The buildings were hidden by the leaves save for a slender white steeple emerging from the canopy. It was the same from below, everyone knew the house was here, but privacy was enforced by foliage. From its place on the hill the house commanded respect.

In the winter when the leaves were gone, William imagined the wind would slice right through you. The road to town would be impassable in heavy snow. The inhabitants of this house would be sturdy and self-reliant by necessity. Perhaps they were just too stubborn to live anywhere else.

It was the image of her postcard, tempered by time. He laid his hand against her back and she turned to him and cried on his shirt.

Millie straightened herself quickly, smoothed her hands over her hair, wiped her eyes, and pulled down the hem of her skirt. She smiled at him and put her hand in his. "See?" And she led them onward.

## CHAPTER SIX

### The Homecoming

The fool dog was barking up a storm in the front yard. This struck Eleanor Abbott as odd, because Jessup usually only alerted like this when the fox came in the night. It was late afternoon, nearly evening and usually this hour was a quiet one as the day wrapped up to prepare for sleep. She hadn't heard anyone drive up and they didn't get many passersby way up here on the hill. Still, he persisted long after some passing creature would have been merrily chased.

Eleanor sighed and wiped her hands on the cotton tea towel near the sink. She had been scrubbing her hands for a good ten minutes and she'd probably not get all the soil from beneath her nails if she kept at it for another hour. It was lucky for her she didn't have anyone to impress; the chickens certainly wouldn't notice when she closed their coop later.

At the edge of the road, just inside the low stone wall, barely on her property, but near enough to be considered a trespasser, a tall muscular man smiled at the activities on her front lawn. Jessup was racing around the yard, yipping and wiggling and dropping down with his front paws out in front of him in an invitation to play. There on the grass, face down near the forsythia bush, a young girl lay on the ground as the dog danced around her and licked her face. The big man was ignored by both dog and child. Eleanor however could not look away.

The tableau before her made no sense--the enormous, still man, the laughing girl, the exuberant dog. Eleanor wished she had thought to carry her father's shotgun outside with her. She wished she had not come outside at all. Still, doing nothing was cowardly and wrong.

"Jessup! No! Hush!" she hollered as she opened the screen door onto the steps. "Just hush! Come here," and she whistled as she stepped onto the overgrown grass.

"I'm so sorry," she said as she shooed the dog away and helped the child to her feet.

"Eleanor!" Millie cried as she flung her arms around her neck. "I'm back! And the dog's gotten so big. And the bush is bigger too, but the house looks smaller, but maybe that's just because I am taller now."

Eleanor couldn't find her breath to speak all the words jumbled in her brain. "Millie," was all she could say.

She crushed the little girl against her chest, squeezing as if she could make up for years of missing someone by the sheer strength of her arms. Eleanor wasn't prone to hysterics, to tears, but this was beyond her control; emotion poured from her and she shook from the impact of her surprise.

"Millie, where are your parents?" she said and craned her neck to look down the road from town. No one else was coming.

Millie went limp against her, and clung like a feverish infant. "It's a terrible story. Can I tell it later?"

Eleanor glanced over at the strange man who stood quietly watching her family reunion. He kept a polite distance, but was still too close for her taste. Her nearest neighbor was a significant ways away. His face, when he turned it, was crooked and mangled and horrific. She hugged Millie tight, ready to pull her to the house. "Millie," Eleanor whispered, "Who's that man?"

Millie perked up, stood, and patted her dress down where Eleanor had wrinkled it. "That's William. He's my friend. He helped me get here."

Eleanor kept her voice low. "Is he part of the terrible story?" she asked.

Millie also spoke softly, "He's the hero. He really is."

"Honey, why don't you go inside and freshen up? I found a little doll house in the attic that your mother and I used to play with. I've missed seeing you these past few Christmases, but I saved it for you. Still has a bow on it! I put it right by the dresser. I'll fix you something to eat, then you can tell me all about your trip." She hugged her niece tight, before she let the squirming child run inside to see her new toy.

Eleanor took a deep breath through her nose and rose slowly from her crouched position. She looked toward the screen door, still vibrating from the force of Millie's slam and imagined she could just go in and shut the heavy front door behind her, maybe push the book shelf behind it, barricading them both inside, safe.

She turned to the big man, half his face was ravaged by terrible scars. It was menacing by design but his actions were slow and tentative, almost insecure, like a mistreated draft horse.

"Where is my sister?" Eleanor asked when she finally found her voice. It surprised her that it didn't come out like a squeak, the sound of a terrified little rabbit cornered by the dog behind the wood pile.

"I don't know, ma'am." His voice was calm and low, no drawl or accent, no clue as to where he came from or what he wanted. He answered, and then stood there, waiting for the next question. Or not. Left to him, Eleanor imagined the subject could remain unresolved indefinitely.

"My brother-in-law?"

"I'm sorry, ma'am, I don't know that either." He stood straight at the edge of the yard, facing her directly with his body, but with the scarred side of his face turned away. The top of her head would barely come up to his chin, yet in this exchange it was as if he wanted to be smaller, like he intentionally didn't want to appear intimidating, though his physique didn't offer many other options.

"Mister...?"

"Hart. William Hart." He said his name, nothing more and didn't offer to shake her hand, but kept both of his hands firmly in his pockets. His clothes were dirty and rumpled now, but of good quality. His boots were scuffed, but sturdy and recently soled.

"Mister Hart, this is John Abbott's farm. We don't tolerate a lot of nonsense around here. Where did you meet Millie?" Eleanor felt the headache growing behind her eyes and hoped he couldn't see her apprehension.

"Chicago." Jessup trotted up with a stick in his mouth, nudged William Hart with it and a waggle to play. William quickly withdrew his hand from his pocket and gave the stick a mighty heave way down past the herb garden. The dog gave chase in a mad scrambling rush and William thrust his hand immediately back out of view.

"So Millie was in Chicago, Mr. Hart. What was she doing in Chicago, if I may ask?"

"I don't know, ma'am".

"What were you doing in Chicago?" A hint of frustration and anxiety crept into her voice.

"Not much, unfortunately." The dog returned, nudged the slimy stick against him which was thrown without hesitation and his hands pocketed once again. "Millie was alone when I met her, Miss Abbott. She wanted to come here. She said you were family." The dog didn't return, he lay in the sun at the edge of the yard, exhausted, panting as he gnawed happily.

"Who was looking after her?"

"Maybe you should ask her, ma'am." He looked back toward the dog, who made no move to rejoin the conversation.

"Do they even know she's here?" Eleanor stole another glance at his terrible face. His left eye was completely gone, replaced with a lump of scar tissue like an insult. It was the kind of injury that changed a person, made them humble or made them mean and she couldn't be sure which she faced.

"I don't know....."

Millie erupted into the yard then, full of excitement. "Thank you! It's wonderful! Can we make some more tiny clothes for the dolls?"

Then she was off, crossing the overgrown grass to pull William's hand from his pocket. He was reluctant to bring it, but soon acquiesced to her tugs. "Come on. I'll show you! The dollhouse is so adorable and there's a little rocking chair that really rocks!"

Eleanor fought to make sense as Millie pulled the big man toward her front door. "Millie, hold up," she croaked out at the last second. His foot was already on her front porch. "How do you know Mr. Hart?" she could barely draw breath to form the question. He withdrew his boot from the step.

"I told you. William saved me. He's a hero!" Millie extended her other hand to Eleanor, bridging the gap between her and the stranger. "I was so lucky he was there to rescue me. And then he helped me get home! Everything is fine, Eleanor," she said with absolute certainty. She smiled at Eleanor with an expression so calm that it made her want to believe Millie's childish optimism. "Come on, William. I'll show you my room."

The screen door closed behind them without a ripple. William Hart closed the door so gently it left no evidence of his passage into the dim interior of her home. Eleanor opened the screen, it squeaked when she did it, and stood a minute in the cool dark of the porch. The furniture here was dusty from lack of use. Some of the chairs were turned over, her mother's favorite little table was covered in a white cloth. That table should have come in last winter; the dampness of the season couldn't have been good for the inlay around the edges. The delicate Greek key pattern was likely ruined from neglect.

She realized that thoughts of old furniture were ridiculous. As were thoughts of preparing dinner, but that's where her dazzled mind headed next. She was over her head, thrilled to have Millie home, anxious about the stranger, concerned for her missing sister, and Richard.

Millie's footsteps pattered across the front parlor, followed by the slower steadier pace of her companion. Eleanor listened to the sounds of their ascension-- the center step of the steep, narrow staircase creaked as always. Millie narrated the grand tour of Eleanor's room, then Caroline's, then Johnny's. The closet doors were opened then shut with Millie's characteristic vigor. The squeak of the weight of the large grown man settling onto Millie's twin bed sent Eleanor flying up the stairs.

"Everything all right in here?" Eleanor asked, striving for chipper, breezy, relaxed, but failing. She stood stiffly with her back against the wall.

William scrambled respectfully to his feet as Eleanor entered, sending the tiny chairs that Millie had set on his lap clattering to the floor. It was a small room, made smaller by his full height.

"We're fine. What time is dinner? I'm hungry!" Millie's clear voice showed no distress. She knelt on the floor and demonstrated the structure of the little cabinet from the doll kitchen. William didn't object when she pressed it into his hand and moved on to examine the next object. He made no comment other than mild appreciation for the craftsmanship of each piece of miniature furniture she showed him.

Eleanor lingered, listening, watching, wanting to gain insight, perspective, and details of Caroline and Richard's absence. She wanted assurance of Millie's safety with William Hart. All her observations earned her were the names of the newly christened dolls, Winifred and Guinevere, sisters like her and Caroline. Millie talked of the dolls and potential adventure they could have and the need to obtain a tiny dog for their household. William Hart said nothing and didn't move. The sounds of Millie-- stepping, climbing, dancing-could be heard clearly. Eleanor could close her eyes and pretend that the big man was just gone, disappeared as if he had been merely a dream.

#

Eleanor pulled a bowl of chicken from the icebox, chopped onions and carrots and prepared a salad with some spring lettuce and escarole and spicy radishes. She sliced the oatmeal bread she'd made last night and pulled a crock of butter from the larder. She set the table with her good dishes after giving them a quick wipe. They hadn't been used in nearly a year. It hardly seemed worth it for just her. She used the same plate for every meal; an old blue willow set of plate, bowl, cup and saucer with a little chip on the dinner plate. The rest of this china stayed in a glass front cabinet and waited. Today she used her mother's favorite set of white bone china with leaves embossed around the edge. It was delicate and elegant and too fine for a simple farmhouse luncheon, but today called for a celebration and she didn't skimp. She used her mother's linen napkins with the blue scalloped edges too and picked a few sprigs of lilac from the door yard for color.

Millie exploded into the room from her exploration outside and hugged Eleanor hard around the waist. Eleanor patted her head, admiring her soft brown hair with her hands. "You've cut it short since I saw you last," she said. "This is such pretty hair cut for the grown-up girl you've become." Eleanor found herself tearing up a little bit as she thought about the years she'd missed in the child's life. She chided herself not to dwell too much in the past.

Eleanor herself hadn't changed much in the interim years. She had always been plain, her brown hair was pretty enough, she wore it cut short in a simple bob that she parted to the right and pinned back to keep it out of her eyes. Her eyes were green and a little close set, giving her the effect of always carefully scrutinizing her surroundings and companions. Her lips were thin and tended towards pale. Millie had Eleanor's green eyes and brown hair but she favored her mother, long lashes, big eyes, full lips with a cupid's bow of continuous surprise and delight. Millie was destined to be a great beauty like Caroline, but Eleanor hoped that she would avoid some of her mother's foibles.

She gave Millie another tight squeeze. "Go sit down and we'll eat. Milk or peppermint tea?" She shifted her attention to William, who lingered in the doorway to the parlor, trying not to intrude. She warmed her smile despite her concerns, "Please sit down."

The big table in the kitchen could comfortably seat eight. Today it felt crowded by questions and absences. Eleanor felt she might explode with curiosity before too much longer.

"Millie," Eleanor started as the little girl began to eat. "I need you to tell me about how you met Mr. Hart."

Millie was put off by this question. He could see the calculations working in the child's head, an analysis far beyond her years---lie, tell the truth, soften it, spill it all. Millie had been holding her breath trying to decide what to say next.

William laid his hand, his half hand, on Millie's arm. "Tell her. Tell it all."

He was resigned to Eleanor's reaction. He would do whatever she wanted. He had nothing and everything to lose.

"This dinner is really good," Millie said.

"Tell her," William urged.

Millie drew in a breath, a big gulp like she was a singer preparing to deliver an aria or a diver preparing to enter the sea. "First," she paused for effect. Her voice was lower than usual and she enunciated carefully. The final 't' in 'first' snapped like a dry twig. "First, believe that Scarecrow was no good."

"Who's Scarecrow?" Eleanor asked, amused.

Millie shot her a quelling glance. "Scarecrow is the villain. It's a nickname. That's what everyone called him." She continued, "Scarecrow was no good. He was a very bad man. That night thick mist covered the cemetery. The gravestones cast shadows in terrifying shapes. We girls often cut through, but it was different during the day and not scary at all when your friends were around. That evening I walked alone, solitary. I hurried as fast as I could, but it wasn't quick enough. I was being followed. I could hear someone coming but I couldn't see who it was."

"Scarecrow?" Eleanor couldn't help but ask.

"Scarecrow." Millie nodded solemnly. She had William's hand, his damaged hand, clasped in her tiny fist.

"It's ok," William said evenly. Millie scooted over and whispered in his ear. "What's done is done," William said quietly to Millie. "You're fine now, right?"

She nodded and carried on with her story. "Then, from out of the fog he came. Scarecrow!" Dramatic pause. "He grabbed me! And he threw my book bag. Then he tried to kiss me! His breath was disgusting and his teeth were brown. I told him to get his paws off me, but he wouldn't, not at all. He just kept pulling me and he ripped my shirt. I had to bite him to get him to stop." Millie's eyes were closed as she relived the traumatic moment. "But that just made him madder. Then he knocked me down, and I got wet and dirty because it was starting to really rain. I was down on the ground and he started to drag me by the feet toward...." She paused and looked to William. "What's that little building called with the statue on top?"

"Mausoleum?"

She nodded. "Yes. He dragged me closer and closer to the mausoleum. It was filled with spiders!"

Eleanor held her breath. Millie was a child, ten years old, and a little underweight. She weighed maybe sixty pounds. The sip of tea she swallowed did nothing for Eleanor's dry throat. "Scarecrow is a grown man?"

"Yes! Tall. Taller than William!" Millie placed her hand three inches over William's head as he remained seated.

"Continue," was all Eleanor could manage to say. William sat perfectly still but the muscle in his jaw clenched and unclenched. Both his hands were on the table. His right index finger tapped the enamel surface. The meal sat untouched on the plates. A single fly buzzed and swooped over the chicken.

"Suddenly!" Millie boomed as she shot up and banged her

palms on the tabletop, upsetting plates and silverware. "Oops," she said, temporarily tempered, but undeterred from her narrative. "Suddenly," she repeated in a softer, more dramatic voice. "William arrived for the rescue! He pulled Scarecrow off me." Millie did a full reenactment in the kitchen, playing all three parts: the hero, the villain and the victim. "Scarecrow was forced to let me go. And then I fell back and hurt my head." She pulled her hair up to show a small, healing scab at the base of her skull.

"Then William heaved him to the ground. Threw him pretty far, really far, and then he hit Scarecrow right in the face! Pow! Crack!"

Her repetition of "pow" went on a sickeningly long time. She continued in a low, confidential voice, "I could practically see the halo surrounding William's head! The avenging servant of the Lord sent to protect the children. It was magnificent. I knew he was an angel right away. I did!" She stood behind William's chair and looped her slender arms around his neck. She laid her soft cheek against his scarred one and kissed him reverently.

"I'm not an angel," William said gently as he pulled her off him. "Sit down and eat your meal," he said.

Millie mouthed the word "angel" to Eleanor across the table and finally managed to sit still long enough to eat.

Eleanor couldn't eat anything. She couldn't even pick or pretend.

"What happened to Scarecrow after that?" Eleanor asked looking back and forth between Millie and William.

"I'm pretty sure he was dead," Millie said as she drank her milk. "Right, William?"

"He was dead," William said softly.

When Eleanor looked in his eyes, eye, she didn't see any glee

95

or bravado. He didn't preen under the glow of Millie's praise. He was clearly uncomfortable in the role of the hero. "He would have hurt her?" Eleanor asked him, adult to adult.

"He really did hurt me!" Millie lifted her hair again to show the abrasion. She pushed up her sleeves revealing the fading, fingerprint-sized bruises of her ordeal-- the attacker's fingers were all intact.

"Scarecrow would have hurt her without a backwards glance and then gone off and done it to some other kid." He added emphasis to the word 'hurt', wrapping it with his voice to make it ravenous and twisted. Eleanor shuddered and stared at him so long he turned away.

"I'm glad you're safe now, sweetheart." Eleanor covered her plate with a towel and put it in the icebox, though she couldn't imagine being hungry any time soon. She delivered a piece of strawberry pie and set it down at Millie's place. Millie dug eagerly into it. A piece of the soft, red filling plopped onto the white china plate. "I've heard how you met Mr. Hart. Now I need to know where your parents are."

Millie slumped into her chair as if she were nothing but a pile of ash. "My mother got tired and sick and now she's in heaven with the angels. I'm not sure where my father is right now."

Eleanor wouldn't have expected the news of her sister's death to hit her so hard. When pressed, Millie whispered the barest elements of her mother's death like ancient myth; something that happened a long time ago, and to someone else. It had been years since Eleanor had seen Caroline, longer since they had been close. She felt as if the whole world were dying around her. No time to get wrapped up in that. Details of Caroline's death and Richard's absence were another of Millie's terrible stories. Eleanor didn't think she could hear any more of those tonight. When Millie asked if she could show William the bee tree, Eleanor didn't have the heart or stomach to insist on anything else. Soon enough she would learn more particulars of her loss.

"Why don't you go up to the paddock and say hello to Chester first. I imagine he'd appreciate an apple," Eleanor said. "Mr. Hart will join you shortly." With two of last fall's remaining Winesaps in her pocket and a quick peck on the cheek, Millie was gone.

The silence was thick in the kitchen. From Eleanor there was no movement, no fidget, no words, no eye contact. She just sat with her eyes closed. Outside she was aware of the flutter of birds in the tree nearby, the breeze through the screen door. The scent of bee balm, sweet and minty, drifted in. From the front room came the steady tick tick tick of the clock on the wall. She still didn't move or talk, only breathed soft and slow. He wouldn't get up until she did and she made no change, just sat and sat and sat.

"Was that story true?" Eleanor asked.

"It is." He was conservative with his words, but Eleanor didn't really expect him to be otherwise. The residue of Millie's story lingered like smoke from a grease fire, choking all other conversation.

"Hey William!" Millie hollered from the yard. "Are you coming?"

He hardly moved, not to answer the little girl's summons, not to leave of his own free will, not to threaten Eleanor. Her entire life Eleanor had wanted to protect her niece, but in reality the big, damaged man was the only one who had succeeded at the task.

"Those bees have been especially aggressive this year," she said. "Make sure Millie doesn't get too close."

"Thank you for bringing her home," she said but received no reply. He had already left her quiet kitchen.

The summer her sister Caroline met Richard Cage, Eleanor

Abbott was sixteen years old. Her family was still reeling from the death that winter of her brother, Johnny, and their mother eighteen months prior. Johnny had been tall like their father and calm and even-tempered like their mother. From an early age he had taken to the tending of the animals, never flinching or squeamish in either their care or their slaughter. Their father had pinned all his hopes for the continuation of his legacy on the fragile frame of his fourteen-year-old son. When Johnny had fallen to influenza her father, John Abbott, hardly spoke for weeks.

A girl in a farm household had value, certainly when her mother was alive she had worked hard to make their farm the great success it was, but a son, a son you could build plans around. With the girls her father hoped they would marry well, perhaps to young men who had a stake of their own, perhaps to strong young men who could help grow the Abbott holdings. Unfortunately in Caroline's choice of husband, he got neither.

The persistent clang of Blossom's bell and the bleats of two young nanny goats reminded her that the farm had no patience for her memories. Eleanor cleaned off the table then went upstairs to gather clean towels and sheets for Millie. And William.

The back bedroom had a low sloping ceiling and deep shelves under the gabled windows. This had been her brother's room, and it still held evidence of its prior occupant; a lucky horseshoe over the door, a glass jar of colored marbles, a rough whittled wooden elephant the size of the boy's fist. This memory too, she pushed aside in favor of action. She took an extra quilt from the closet and tucked it under her arm to bring up to the hired man's quarters. The nights still get chilly up here on the hill.

Millie's room was fresher than Johnny's. Eleanor visited this room often and opened the window wide when the weather was good. It soothed her to sit in here when the evenings were too quiet. The room in the front overlooking the street had a high rectangular window and was just barely big enough for a twin bed and a small white chest of drawers. The walls were painted the same delicate pink as the smooth glossy interior of the giant conch shell that sat on the mantel downstairs. Millie had always been fascinated by that shell and she swore she could hear a typhoon when she held it to her ear. Millie had celebrated her seventh birthday with the picnic tea party on the back terrace. The Milsap girls, her little friends from Sunday-school attended. Eleanor had served the girls, all in pretty dresses with white gloves, raspberry tea in real china cops and a round cake covered with strawberries and rose petals. The girls pretended to be elegant ladies, pinkies extended and so forth, as they called each other 'your majesty' and said everything was divine.

Eleanor pulled a blue crocheted blanket from the top of the wardrobe and spread it on the foot of Millie's bed. She hurried to finish her chores before the animals became too impatient.

She was in the barn milking Blossom when she heard the crunch of one set of boots come down from the back field. Millie had been back in town for less than a day and already Eleanor felt a little nervous at her perceived absence. The sound of boots, a singular set, drove her from the dim of the stall to see what was what.

William carried Millie on his back like she weighed nothing. Her arms hung limply over his chest. With his right arm he gripped her legs around his waist. He smiled a crooked smile when he saw Eleanor approach them.

"One minute she was talking about tadpoles and the next she was asleep on my shoulder." He nodded graciously as Eleanor took the little girl from his back. He took the bucket of milk she had set down on the ground and followed her to the house.

Eleanor set Millie on her bed and spent a long time tucking her in. She carefully arranged the pillows and the little gingham doll Caroline had made when she was expecting. The first baby always seems to make women nest a little, it made her sister, for a brief shining moment, domesticated and settled. Having children made some people believe that this kind of life could suit them, even if all evidence was to the contrary. To her knowledge, this optimistic little rag doll was the only thing her sister Caroline had ever stitched. Eleanor patted the little doll one more time, a kiss good night for Millie, and quietly exited the room.

#

William sat at the kitchen table with a heavy white mug steaming in front of him. His right hand was on the mug, embracing the comforting warmth. His left hand was out of sight on his lap under the table. She had seen the hand earlier, but had been too polite to ask. William was so quiet it was unlikely he would offer any explanation. Eleanor could envision a scenario in which no information at all was conveyed between them.

"I hope it's all right I made myself some tea," he said.

She let the sweet tang of lemon balm tickle her nostrils. She liked to drink it in the winter as it always reminded her of June. A big patch of it grew around the edge of the stone wall; it sprang up uninvited among the tall brown iris pods. Every summer she would go out with her grandfather's sharp bone-handled knife and cut the fragrant leaves, bundle them with string, and hang the bunches in the back shed to dry. When she drank lemon balm tea she felt like she was drinking last summer. William Hart sat at her table and drank that summer too.

Last year Eleanor spent the summer attending to her father as he died. All the smoothness had gone out of him in the months before he passed. It was as if every unkind thought he had ever had was lodged in his chest waiting to be hacked up in a bitter wrenching cough. Most of his anger was reserved for Richard Cage, but there were still plenty for Eleanor.

"This stew tastes like sewage, Eleanor," her father said as he dumped the contents on the floor near his chair. "If you were half the woman your mother was, I might have attracted a husband for you by now and I wouldn't be in this state."

That summer Eleanor only drank savory and pungent tea-oregano, thyme, and cayenne with plenty of honey. Mrs. Johnson told her the blend would protect her from her father's illness. Eleanor felt that the sharp bite protected her from losing herself that terrible season.

Tonight she was in the present as fireflies blinked in the yard. Her chores were done and a sweet little girl slept upstairs in her pink bedroom.

She pulled another cup, a delicate fluted vessel with violets painted on it, and poured herself a cup of tea as well. Lemon balm.

"Did you need anything? " Eleanor asked. "Are you hungry?" She used food as a replacement for conversation or interaction. She knew this was a shoddy substitute but sometimes it was the best she could do. She didn't wait for a response from him; she just brought him a plate with cornbread and hoped it would convey her meaning, gratitude combined with caution. He ate it eagerly.

She considered the action of spinning raw fleece into yarn. It requires not force or abrupt movement, but a slow steady pressure. Pulling too hard, too fast is guaranteed to break the thread and force one to start from scratch. Patience she could do; Eleanor understood the subtleties of silence.

"I'll just bunk in the barn, if that's all right. Been a long couple of days," William said. The sky outside was mostly dark and she would need to light the lamp on the side board if she planned to linger herself. The kitchen seemed small in the dark, intimate. "I'm glad Millie has a nice place like this," he said offhandedly, over his shoulder, like it wasn't the most important thing he'd said all day. Like it wasn't the nicest thing anyone had said to Eleanor in a year.

She moved to rise. "We have a bed for you," she was embarrassed she hadn't mentioned it earlier.

"Barn's fine," he said. "Good night."

Eleanor didn't light the lamp. She sat there in the kitchen, in the dark, and listened to the crickets. Eventually she carried the cups to the sink and went quietly off to her own bed.

When Eleanor awoke in the morning she realized she had been dreaming about Richard Cage. In the way of all dreams, it was a convoluted jumble of times and places. In her dream, Eleanor and Caroline strolled the main concourse of the Mass Aggie County Fair. Johnny was busy fussing over his prized Holstein heifer. Richard came and walked between them, one Abbott girl on each arm.

Richard had a way of making Eleanor blush. She felt it in the dream, the way she felt had rushed over her cheeks, and the way she giggled at every little thing he said. The world seemed a bit brighter when Richard Cage was around.

In the dream people, dark and ugly men, kept popping out of the crowd to talk to him. Eleanor and Caroline kept walking and laughing as Richard was drawn into increasingly loud conversations with increasingly ugly, dirty people. They strolled and the fairway seemed to go on and on and Richard always ran to catch up, always talking, always joking, but each time he returned he was a little more tattered and grimy at first; and then he magically was restored to his usual pristine state.

She scrambled up from sleep, patting the memory of the past down with force as she made her bed with rigor. She pulled the sheet tight with hospital corners and smoothed the tart green quilt until it was as smooth as glass. The pillow was aligned at a right angle to the mattress and her house slippers sat carefully side-by-side underneath. She reminded herself she had too much work to do to be bothered by ghosts and she set off as quickly as possible to go do it.

As it was, she had slept later than usual. She could hear the animals getting restless outside. She had some peas to harvest, tomatoes to transplant from the cold frame, early spinach to thin, eggs to gather, soil to till, trees to trim, barns to paint, and on and on and on. The work around the farm was never-ending and Eleanor didn't feel up to half of it.

#

When she was a girl, Eleanor planned on being a teacher. There was a teacher's college in Springfield and another one up in Amherst. Her old teacher had helped her complete the application and had proofread the essay she'd written on Ralph Waldo Emerson. The admissions office had given her the address of a clean, respectable boardinghouse where a lot of the girls stayed. All she needed was the application fee, which her father refused to give her. Eleanor believed things would have been different if her mother was still alive. As it was, she was needed here at the farm.

It was warm in the hen house when she opened the door to the coop the next morning. The chickens fluttered out in a chattering rush, eager to exchange gossip and see what was new in the world. They were always funny with their own individual personalities and quirks, the one with the crooked comb who always ran frantically all over the yard before settling down to explore one small square for the rest of the day. The one who followed Eleanor like an acolyte as she did her chores, the one who cackled and squawked from morning to night. There were a dozen of these mature layers she called the ladies as opposed to the young chickens to be eaten or sold for meat that she called the girls. With the girls she kept an emotional distance so as not to become softhearted when it came time to slaughter.

With the hogs and the beef cattle attachment was unavoidable as these animals stayed on the farm for a year or more getting fatter and living just as happily as creatures kept for pets or work. They were fed well, sheltered, protected from disease and predators. When their final days came Eleanor liked to imagine it was painless and peaceful, but that wasn't always possible. She hoped that in the afterlife these souls remembered that during their time here they were treated with kindness.

Maybe Millie had the touch with animals that Johnny had possessed. At the very least the child could look after the chickens and save Eleanor a half an hour in the mornings. Caroline had taken care of the chickens, feeding them and collecting the eggs, even though she hated it and refused to do any of the other tasks.

Eleanor walked by the cows and returned to the house with the pail of milk and a basket full of eggs. William Hart sat quietly on the bench near her kitchen door. He rose smoothly as she entered and took the milk pail from her and closed the door in her wake.

Eleanor didn't yet know what to make of him, didn't know how to be easy around him. Eleanor didn't have much experience with men her age. Or, if she were truthful, of women her own age. She didn't have experience with people her own age. Hemford tended to be a community that young people left at the first opportunity. Farm life was hard without much financial incentive. After the mill fire and the failure of the railroad connector line to go through, all hopes for a young person's advancement had dried up with the jobs in the industry in town. A few of the bigger farms took on extra hands and a few of the farmer's wives had opened little shops, but jobs in town were at a premium. Unless you are born into a career here it seemed unlikely that anyone would come to Hemford to find one.

Eleanor wondered when William was planning to leave.

She didn't think he had grown up on a farm. He had the strength for it certainly, but he didn't have the rhythm of it. She pegged him for a city boy, always in a rush. Farmers didn't rush the same way. They knew the work would never be done. Even if they completed all the day's tasks, there would be a repeat for tomorrow, animals to care for, seeds to plant, rows to hoe.

There was always something that you didn't get done yesterday that you hoped to get to tomorrow. Eleanor didn't want to think that she was wasting her breath complaining, but rather she thought she was facing facts.

"How do you like your eggs?" she asked as she fired up the kitchen stove. Her garden boots were wet from the dew on the grass. A stranger with scars sat at her kitchen table.

"Anything is fine," he said. "Thank you."

"I don't have coffee. But I've got some peppermint tea if you'd like." She didn't wait for him to answer. She brought a bowl of cooked potatoes from the larder and chopped an onion, added this to frying pan with some butter, and began to fry up some home fries. Without a word, she went out to the kitchen garden and returned with chives, chervil, and parsley. She pulled a wheel of cheese and set it on the counter. Her favorite bowl was creamy white with a pale blue stripe on the rim. It was heavy and sturdy and it was shaped so that it was impossible to accidentally tip. She broke half a dozen eggs into the bowl, whipped them with a whisk, and poured it into another buttered skillet. She poured the eggs in a thin layer, added herbs, cheese, and gave a deft flip with a spatula. She turned this out onto a plate she had warmed on the back of the stove and added potatoes and presented it to him with a steaming pot of tea.

He was staring at her when she sat down next to him. She was flushed with the heat of the stove and the heat of her actions. He hadn't touched his food. She picked up her fork without a moment of hesitation. "Please eat," she said. "Enjoy."

Eleanor was unsure of the motivation behind his hesitancy, but she paid it no mind. She was hungry, and if he were going to complain, at least she would hear it on a full stomach.

"Thank you," he said and he ate his omelet in five big bites, then attacked his potatoes with equal enthusiasm. When no complaints came, Eleanor relaxed a bit and enjoyed her own meal and the warmth of the tea.

Millie padded in as she finished and Eleanor was right back to the stove preparing more potatoes and fixing Millie an omelet and another for William. She poured each a big glass of milk.

Eleanor had always been a delicate eater. Her mother had trained her and her siblings to exhibit proper table manners, even if they were only in a simple farmhouse. Eleanor's mother had been a nanny's helper for a family of wealthy industrialist's children in Hyannisport before she married John Abbott and she always determined that her children would stand out with impeccable table manners. Millie and William ate in a rush, like they expected this would be the last meal that they would ever have and that it was likely to be taken away at any moment.

"This food is so much better than what we had at the orphanage," Millie said with enthusiasm. She gulped down her milk. "May I have some more milk please?"

Eleanor took a moment to draw the breath that had been sucked out of her chest; an orphanage. She pictured something from Dickens, bleak and gray, no food, hard labor. The thought of Millie in such a place was almost too much. She lingered in the larder calming herself.

William came up behind her and spoke softly. "I think it was a good place. Plenty of food, warm and safe."

He was trying to be kind, but his presence, his closeness, had the opposite effect. His very existence was an irritant at the moment and she brushed past him with the milk jug into the light of the open kitchen.

"Here you go, honey," she said as she filled Millie's glass and William's. She sat then and William joined them, careful not to make eye contact. "Millie, honey," she spoke softly and leaned in close. "Where is your papa? Why were you at an orphanage?"

Eleanor knew that some people, mothers who have lost their husbands mostly, had to give up their children after they had lost their homes and all means of support. These were sad and desperate people who gave up their babies so they wouldn't starve to death. Richard Cage had never been that desperate or selfless a day in his life. If he had given up Millie it was to suit his own purposes or it meant that he was dead. It went against her general character, but Eleanor secretly wished that Richard Cage were dead. But first she needed Millie to explain.

"Papa told me to stay there, cause he had to go do a deal and get us some money. He told the Sisters he would be back really soon, but I didn't exactly believe him so I came here instead with William." She said it with finality as only a child can. Ever her father's daughter, Millie had distilled the situation down to its essential elements and decided that Richard Cage was a risk not likely to end up well for her. The sad part was that Eleanor thought that Millie had probably assessed the situation well. Richard didn't and never would have her best interests at heart.

Eleanor quickly shook it off, reminding herself to focus on the present day. "Well, I'm glad you had that good idea and I'm glad that your friend was able to help you." She knew again she couldn't force the story out of the child. She knew that Millie probably didn't know many details of what happened to the money Richard had stolen from countless good people along the way. Eleanor needed a slow and steady pull on the thread of the truth. Or she could just forget it, like the remnants of a bad dream that happened a long time ago. Millie was here now.

She rose and went around the table to Millie again. "You both finish your breakfast. I'm going to go upstairs and find some clothes for you and Mr. Hart. Millie, I want you to have a bath while the cook stove is still hot. Mr. Hart, when you're done if you wouldn't mind getting a few buckets of water from the well. Sorry, the indoor plumbing isn't operational. Next summer maybe. Later this morning you're welcome to use the tub while Millie and I go down to deliver some eggs and pick up a few things in town." She said it fast, like it was a certainty, as if it were a plan of action that couldn't be deterred because to talk this way soothed her. In a world of mad uncertainties, sometimes pretending that everything was ordinary was the best she could do.

"That would be fine, Miss Abbott," he said. He ate the remainder of his breakfast slowly in a relaxed manner. The initial need had been sated and now he was just enjoying the flavors.

Upstairs there was a closet set into the long hallway between the front bedrooms. Hanging in the closet were abandoned clothes of the missing or deceased. She leafed through the offerings and selected a few sets of her brother Johnny's clothes for Millie to wear around the farm and several of Caroline's girlhood dresses for her to wear at school. For William she chose a few of her father's shirts she thought might fit and a pair of Richard's trousers. Her father's work pants and overalls had long since gone to the rag bag; he had worn them hard, past what could be mended. Richard's trousers were light cotton khaki, untorn, unstained, barely worn. The day Richard left he had worn his dark expensive suit and carried a second one. Those two suits probably cost more than all the rest of the clothing in the house. Richard was never cut out for farming life.

When she came back downstairs, William and Millie had raised the heat on the stove and had two big pots of water heating. Millie chattered and danced around in her bare feet. She showed William where they kept the big galvanized washtub. Eleanor stood in the doorway and watched them. Millie seemed completely at ease with the big man, in a way Eleanor hadn't seen with Richard or John Abbott. Around those two, the little girl had watched her tongue and minded her manners, on edge, waiting for some drama or criticism. Today she was just a happy little girl playing around foolishly. William seemed more relaxed too in this setting. He lifted the big kettles off the stove with ease and poured the steaming contents into the tub, then refilled the pots from the buckets and set the empties by the door. He was handsome when he smiled, which didn't happen often she suspected. Like many folks these days, he looked like the weight of the world was on his shoulders much of the time.

Eleanor stepped into the kitchen. "Looks like you two have done a great job," she said, trying not to bring the light spirits of the room too far down. She delivered some rose scented soap to the little girl and patted her hair sweetly. She tested the water with her finger,

"Will you join me outside?" she asked William. She was polite by default. "See you in a bit, Millie." She laid the clothes and the towel on the table.

Outside the sky was blue and dotted with perfect white clouds. The air was still, her mind was not. Eleanor had thought they could sit near her irises and herbs and act as if this day was commonplace. It was not and she couldn't stay still and pretend it was. Her discomfort was like a rock on her chest. "I need to go look after something," Eleanor said, trying to make a graceful exit.

"I don't know much about farming."

That William had spoken at all surprised her. That his voice sounded so small gave her pause. He was clearly still exhausted from the trip, but he looked at her gardens, and their hill, and her father's orchards like a mystified and delighted foreigner.

Amused, she confessed, "I don't know much about farming either. Walk with me if you like."

William fell into step beside her, but keeping some distance. His damaged hand was in his pocket, his ruined face turned away from her view. They were probably close to the same age, Eleanor was nearing thirty, but they both seemed much, much older--tentative and brittle like the yellowed pages of a book that no one read. She tried to smile.

"I'm just trying to keep afloat. My father never believed in training girls to do much around the farm, other than preserve the harvest and keep the place neat and clean. I guess the joke's on him that I am the last one left. I think my father expected to live forever. It made him angry to die when he did." She realized she said too much. No question had been asked. "A New England farm is different from the big tracts out in the Midwest. Here we do a few different things and have different crops each season. We've got chickens, hogs, cows. We've got apples in the fall. We've got a big sugar wood for syrup in the spring, and fruits and vegetables in the summer."

The chickens clucked around the yard, following Eleanor hoping for some food. The milk cow and the calf nibbled grass in an enclosed pasture while a solitary horse trotted up to the fence in greeting. The barn was large and could easily accommodate many more animals. The interior was dark and cool, smelled of hay and manure. In one corner a farm truck sat covered with a dusty tarp. Overhead a loft half filled with hay ran across the back of the space. The plow, shovels, rakes, and hoes leaned up against one wall in a rack. They exited through a door at the back and went around to the hired man's quarters. This was a large room with a potbelly stove, table and three chairs, two single beds, and two bunks. The room had been vacant for a while and had the air of abandonment.

"You don't have any help?" he asked, carefully assessing the place, looking out the window and sitting on one dusty bed.

"Not this season," she said. "When the apples come in we usually have a few men to help with the picking and cider press."

As she looked around the room Eleanor couldn't help but tick the hours of work in front of her. Each invisible mark she made wore her down a little further. Each mark was a small failure; the leaking roof, the unfilled beds, the crops that withered in the fields because of lack of tending, the rust on the unused tools, the unpruned apple trees bearing only half the fruit that they should, the un-used truck that she couldn't afford to have repaired. As she continued, leading him through the property, she looked at it through a stranger's eyes. The uneven rows of brussels sprouts and broccoli, green peppers and tomatoes, the clover gone over in the backfield. The weeds everywhere. It mocked her; this farm had gone awry and had grown monstrous in its sucking needs. There was no way she could keep up with it all, even if she worked from morning until night.

"I'm sorry," she said quietly, under her breath.

William wasn't close enough to hear her. He seemed to be lost in his own thoughts. He reached down with his good hand and plucked a shiny green leaf of romaine lettuce and popped it into his mouth.

"We should get back," Eleanor said resolving once again to just face the immediate tasks in front of her, the present. "Poor Millie will be one big prune if she is still in that tub after all this time." She led them down the path at the end of the field and back toward the kitchen door.

Millie was done when they got back. She had chosen one of Caroline's old dresses tied up with a ribbon to make it fit. She smiled and twirled herself to model her outfit.

She reminded Eleanor of Caroline as a girl, pretty and competent. The world had opened up to her. Caroline was smart and clever with words and pretty and unafraid. Caroline loved to sing and dance and be the center of attention while Eleanor, the plainer sister, had played the piano in accompaniment. The girls, with Johnny telling jokes and cracking wise, were talented children, but it was clear from an early age who was the star. As the oldest, Caroline had always felt comfortable in the spotlight. Eleanor felt better in the background. Millie had Eleanor's coloring but she had her mother's flair and charisma.

"It looks very nice," Eleanor said to Millie. "Let's go do our errands and we can stop at the library on the way back if you'd like."

"Yes please!" Millie said as she hugged William and then pranced out the door in her mother's pretty dress.

"It's a good place you've got here, Miss Abbott. Real nice place," William said. Her response was interrupted by Millie's knock at the kitchen window. She had her nose pressed against the pane like a pig and her lips pursed like a fish. "We'll be back shortly," Eleanor laughed as she exited. It was good to have Millie home.

#

On the way down North Road Eleanor pried gently at Millie, trying to get more insights on the events of the Cage family's exodus since they had left three years ago. But all she could gather by the time they reached the town was that Millie had lived in five or six different places in the past three years, meaning that they had lived about six months in each location. This seemed to fit with their usual pattern. Richard Cage was a grifter, a flimflam man, a professional liar. He liked to work in one area for a while and just before he got caught they pulled up stakes and left in the night. Millie informed Eleanor that sometimes their last name was Cage, sometimes Gage, sometimes Gagnon, sometimes Cagney.

"But Cage is what it says on my birth certificate, right? So that's what I want to be at this school." She grasped Eleanor's hand and squeezed.

When John Abbott had met Richard Cage he was not

impressed. John was a simple hard-working man. The furthest he had ever traveled was seventy-five miles to Boston to buy a new plow harness and attend the symposium about crop rotation and newfangled planting techniques. He decided almost immediately that a college degree didn't confer a lick of sense when it came to growing things, but he thought that harness made the trip worthwhile. Boston seemed as foreign to him as Siam, another world, and when Richard arrived on the scene with his fancy suit and his city ways, John approached him as he would a Ming vase, pretty and expensive but relatively useless in getting things done.

Richard won his future father-in-law over through slow steady persistence. Caroline was in love from the first, in the only way a sheltered nineteen-year-old can be; with her whole heart and soul, with complete trust and abandon. As he was a guest at the Abbott family table, Richard slowly drew John in among his supporters. Without the skeptical reasoning offered by his wife, Eleanor's mother who had passed two winters prior, and still mourning the more recent loss of his son Johnny, Eleanor's father was susceptible to a glittering dream dangled by a smooth talking man.

In 1921 there was still talk of a railroad connector line to the Boston and Albany Railroad that ran through the center of the state. A railroad meant progress, industry, opportunity, and jobs. Given the topography of the landscape, options for the route the tracks could take were limited. Some folks, whose land was in the right place, would flourish; others would shrivel as the world would pass them by. Richard Cage understood the world of possibilities and promises. In a town made up of farmers and craftsmen, he seemed like the natural choice to lead a consortium of investors. He was shrewd and well dressed. His involvement with the Abbott farm lent him an air of trustworthiness that time would prove he hadn't deserved. He held meetings at the town hall, armed with a prospectus so thick with fine print that no one found time to read it. If they had, they would have seen that Richard and a silent partner had sole control of any proceeds and expenditures of the endeavor. Investors would only receive a share if the project reached certain elusive milestones. As deadlines were missed, and no railroad appeared, further examination showed that the initial investments the townsfolk had contributed had been eaten up by various administrative fees--consultations, travel costs, and miscellaneous expenses.

"Better luck next time," Richard said. "There is risk inherent in any investment, you realize that."

Of course they hadn't realized the risk, but were too proud to admit their ignorance.

Eleanor was seventeen at the time and still dreamed that someday she would have a husband as smart and handsome as Richard Cage. In her heart for a long time she believed he had been misled, just like the rest of the town and needed her aid and compassion. She gave it by helping Richard and Caroline pack up their things and leave in the middle of the night.

#

As they neared the bottom of North Road, Millie caught sight of the small jungle gym and tall metal slide at the side of the school house. She knew the playground was here, of course; Millie had been visiting Hemford intermittently all her life and had played here many times. But their approach today was the first time she came with the expectation that she would attend class here in the fall.

"Swings!" she yelled with proprietary volume as she raced ahead toward the gnarled, broad oak. There two flat boards were attached to the branches with sturdy, weathered rope. Millie took the swing furthest from the road and, after pushing off with one leg, began to pump furiously. She soon achieved a height over the top of Eleanor's head. "Come on and join me, Eleanor. I know you know how," she cajoled and then let out a howl like a wolf.

School was not in session and the yard was deserted. Eleanor walked, not ran, but she took a seat on the swing next to Millie. She twirled at an idle pace, enjoying the sounds of mourning doves and rustling leaves. Millie cackled with laughter.

Eleanor had rarely visited the school since becoming an adult, no need. She remembered it though, as she approached with Millie, in a deep way she hadn't expected. She recalled the precise location of her girlhood desk, the smell of chalk, and the aching disappointment when circumstance didn't allow her to continue her studies. Eleanor had been a good student, but the farm had needs. The school was a plain wooden structure painted a mustard brown, straight and symmetrical with a white bell cupola on the top to call the children to school. Inside were two identical rooms, a nod to the town's population growth a decade ago, one for the upper grades, one for the lower, each with a blackboard displaying the lessons and desks radiating back in straight rows.

"What's all this?" a voice called from toward the front of the building, clearly displeased. Eliza Willoughby had been a year behind Eleanor at school, her brother Johnny's peer. They hadn't been close friends, but growing up in the limited social circles of a very small town, they knew each other from young children. Eleanor rose quickly from the swing and remembered that Eliza had gotten married a few years back to one of the Baxter boys. She smoothed down her dress and forced a smile.

Eleanor hoped that her hesitancy didn't communicate to

Millie. She wanted the little girl to enter this building as confident as she was right now. Eliza Willoughby had been quite young when Richard Cage had last swept through town, but her father had lost a lot of money and died of a heart attack soon after. Eleanor hoped that she still retained some of that blissful ignorance of youth.

"Millie, come on down here and say hello, please." Eleanor took a step forward and extended her hand in greeting. That her handshake wasn't immediately taken did not escape Eleanor's notice. She persisted, holding polite civility in the air between them.

"Eleanor," Eliza Willoughby Baxter droned. Her voice was an octave lower than normal and laced with derision. "Who do we have here?"

Eleanor wanted to flee, wanted to take Millie far away, but she stood her ground. "Millie, Mrs. Baxter will be your teacher in the fall. Eliza, you remember Caroline's daughter."

"Oooh!" Millie exclaimed as she executed a deep curtsy. Her hair was mussed and little beads of sweat spotted the bridge of her nose, but she presented herself like a princess. "I'm so pleased to meet you, Mrs. Baxter! I finished fourth grade. Almost. I was in the advanced reading group. And the advanced math group. Penmanship is my weakest subject. My last teacher said I needed to slow down and focus, but that is terribly difficult for me. Terribly difficult."

Eleanor had expected icy criticism from Eliza Baxter in light of their shared family histories but all lingering bitterness melted in the warmth of Millie's contagious enthusiasm.

"Nice to see you again, Millie. I knew you when you were just a baby. I can see you are going to be an asset to our classroom this year. Would you like me to show you around?" She took the little girl's hand and led her inside.

Eleanor was forgotten. She was grateful to be ignored and sat on the wooden bench near the door resting in the sun until Millie burst through the front door.

"They have a shark's tooth! A real one! It's so sharp it could almost cut your finger right off."

"Dangerous," Eleanor said with a smile.

"Not really. I was careful," Millie assured her.

Eliza Baxter was unprepared for the hug launched at her midsection, but she recovered quickly and rubbed her hands against Millie's head."I'll see you at the beginning of September," she said before going back inside.

Eleanor and Millie continued down the road to the general store. Main Street Mercantile sold foodstuffs and dry goods. It was a tall building, whitewashed, with the store on the first floor and the shopkeeper's rooms upstairs. This time of year pots of red geraniums and trailing blue lobelia decorated the front porch. The heavy front door was open to let in the warm afternoon air. The interior now boasted electricity, a recent addition, and the store was unevenly lit with flares of glaring light surrounded by pockets of shadows. A long wooden counter ran along the west wall with a gleaming brass cash register at one end. The register looked like it belonged in a much grander place; the rear panel was bas-relief of an eagle grasping an olive branch in its talon and a flowing ribbon in its beak. The numbers were elegant italic font on high glassed-in buttons and it rang a robust, cheery bell as each transaction was completed.

Eleanor set her basket of eggs to sell on the counter. Millie had disappeared into the back corner of the store. Eleanor found her looking at the bolts of colorful cotton cloth. She had selected a fiery red print with blue flowers and unwrapped a few feet from the bolt. Millie held the fabric up in front of herself, sashaying in her makeshift skirt.

"That's pretty, isn't it?" Eleanor asked as she approached. She hadn't had much use for her sewing machine lately; she was too tired at the end of the night to work on the quilt she had begun. It would be nice to have something new for Millie. Maybe she could even teach the little girl to sew; Lord knows Caroline never took to it. She wondered if her niece would. Millie had always excelled at fine work; puzzles and drawing and such. Of course Eleanor hadn't seen or spoken to Millie for three years, forever in a child's short life.

"Oh yes," Millie said dreamily. Eleanor plucked the bolt from the barrel where it rested with others: orange, pink, pale mint green.

Millie quickly turned nervous and embarrassed. She spoke in a quiet voice. "It's very nice, but I don't need it. I can make do."

"Of course you can make do," Eleanor said smoothly, "But you don't need to." She was filled with anger at Richard and Caroline for a lifetime of extravagances that didn't extend to their own child. She knew that her dearly departed sister was one of the most selfish people to walk the earth and her husband was no better. Eleanor would give anything she had to buy Millie a hundred dresses if it removed the hurt from her niece's eyes. She could easily afford to buy enough fabric to make one.

"What I've already got is plenty. I have much more than some people do."

Eleanor looked down at the dress Millie was wearing. In addition to it being too big, Caroline's old dress was impractical and ill-suited to life on a farm. The color was a buttery yellow, trimmed with white. Already the lace at the hem showed a dirty tear from Millie's vigorous play. The fabric itself was fine and nearly sheer with a slight sheen. Eleanor glanced at her own reflection in a small mirror on the wall. Her dress was brown--the color of dust, or wheat, or hay. The texture was rough, one step away from the feed sacks delivered with grain for the hogs.

Eleanor held the colorful material to her chest. Millie looked at it longingly and whispered, "I do have a few pennies."

Leaning down to speak into Millie's ear she said, "Here, we pay with eggs! You'll help me with the chickens, won't you?"

"Yes, Ma'am!"

Eleanor set the fabric, a few candles, a packet of needles, and some coordinating thread on the counter. "Eleanor," Mrs. Jensen greeted as she carried some bags from the stockroom in back. She was a sturdy woman, very short and nearly round. She cooed over the eggs as she caressed one in her palm. "Eleanor, your eggs are always the best in town."

"I get to help with the chickens!" Millie said. She scanned the store for future purchases. Millie and Mrs. Jensen fell into easy conversation about animals and summer plans. When Mrs. Jensen inquired about Caroline, Millie gave what Eleanor was learning was a programmed, practiced response. "My mother is with the angels now." She rarely said anything different in explanation. Eleanor resolved to let it rest.

Eleanor offered no commentary, just a smile. As the day wore on she was increasingly distracted and everything was tinged with a pervasive, low grade anxiety; William Hart, Millie, Richard Cage all grappled in her head to the exclusion of all other mundane conversation. Mrs. Jensen looked concerned but made no comment. She simply counted the eggs, made in notes in her account book, and put the smaller items in the empty egg basket. She unrolled a little fabric from the bolt. "How much will you need?"

"Three yards, please," Eleanor answered.

"It's for a dress for me!" Millie almost squealed.

Mrs. Jensen laid it along the counter yardstick and cut it with a long heavy pair of black handled scissors. She wrote the total in her account book and slid it back into the drawer. "Always nice to have children around, isn't it?" she said to Eleanor before returning to the stockroom with a wink and a wave for Millie as she left.

When they were younger, Eleanor and Mrs. Jensen's daughter, Teresa, were fast friends. Eleanor spent many afternoons upstairs in the Jensen apartment playing dolls or playing dominoes. She liked to go there on rainy days because of the echo of the rain on the roof. They lay on Teresa's bed and daydreamed of the handsome men they would marry when they were grown.

On sunny days they wandered up North Road after school picking wildflowers on the edge of the road as they walked. They presented these grand bouquets of weeds to Eleanor's mother who always smiled as if it were a prize fit for a queen.

"Orchids," Sarah Abbott would pronounce. "Roses, gardenias, frangipani," she would exaggerate each syllable, rolling her consonants as she plunged her nose into goldenrod, dandelions, and purple loosestrife. The girls collapsed into giggles pretending they had all types of glamorous flowers they could hardly imagine.

Eleanor and Teresa were inseparable as children and most nights dinner would have a place set for the extra daughter at one house or the other. Caroline, as the older sister, always set herself apart; her sights were on loftier goals. The year that Caroline met Richard, Teresa found her own handsome husband and the next year moved over to Indian Orchard to his family's farm.

Millie didn't say much on the way back up North Road, not

even to comment on the abundance of shelf mushrooms on a fallen log, not even to admire a heart-shaped rock that Eleanor put in her pocket. As they neared the house Jessup meandered out to greet them, but even he didn't race or bark. The excitement of novelty exhausted them all despite the joy of reunion. Eleanor longed for the quiet of routine. Tonight they would all drink chamomile tea. Well, she and Millie would; William Hart's course remained undetermined.

## CHAPTER SEVEN
William on the Farm

William enjoyed being alone. More than that, he required long periods of solitude to maintain his sanity. He disliked small-talk even before the war, but after he came home, it was almost painful. He thought about his face and his unwillingness to subject others to it. He thought about the ridiculous things that most people wanted to talk about. He could tolerate conversation for a little while, but sooner or later his mind drifted, usually to somewhere unpleasant. Better to stay busy, and alone. Here on the Abbott holdings, he was miles away from another person.

After he finished his bath, he emptied the tub and put on the clean clothes that Eleanor had provided. He set aside the clothes he had arrived in; it was likely that Scarecrow's blood would never be completely eradicated. The shirt fit him well, soft cotton in a somber green plaid. The pants were practically new and a little too loose. He pulled his belt through loops and fastened the buckle. In the left front pocket he felt the crisp coolness of currency. It was a twenty-dollar bill, a fortune to someone like Eleanor after the crash, but apparently inconsequential to the owner of the trousers. He folded it back up and tucked it in under the canister for salt where she would find it.

The farm made him itch. It was like the missing parts of him could see the work threatening to swamp the place and were eager to take some action. William sometimes felt his missing fingers. In his dreams he was always whole. When he petted Eleanor's dog Jessup or his old landlady's cat he always felt his hand all the way to his pinky. The softness of the fur seemed to activate his memories and while he stroked the animal and closed his eyes he could pretend he was all still there. For hours after he liked to exercise them; pointing or putting on an invisible ring.

With his missing eye he felt philosophical. He felt that he could see things as they ought to be; people with jobs and food, Millie reunited with her family, Eleanor's farm set to rights. He sat in the kitchen chair and closed his good eye and looked through the deadeye to see wood chopped and neatly stacked by the barn, he could see trees red with apples, fields full, green, and lush and the vines bent with the weight of the fruit, the barn noisy with livestock.

And he saw himself in the image, whole and handsome again, with a smiling Eleanor at his side while Millie played in a big pile of autumn leaves.

He didn't know anything about farming, but even an amateur knew that the Abbott farm was not as it should be. He didn't even know how to begin mending things. What he did understand was wood. On the near side of the barn were three cords of firewood. It was good quality, hickory and maple mostly with a little bit of oak mixed in, but in chunks too big to be of any use. It had been here a while and little sprouts of grass and weeds sprang up between the pieces. It was a massive amount of unusable debris right now. Once split, chopped, and stacked it would heat the house for the winter. Against the side of the barn only a few pieces of wood lay atop a layer of pea stone for drainage. As it was, this huge pile was just an eyesore.

In the barn he found an ax, a mallet and a splitting wedge. All the tools were good quality. Everything was old but well maintained and sharp. The mallet had a new handle a few years back. Right now the tools were guarded by spider webs and cobwebs. He wiped everything off and hefted the weight of the tools. He practiced a swing outside. He had grown up around trees and tools, but he hadn't wielded an ax since he had come back from France. He suspected that his damaged hand would throw off his swing and he decided the mallet would be a safer choice for this experiment.

The right hand went higher up on the handle and applied most of the force. The left hand, the half hand, applied some force and helps with guidance, a rudder. He gave a few tentative swings, warmed up the muscles in his shoulder and back. It felt different then he remembered, but soon he was used to it and he was ready to get into the meditative rhythm of the wood pile.

He didn't see a chopping block. Usually once you found a log sturdy enough and even you saved it for the season. Not dissuaded, he selected a big round chunk of oak about the right size and he rolled, tipped, and dragged it to an even place in the yard. Once he was satisfied that it wouldn't tip or rock under pressure, he selected a good sized chunk and set the wedge. This too had to be relearned for the missing fingers, but he soon had the hang of it.

The clang of the steel mallet hitting the steel wedge reverberated in the air. He lifted the heavy oak handle with a mighty mallet head to above his shoulder, lifted it over his head and let it fall, ringing metal on metal, lifted again, then fall, the ring of steel--lift, fall, ring. The key to splitting was regulated speed. The rhythm could work in your favor if you timed it right. It became almost a dance, meditation, like saying your prayers. After three good hits the wood split in half with a satisfying rip. Each piece clattered to the ground and if it were small enough for Eleanor to handle, he tossed it into a smaller pile to be stacked. The larger pieces returned to the stump and were split again. He kept this rhythm lift, fall, ring, toss for a good while. He wasn't a person to wear a watch, he woke with the sun and worked until it was done or somebody told him to stop.

His shoulder started to sting from the motion, so he moved to stacking. Wood left on the ground was susceptible to rot. Also wood left on the ground would be covered with snow come winter, making it hard to get to and hard to get burning once you got it to the stove.

William liked stacking. It was like a puzzle, each log had a place it wanted to be. He rotated each piece to stay where it would fit snug with a minimum gap from the piece next to it. As he worked, the motion came back to him, natural as breathing. He grasped and turned and set and the mosaic he made grew ever taller.

He contemplated nothing more trying than the bite of the ax head through the wood. It was the same motion as with the mallet and wedge, but a little easier as he didn't have to navigate holding the wedge at first. The ax was also a little lighter and he was able to speed the motion. He liked how he felt the bites of the ax directly into the wood.

He moved to the stacking again, quicker this time. His back and shoulder would be sore tonight. The last job he had was over a month ago at a toolmaker's warehouse packing hammers, wrenches, and saws into boxes and loading these into trucks. Even when times were bad, a willing laborer was always in demand.

He was stacking wood, making a game of it by seeing how quick he could do it and still have it packed tight when Millie and Eleanor came up the hill.

"Like Paul Bunyan!" Millie laughed. "We saw you with the ax

from way down there. You chop so fast! Is it sharp?" She approached the tool cautiously, sensibly, and touched the blade with her fingertip.

"A good ax is supposed to be sharp," he said, and reached over her to get the shirt he had removed while he was working. He was dripping with sweat and grateful for the cool breeze. He wiped his brow with his shirt before he buttoned it up.

"Millie Cage, you soar like a hawk." Eleanor was out of breath as she tried to match Millie's pace up the hill. "Oh my," she sighed as she saw the knee-high stack of wood that spanned the length of the barn. "Millie, use some of that energy to go fetch Mr. Hart some water. He must be parched."

Millie stopped and saluted and raced down to the house.

"Bring the yellow pitcher," Eleanor yelled behind her. Millie waved one hand but didn't slow a bit.

"I can't pay you," she said with seriousness. It pained her to say this. She looked down at her shoe. She turned to look toward the house as if urging Millie's return. So serious, this Eleanor, it was like she was always waiting for something to be wrong, to be scolded, to be disappointed. In truth, he would have paid her to chop this wood. When he looked back over the past few hours, he realized that this was the most content he had been in a long while. He looked forward to chopping more tomorrow. If she would let him. He wondered at their strange pairing of expectations.

Eleanor couldn't stand the silence. She had run out of nervous little ways to fill the time. "I mean, I have only a very little bit of money. I don't mean to imply that I would cheat you. I appreciate your work. I don't see how I could have managed."

"Don't worry. We can work something out," he said with a chuckle. He was looking forward to chopping wood; if he had said that as a kid he would have been carted off to the nut house.

Eleanor wheeled around to face him. Her face blanched and her nostrils flared with anger, then the anger faded to defeat. She looked at the massive mound of unusable wood behind her and the smaller pieces stacked neatly against the barn. She looked small then, frail, and tiny, like she was paper thin and could be blown away in the wind.

#

When that firewood arrived her father was still alive, but ailing. Most afternoons he took to his bed in the back room right after lunch and didn't emerge until the next day. Most people knew he was sick; they no longer came around as much to talk to him, but still on the face of things, John Abbott continued to be very much in charge.

He had ordered the wood as usual, in the spring when the memory of the previous winter was still fresh in his mind. The year before he had ordered too much and the winter was mild and so they had burned it slower. Eleanor had used this miscalculation to her advantage and utilized what was left over while her father was so sick and could no longer help. This load of wood arrived in late September with Billy Harris, whose father owned a store in town. That day Billy was helping Mrs. Hanson from over in Munroe. The Abbotts had known old Pete Hanson very well, Eleanor remembered the silly black dog who rode up front in the wagon, right up on Mr. Hanson's lap as he tried to steer. When old Mr. Hanson brought wood, he always brought a piece of molasses candy for the children; Billy Harris came only with a sneer and an air of superiority. He had lost some money playing poker with Richard and he had a crush on Caroline. He had taken it badly when she married an outsider. Billy felt that the world, especially the Abbotts, owed him something.

That fall Billy Harris had driven up the hill with his team of four strong horses, his helper, Charlie, a wagon full of wood, and a bad attitude.

"I'm sorry to hear your father's taken ill," he said, not really sorry. Billy had gotten fatter since she had last seen him. His cheeks were distended like a squirrel gathering seeds and the buttons of his vest strained against his expanding girth.

"I guess the sickness made him forgetful," Billy said, not coming down to talk face-to-face. He towered over her. "He forgot to pay me to unload the wagon."

The way he said it made Eleanor think instantly of goldenseal root. It was a gnarled and twisted rhizome that grew in dark and shady corners. When you broke it open, it left a bright yellow stain on your fingers. It was a powerful medicine for colds and certain stomach problems but it had a harsh and bitter taste that nothing could mask. Eleanor could barely swallow it and she couldn't stand the smell. She knew whatever he said next was going to be bad, but they needed that wood.

He reached down and gave her a handwritten bill. The writing was sloppy, like a young child, big block print with a mixture of capital and small letters in no apparent pattern. The sum at the bottom far exceeded the money she had left.

"Is that going to be a problem?" Billy Harris asked. He looked away from her, averted his eyes. When old Mr. Hanson was alive, he and her father had done business without a scrap of paper between them. They shook hands like men, balanced transactions over a long-term relationship of trust. Now Pete Hanson was dead and John Abbott nearly so and it had all come down to Eleanor relying on the good sense of an overgrown boy who had none.

"I could make payments," Eleanor said, trying to sound confident.

"No credit. Richard taught me that," he said her brother-in-law's name like it was made of sawdust.

"You could have one of the hogs when we butcher it," she said.

"No."

His smile made her inexplicably queasy. It spread across his face like mud. There was no brightness or life in his expression, instead it was the face of a schoolboy who had lied to his teacher and gotten away with it.

"Go get lost for a while, Charlie," he said to his helper. Charlie Mitchum was a little bit simple. He was strong and tall like a man, but more like a child in temperament and intellect. She had never known Charlie to be knowingly cruel, but his size and lack of sense made him clumsy and rough sometimes. Affably, he grabbed his tobacco pouch and his fishing pole and headed back to the pond to look for catfish. "Come back when I holler and not before," Billy Harris said.

He jumped off the wagon as soon as Charlie had faded from sight. As uncomfortable as Eleanor was at his being so high above her, him standing on the ground was worse. Up close she could hear Billy Harris chomping his teeth up and down with agitation. He shifted from foot to foot like he had to urinate.

"Eleanor, I think we can work something out," Billy Harris said. He was a short man, now grown fat, so he would look like an egg with beady eyes before too long. He tried to add to his stature by being cruel and dominant, like a rooster bossing and fussing all over the yard. Eleanor knew she had no champions now. No options. She would have to agree to whatever "something" Billy Harris had in mind. The thought made her feel sick.

Before she could question or speak he grabbed her hard by the arm. Before she could react or protest he pulled her behind him to the barn. He swung the heavy red wooden door shut behind them. The interior was warm, and the air was close. Flies covered a pile of manure in an un-mucked stall.

In that moment she was two people. No, in that moment she was more like half a person. She was barely her physical self; Billy's rough fingers digging into her flash, her feet stumbling as he hauled her behind him, the feel of the straw as it scratched her knees. The part of her that baked, that brought her father soup, that nurtured, or loved, or respected herself – that part floated above Eleanor like a thin film of smoke.

When it came, she was only vaguely aware of Billy fumbling with his trousers, then the sensation of her mouth being filled to the point of gagging suffocation, then his hands pressing hard at her hair.

She hardly heard him say, "You're almost as pretty as your sister."

When it was over, she sat in the far back of the stall and listened as Billy called Charlie and the two men threw the wood down in a tremendous pile. From her place in the barn, the walls rattled and shook as a thousand pounds of wood rained down in the yard. It was like an avalanche and Eleanor was both the body buried beneath and the cloud of dust left behind.

#

"Wait," William started toward her. She took an instinctive step backward, away from him. "Whatever you think I said, I didn't. The wood is no problem. Really."

Over her shoulder he heard the slam of the kitchen screen door and saw Millie carrying a big pitcher of water in her two hands. She had three mugs looped over her fingers. The assemblage was awkward and the water was heavy for the little girl. In her eagerness she walked as fast as she could and even from this distance he could see the water sloshing over the top of the vessel with each step.

"Help!" came the plaintiff cry from down the drive. "This is really heavy." Eleanor hurried down toward the house to assist with Millie's burden. She glanced back at William, then looked immediately away. When they returned to the barn, Eleanor had tamped down any trace of emotion and beamed a serene smile at her niece.

Millie presented him with a mug and a curtsy before setting the other mugs on the chopping block and racing back toward the back door, leaving Eleanor and William alone once again.

"I...," he started to speak after downing a cool glass of water.

"I'm being foolish," Eleanor said abruptly, though clearly something had upset her. William had spent the past dozen years in the company of men and machines. Or alone. He had offended or distressed her, but wasn't sure how. He stood there speechless as the sweat from his labors dried on his back. He looked longingly at the wood waiting to be chopped.

"Just foolish memories inside my own head," Eleanor said. She had turned solemn and was clearly trying to allay some demons known only to her. She took her cup of water to stand over near the paddock under the big chestnut tree. She turned away from him and talked exclusively to the horse, who wandered over to have his nose scratched.

William came up next to her on the rail, close enough to speak quietly, yet just out of reach in case Eleanor decided she needed to swat him for something. "I'm sorry I said something out of line, ma'am.

Actions are much easier for me than words. Sorry for my misstep."

She looked as if she might cry. "Foolishness inside my own head," she repeated. "You've done nothing wrong. I just need a moment. Please. Before Millie gets back."

He nodded and retreated, unclear about the benefit of any other course of action. He picked up the ax again.

Millie came backwards out of the kitchen door with a painted wooden tray in her outstretched hands. On the tray rested several plates sliding gently back and forth as she walked. All her concentration was focused on delivering her assortment. She bit her bottom lip in the effort not to send anything scattering, as did Eleanor in support from her place at the fence post. They were a matched set, two pretty girls in cotton dresses just below the knee, warm brown hair, cut short in a bob pulled back on one side with a pin. Eleanor wasn't beautiful; Millie would be a stunner when she was grown, but she was attractive and strong. She was a little thin right now, tired in a way that just a good night's sleep couldn't cure. Eleanor Abbott was worn, weary, burdened, and overwhelmed.

Millie and Eleanor shared the same expression of deep intense determination. William's first instinct was to jump up and handle it, balance it, but he suspected that neither of them would appreciate his intervention. He bided his time, set down the ax, and had another cup of water.

"Picnic!" Millie declared as she set the tray on a sunny patch of grass right between them. William smiled at this small twist; Millie was always the conciliator without even meaning to. She had assembled a plate of biscuits with a little pot of jam, some molasses cookies, hard-boiled eggs, and an unopened jar of bread and butter pickles.

He had built an appetite as he worked and now his stomach grumbled involuntarily at the sight of food. Back in Chicago, even for someone who had money, there was a feeling of scarcity, a few less choices, and slightly smaller portions. In the air there was seemed to always be the threat that this would be your last meal for a while and it might be wise to save some for later in case you needed it. He knew this food didn't come easy, someone had to work to make this bounty possible. He knew just how Millie felt when she wandered into Eleanor's full pantry. It felt possible that everything would be okay.

"The library here is small but I found a copy of Black Beauty. I read it before but it's good and so sad at the beginning." Millie talked with her mouth full and rarely paused. She commented on the jam, (blueberry), and the eggs, (Eleanor had boiled a few yesterday morning), as crumbs rained down on the skirt of her dress. Millie took her shoes off and wiggled her toes in the grass, then redirected her attention to eating and struggled to open the jar of pickles which she handed off to William while she urged Eleanor to eat a cookie.

"They're delicious," Millie was firm and pressed one into Eleanor's hand. "Cookies are meant to be enjoyed."

Eleanor had barely spoken since she sat down. She nibbled around the edges of the sweet. The cookies were good, crisp and buttery, with a thin layer of icing. William had eaten one without thinking, gobbled in two greedy bites, but as he watched, Eleanor approached hers as if under the burden of a great sadness and regret.

"Hey Millie, we need a fork or something to fish these pickles out".

"Oops," she sprang up and set off toward the house, pausing to do a cart wheel on the grass on her way to the door.

"Eleanor," he started, then started again. "Miss Abbott. I get ahead of myself sometimes. The wood was there. I chopped some. I wasn't thinking. I should have checked with you first."

"Don't be silly," she cut him off. "The wood wasn't doing anyone any good as it was. My thoughts went elsewhere. I appreciate all you've done." Her cheeks were flushed and her lips were pale. She looked like she wanted to rage or scream but felt she couldn't. She sat primly on the other side of Millie's picnic, spine straight, legs pressed tightly together.

William saw it then, the fear and the disgust. She had been hurt. He felt his own anger springing to her defense. "I'm sorry," he said, even as he knew his sentiment made no difference. He struggled to calm his heartbeat and realized he had no help to offer her; she alone was tied to this private, onerous past. "I was happy for some work."

"Millie and I sincerely appreciate it," she said, rising slowly from the ground as Millie pounced back to them. She brushed off the back of her dress and popped the last of her cookie into Millie's mouth. "I've got chores. Tomorrow, young lady, I'll show you how to gather the eggs and look after the chickens. Make sure you straighten this up when you go inside." She kissed the little girl on the top of her head and left barely acknowledging William beyond a small smile and a nod of the head.

He lay back on the grass while Millie fed him pickles, identifying each chunk as she presented it to him: cucumber, cauliflower, onion, and zucchini. The vegetables were crisp and the brine was a mix of sweet and sour. With his good eye closed, through his dead eye, he tried to see the possibilities. At this moment he couldn't, he could only listen to Millie tell him about her new school, feel the sun on his face, hear the lows of the cows and distant slow clang of a somber bell. The air felt heavy, telling him there might be rain tonight.

From the interior of the barn came a great clatter of tools with an outraged cry. William was up in seconds as the muttering continued to echo in the near empty barn.

"I'll see to that," he said gesturing toward the barn. "You go ahead and bring the tray inside. You spread a good picnic, Millie. Thank you."

He hustled into the barn to find Eleanor on the ground gathering up an arm full of dropped stakes and a hoe from the floor. He bent to pick up the implement that had fallen nearest.

"Thank you," she grasped the stake from him and turned to exit the barn. He could see she had been crying.

"Miss Abbott...

She didn't turn, didn't speak. She left with the awkward items and walked toward the back garden without looking back his way.

William went outside and the picnic was gone. The water pitcher and a single mug sat in the afternoon shade at the edge of the barn. He went back to the mound of wood, lifted a big heavy log on the block, set the wedge, lifted the mallet, and let the metal sing.

He worked through the afternoon lost in the rhythm of what was in front of him. The pace he set didn't allow any space for thoughts. He didn't see or know anything beyond the knowledge of how the sound of oak falling on the ground was different from the sound of the maple. He paused periodically to drink and wipe the sweat off his face, then returned immediately before any idle thoughts or pondering could creep in.

Millie came up behind him, not jumping or talking or singing. "Eleanor says to come in for dinner. Wash up at the pump first she says." He took a minute to bring the tools in and set them in their place.

The air felt cooler now and gray clouds congealed in the sky. Millie was his shadow, carrying the heavy wedge behind him. She let it drop with a thud to the hay below the tool rack.

"Eleanor says you're leaving soon," Millie said as she trailed behind William out to the paddock to bring the horse in. "Come on, Chester," she said to the reluctant animal and reached up to grab his halter. "We've got carrots."

William realized he didn't know what to do with the horse other than protect him from the rain. Millie seemed to, so he followed her lead, standing dumbly behind the little girl and the sway backed horse. "Get some water," she said as if this were obvious. He went to the pump to wash his face and hands and filled a bucket. She took it from him and set it in the corner, closed the stall, and pulled a carrot from a basket near the door. "Good night Chester," she said and took William's hand, his good hand, and led him toward the house.

"Are you really leaving soon?" she asked him again.

"Probably leave eventually." This response didn't satisfy either of them but they let it stand for now. They walked down to the house, silently and hand in hand.

In the kitchen Eleanor had laid the table with plates, cups, and cutlery. In the center of the table a steaming chicken pie waited to be devoured. Creamy gravy bubbled up through the starburst of slits cut into the golden brown crust. The savory dinner was baked in a cobalt blue pottery casserole dish. She had set a little vase of white flowers at the end of the table between a matched set of candlesticks sparkling against the darkening night. It was like a small piece of art, a still life in a painting.

Millie slid happily into her seat. "This looks pretty and it smells so good."

They bowed their heads in a simple prayer. Eleanor intoned it by rote and Millie swung her feet and bumped them against the rungs of her chair. William put his hand on her leg to stop the pendulum. "Hush and sit still," he said.

Eleanor cut into the dish with a big metal spoon. She served William first, a big portion, then Millie an amount she could probably just finish. The steaming gravy expanded into an ever widening puddle across his plate. In it were chunks of potatoes, chicken, carrots, onions, and peas. It was perfectly seasoned with salt and pepper and herbs from the big garden near the kitchen door. She served herself a portion that would barely keep a bird alive. She picked at it, spearing each individual pea. He guessed that if she were here alone she wouldn't have prepared anything at all.

"Mrs. Baxter says I need some pencils so I can practice my penmanship. She said it was very nice but there was room for improvement. I told her that poetry is my favorite and she said it was hers too!" Millie chattered on about her teacher and all the new friends she would make. Eleanor relaxed and William stayed silent as he cleaned his plate. Without asking, Eleanor heaped another scoop for him.

"Eleanor, did you know that William slept in the barn last night? The barn! He should stay in Uncle Johnny's room. Don't you think?" When neither Eleanor nor William replied Millie explained to William, "He's dead, you know. He died before I was even born! Influenza."

"I think Mr. Hart would be more comfortable in the hired man's quarters. He'll have a little more privacy out there, don't you think, Millie?" Eleanor said.

"Oh boy! I wish I could stay out there. You get your own

stove and table. And," she paused for dramatic effect, "you can sleep on the top bunk!"

"I think I'll keep my feet on the floor, Millie. Thank you Miss Abbott, that will be fine."

#

Eleanor was home when her brother Johnny died. So was her sister Caroline, though she drifted in and out of the house like a leaf on the breeze. At the end, all three of the Abbott siblings were huddled in Johnny's narrow bed. That last week in his small room the temperature fluctuated between freezing cold and suffocating heat. Eleanor felt that the bracing air of late October would bring the freshness of outside into the house and aid her brother's beleaguered lungs. Caroline felt the heat held in by the panes of the closed windows and a warmed soapstone at the foot of his bed would ease Johnny's aching muscles. Neither remedy turned out to be right but the girls felt better for the effort.

Johnny had gotten sick like any other teen-aged boy--sore scratchy throat and a runny, congested nose. But it had been a damp cold fall and several of the animals had been ill or injured. Johnny spent more nights in the barn than in his own bed that last long September.

"Don't be crazy," Johnny said when Eleanor fussed at him at him to come inside. "It's warm enough in the barn with the breath of all those creatures. And the hay! Plus you know I need to be able to monitor that sow with the bum leg and if I'm down here at the house I won't be able to hear her if she's in trouble. You know we're expecting her next litter to be champions."

It all made sense. Johnny's arguments were logical. He was the youngest of the Abbott children, Eleanor's junior by a year and a half, but he already seemed more adult and responsible than his sisters. He was funny and friendly, yes, but never at the expense of his duties to the animals. He had an affinity, a gift, and they, even the goats, obeyed him and went willingly wherever he wanted them to go. When it came to the stock, their father was in agreement with Johnny's every decision. These animals were the future of the farm. Everybody knew that.

Their mother died a year ago, but had she still been alive, she would not have allowed it. She would have observed that Johnny wasn't eating as much as he normally did and that he seemed a little pale. She would have seen that his cough, hacking and persistent, was not subsiding. Sarah Abbott would have kept her son home, tucked up tight near her cook stove so she could feed him soup and drown him in garlic and ginger tea. He would be commanded to nap each afternoon with his chest smeared with mustard plaster and wrapped in flannel. Peppermint oil and camphor would have been rubbed on the soles of his feet.

When Eleanor, age sixteen, noticed that Johnny's cough had turned to a rattle and a wheeze, his fever had already started to rage. A hand placed on his forehead found him to be burning up, but Eleanor was unsure of how to proceed.

Dr. Benson had sterile, modern medicine and suggestions, but these did not surpass the folk remedies that Eleanor knew to try. "It's a pity your mother wasn't here," he said. "She was a kind woman and a great healer. I consulted her myself many times over the years."

Eleanor felt the lump in her throat swell to the size of a hubbard squash. Caroline stood next to her in the parlor, under the ticking clock, and took her hand. Eleanor didn't expect any touch or kindness. Tears streamed down her sister's face in untempered rivers. Caroline's hand was cool and as soft as dusting powder.

Their mother was not there and Johnny was sick. Nothing they had attempted made things better. Nobody offered useful suggestions. Eleanor prayed at her brother's bedside but she was alone in the act. Her father had abandoned religion and Caroline was lost in her own thoughts and wouldn't even sit or close her eyes; she stared out the window at the cascading leaves. Eleanor felt like her voice was impossibly small. In the end, Johnny died a gasping shell of a boy, with one sister on either side of him on his narrow bed. Their father was out attending to the stock.

#

Eleanor pushed her food around on her plate, eating only when Millie turned to face her, half a bite of potato, a sliver of carrot. Millie didn't understand the subtleties of propriety. A single woman couldn't have a man sleeping under her roof, no matter how spacious the house was. Was this the cause of her discomfort? William didn't think so, but he also couldn't ask. Some things would remain a mystery for the foreseeable future.

He wondered at her lack of support here. In small towns one would expect a spirit of community allegiance. Millie had expected her grandfather to be here but learned that the old man had died last winter. He would have expected upon the death of the patriarch and sole farmer, the town would step up and lend a hand. There wasn't much hard currency flowing, but she hadn't even hired someone to come work in exchange for room and board which was common these days.

Millie had eaten her fill and Eleanor took the opportunity to declare the meal done. She took her plate and Millie's and cleared their portion of the table. William scrambled to finish his dinner before she returned and took his plate away too.

"Okay, my dear," she said to Millie. "There are some new

pencils in the tall chest in the front parlor so you can practice. I've got to see to poor Blossom before she bursts with milk, I'll be back in a bit and you can read to me or I will read to you before bed."

"All right," Millie said. "What should William do?"

"He's grown," Eleanor answered. "I'm sure he'll find some way to entertain himself for a few hours." She didn't even look at him.

Millie and the dog accompanied him back to the woodpile, but they quickly became bored and wandered off. The sun was low in the west and showing the first smudges of pink between the gathering clouds at the far edge of the sky. He went back to work to straighten his head. Lift, fall, clang, rip,throw, then stack, stack, stack. Wood didn't have an agenda, it never failed to communicate, made no demands, and had no expectations. It just sat and waited to become useful. As he worked through the pile he found last season's chopping block. It was the trunk of a tree with the roots still in the ground. It was broad, flat, and the size of the tabletop. It had ax marks from last season, maybe even from multiple years in the past. To find it under the a pile of cordwood, where it could not serve its function, seemed to William to be an intentional insult. Whoever had dumped the cordwood here may have been ill-informed about the process, but more likely it was a deliberate show of disrespect.

Eleanor paused on her way back down to the house with Millie at her heels. "You don't need to do that," she said with icy politeness, returning to the role of hostess.

"Listen," he said too abruptly. "Miss Abbott. Please." She slowed her steps. "Please, hear me out," he said.

She halted mid-step. Milk sloshed over the lip of her pail as she roughly set it down. Eleanor turned to him; her pose said she was ready to listen but the position of her eyebrows indicated she was prepared to be repulsed by anything he said.

"I appreciate the opportunity to be useful," he smiled a crooked smile. "I'm sorry I chopped your wood. If I could put it back the way it was to ease your mind, I would."

Eleanor rubbed her hand over her forehead, as if to wipe away a headache. "I know I'm being ridiculous."

William thought about the fresh milk in the bucket at her feet, the chicken in his belly, and another hour of work available on the wood pile. He said, "I imagine you've had troubles in the past and are being cautious now. I'd call that the opposite of foolish."

"Millie brought you up some blankets. Let her know if you need anything else." Eleanor said her piece and nothing more.

When it started to get dark he finally quit. He went to the pump out back, took off his shirt, and let the water gush over his neck and shoulders. He shook like a dog. Jessup had been following him around much of the day, mostly sleeping in the sun, and now watched him in fascination and then took a lick of water at the base of the pump.

Down at the house William entered the kitchen quietly, stealthily, closing the door softly behind him. The kitchen had been put to rights and it was as if he had never been there, his presence erased. The breakfast table was set for two, Eleanor and Millie.

He grabbed a kerosene lamp from the sideboard and a few wooden matches. Thoughts about the state of the farm and the community still nibbled at him, tore at him, but he couldn't work anymore today. His muscles wouldn't take it and the light was all used up. The best he could do now was sleep.

The moon was full as he walked up to the barn but the clouds had conspired to block it. The rain was inevitable as the air was so heavy that it dampened sound and memory and thought and worry. He entered the room around back and didn't light the lamp. He just lay down on the bunk nearest the door and he slept.

## CHAPTER EIGHT
## What William Thinks in the Night

In 1922 William had been home from the war, broken, for three years. He was still a young man, only twenty-two, but most days he felt ancient. In Baltimore, William had worked at the docks. Industry was bustling then. Fire had destroyed the whole city some years back and they were rebuilding at a frantic pace. Money flowed, jobs were plentiful, and people were in high spirits and optimistic.

William liked working at the port because it was exhausting. He remembered books as a boy, Sherlock Holmes and such, where the docks were the haunts of riffraff and hooligans. This romantic image of masculinity drew him there, imagining he would be moving wooden crates with hemp rope and perhaps run the risk of encountering pirates. In reality, the docks involved meeting huge ships, unloading hundreds of identical loads onto trains west or south Then as new trains rolled in they repeated the process in reverse.

Even though the port was not exactly as he had imagined the docks provided him with what he needed; physical activity enough to keep his mind occupied. Driving the forklifts and operating the cranes required all of his attention and the building boom assured him that he would have all the overtime he could handle. The majority of his time was spent working or sleeping. He didn't have or want a social life. He preferred to keep his human interactions to a minimum. He preferred a world of machinery and endless rows of uniform metal boxes.

Nightmares occasionally plagued him. His sixty-three days in the trenches had taken their toll. He knew realistically that only time would erase the memory of those months in the mud. Sometimes he awoke with that smell in his nose, and the threat of tear gas, and the distant crackle of machine guns. On nights when the nightmares took him, he couldn't wait for the memories to subside. Those nights he headed to Cappy's Tavern down the street, which mostly catered to the old-timers. Each man had his own favorite stool at the bar and they all had their routines. The short guy with the mustache arrived each night at 5:30. He sat at the bar near the taps and had two bourbons, neat, and left a tip clattering on the counter. The old bald man arrived at six p.m, he took a seat at the far end and ordered a beer with a whiskey chaser. Most nights these two men exchanged a brief nod but no words of greeting. The bartender, Cappy's son Donald, greeted everyone as they ordered and made a comment about the weather.

"Cold enough for you?" he asked most nights as William entered.

"Yup," William answered, preferring to use one word answers to discourage too much interaction. "Whiskey."

He wasn't a mean drunk or a loud drunk, but he was serious about drinking to oblivion. He drank intentionally so he would be able to fall headfirst into bed and think of nothing.

Most nights he and the guys enjoyed the peaceful respite. If they struggled with their own demons they didn't say and Williams stayed quiet too. The bartender tried occasionally to make conversation but it always fell flat.

On the night of the fight, William entered the bar to find quite a different atmosphere. The interior was the same; same smoke-stained walls and windows, same faded and stained maroon canvas on the seats in the booths. The piano rocked that night; normally nobody played it. The place was filled with the buzz of conversation and laughter. There were a dozen sailors in sharp white suits and more than a dozen women. They were like bright butterflies in the dimness that was Cappy's. The usual old-timers huddled on their barstools with their heads hung down and their arms circled around their drinks protectively. One woman, older than the sailors by a few years, with an emerald green dress, lots of makeup, and gaudy jewelry, repeatedly bumped into the skinny guy with glasses as he sat over his beer and tried to be invisible. She was gesturing as she told a story and she had one of those long cigarette holders that she waved around to emphasize her points. As she told her story and waved her lit cigarette, she danced a solitary foxtrot back and forth. Each time she made the last step back she bumped into the old timer's stool. William could see that the old man cringed at the contact. Eventually he emptied his glass, dropped some coins on the bar, and left.

William needed a drink. The nightmares grabbed him hard the previous night. Even a double shift couldn't shake it. He needed the sweet, dulling power of whiskey. His room was right around the corner and he didn't have the enthusiasm to find another place to drink. He took the bottle from the bartender and settled into a into a corner booth to get drunk.

The sailors and the women changed Cappy's Tavern. Most nights the only sound was the bartender straightening the glasses and sweeping the floor. The only real color came from the bright labels on the liquor bottles lined up in front of a narrow mirror on the back wall. The seats were reddish, maroon like drying blood. Someone had placed little vases on each table with a sprig of silk flowers, but these had long since faded and collected dust. They were the color of neglected houseplants. It was a working man's bar and all the patrons wore practical plain shirts and pants with stains that would never come out. Everybody was tainted by grease and age and nobody really cared.

The men were all content when they came here, a place to be alone and yet in public. If they passed each other on the street they would nod or tip their hats, but say nothing before they went their separate ways.

When William and the old-timers drank they became even more quiet and taciturn. As the sailors and the women drank, they became louder and more animated. The noise level increased until everybody shouted to be heard above the piano and other people. There were probably more words floating around Cappy's Tavern than there had been in the past ten years.

William found it impossible to sit back and watch the frivolity unfold around him. Being with a crowd, even one as small as this one, seemed too much. He was agitated and hyper alert and liquor did nothing to soothe it. He pushed the bottle aside after only three shots. He stood, got his coat, and started for the door.

"Hey!" Shouts erupted in the small room. It was one of the sailors. All the other sailors got up too and pressed and clustered around the old man. At the front was a small, soft-faced platinum blonde. She wore a parrot blue dress that shimmied when she moved. She was tiny; she weighed maybe one hundred pounds. But she carried herself like she was a princess, like she expected doors to open as she approached and everyone should do her bidding. She was beautiful like a movie star but there was something off. She had the same pinched, judgmental expression on her face since she had walked in. It was as if Cappy's Tavern displeased her by its very existence.

The front of her dress was soaked with a drink that one of the old-timers had spilled on her. The old man looked horrified at what he had done. More than that, he looked cowed, like he didn't even have the right to be here, in his usual place, in his usual bar. The old man extended a damp bar towel toward her.

"Are you kidding me?" she asked. She batted the towel away and it hit the floor with a splat. Her voice was sharp and shrill. It would have been unpleasant even in a polite conversation, but raised in anger it was painfully caustic. "This is silk. Do you know what this dress cost?"

Her fury made the sailors even more agitated. They waited impatiently for the violence to start. The bartender felt it too. He reached behind the bar and got the Louisville slugger he kept under the cash register. The bat was covered in dust from lack of use, but the oak was still strong and straight. He put the bat down on the bar, setting it down with a clunk.

The woman didn't stop. She stepped forward until she was almost touching the old man's chest. He was tall, about six two, and a big man. He had been a butcher once upon a time and his body still showed how it was shaped by lifting sides of beef and wielding a cleaver. He hadn't been the same since a fire destroyed his shop and killed his family. He had always been a kind and jovial man. Now he was just a ghost trying to take up as little space as possible. She jabbed her finger into his massive chest. "Who's going to pay for it? You?" she sneered.

"Send the cleaning bill to the bar." The bartender said, as he was trying to stay cool, but the muscle in his jaw was working overtime and his knuckles were white as they clutched the bat in front of him.

The piano player stopped and the last chords vibrated for a

long time. All conversation had ceased. All eyes were focused on the tiny woman in the blue dress confronting the big old man. The sailors wanted something to happen. What they didn't realize was that the old butcher didn't have any fight left in him. She could poke and verbally punish him all night and he wouldn't react. All he wanted to do was run away, but the path to the door was blocked by uniforms. They would pound the hell out of him and maybe kill him and he wouldn't lift a finger in his own defense.

"I think you should pay for it. You." She jabbed him again. He couldn't retreat any further; the barstool was right behind him. "This dress cost twenty dollars. Do you have twenty dollars, old man?" Jab, jab, jab.

The sailors were packed up all around her. There was literally nowhere for him to go. The bartender was restrained by the bar. He lifted his eyes to meet William's across the room.

William was about the same age as the sailors, but they hadn't paid him any attention. Perhaps it was because he wore the same uniform as the old-timers; drab clothes and downcast eyes. He knew guys like this from his days when he was in the Army. Back in boot camp, before he was sent over to France and pieces of him didn't come back, he was just like these guys. The Army had built him up and told him he was an invincible warrior. The trenches had made him humble and vulnerable; training had made him fierce. The first night of leave, his entire unit had gotten into a fight with some townies, an action that landed seven of their number in a disciplinary action that revoked their next leave, and two of them in the hospital for minor injuries.

He recognized these sailors had yet to see any action and they were still full of spitfire. Their eventual assignments would cool some of this for the smart ones, but tonight these were the most dangerous men on the planet.

William diverted from his planned exit and wound his way through the backs of the crowd to get to the butcher. Each time he pressed forward in the sea of bodies, people were surprised. This slim moment of shock worked in his favor. It was one more instant when his actions avoided a violent reaction and it encouraged him to continue forward and to accelerate his pace. Sooner than expected, William was at the old man's side. The woman was prepared for another jab.

"Why don't you write down the address here, so she can send the bill." William said.

"Sure thing," the bartender said as he wrote the address down on a envelope.

William positioned himself between the old man and the woman as best he could without making contact with her. Now that he was this close he could smell her perfume. It was sweet like flowers, but instead of finding it enchanting or attractive, he found it cloying. Layered under this was the smell of alcohol. Not just what had been spilled on her, but it seeped from her pores. She had been drinking pretty heavily all night, maybe all week. "I'll walk you out," he said to the big butcher.

She redirected her anger toward William. "Who the heck are you?" As she said the word "you" a spray of saliva flowed out of her mouth. He felt the old timer slip out behind him and heard the creak of the door as it opened and shut.

"I'm nobody," William said. He assessed the group in front of him. The sailor that the tiny woman had come with was likely to be the first aggressor; he had the most pride invested in this scenario. The secondary threat would come from the big guy to his left; the guy cracked his knuckles in eager anticipation.

William had realized something about himself when he was in the trenches. He wasn't afraid of violence. He didn't seek it out and he wasn't angry, but if it happened he wasn't afraid. So when the woman aimed her jab at William's chest and he deflected it with his half hand, palm forward, he was ready for the punch that came from her date on his right.

The scene escalated quickly and William saw it only in flashes. The first punch he took square in the face. This was unavoidable until he familiarized himself with the players and their strengths and their tendencies. He responded with a sharp punch in the gut and spun around to block the attempt from his left to knock his block off. He checked the potential path to the exit and finding none, he delivered two more mighty blows to another man who entered the fray. The big guy with the bleeding knuckles gathered his resources for another attack. That sailor would be a problem. He was aggressive and he had been itching for a fight all evening. William hoped he wasn't injured so badly that it prevented him from going to work in the morning. He wasn't afraid, but he certainly wasn't looking forward to the beating he was about to endure. He was running hot on instinct, trying to minimize pain and maximize his response, so it would be over soon without crashing the place up too much.

"Catch!" the bartender yelled as he tossed the baseball bat over the bar. William, operating on shear, sweaty nerves, got a good grip and wheeled around, swinging hard. The sound a Louisville slugger makes as it connects with a human skull is unlike any other. When the bat hits a softball there is a bit of give, so the sound is the dull thud. A baseball is harder and the sound is a crack. The sound of the bat hitting a human head is something between the two. There is a cushion of flesh to soften the sounds, then underneath the hard mass of bone, and under that a hollow chamber providing an echo in the surrounding organic matter to make everything sound sickeningly wet.

If William had time to think, he would have aimed lower and merely broken his aggressor's arm to end the fight. There was no time to think. The sound of the blow was followed by the sounds of the body crashing into the barstools, followed by a stunned silence. The expanding puddle of blood got on everyone's shoes. William set the bat on the counter and left without a word. If the police were called, he didn't know. He was on a train headed north within the hour.

## CHAPTER NINE
### Eleanor

As Eleanor read aloud from the stained and battered book Millie had arrived with, her mind raced elsewhere. Fortunately Millie was exhausted and didn't notice that whole pages were skipped. Eleanor suspected that on an ordinary night no omission would slip by without comment or complaint. When Eleanor declared the chapter done Millie accepted the falsehood and nestled into her pillow with a sigh.

The center step squeaked as she descended from Millie's bedroom. In this at least, she knew what to expect. Eleanor entered the kitchen guided by habit rather than light; the night was dark with heavy clouds but she carried no lamp, no need. She was born in this house and had never lived anywhere else. Since her mother died thirteen years ago not even a stick of furniture had been moved in much of the house on North Road. Her father insisted on routine and she had never been one for a battle of wills. Since his death last winter she made a few attempts at change, a rug or a coat of paint, but had never gotten much further than the pantry. The kitchen was her domain and there she did as she pleased.

Eleanor thought about the girl she used to be. The girl she might have been. If her brother Johnny had lived he would be twenty-six now, a man. He was always funny, always smiling and making jokes. He loved the farm. Maybe with Johnny at his side, John Abbott wouldn't have been so bitter. Maybe Johnny might have found a girl who loved the land too and Eleanor's burdens would be less.

#

"Eleanor!" John Abbott, her father, bellowed when he spoke to his seventeen-year-old daughter. Always. She was certain that at one point in her life, he had held some other tone for her, something affectionate. Paternal. Now, he spoke to her exclusively with scorn, impatience, or anger. She hustled along to see what his summons meant this time.

She approached the barn and saw that her father was not alone. Ted Anderson stood next to him. Ted seemed tall enough to Eleanor when he walked her to the bottom of the hill. Sometimes during their long, lingering afternoon strolls she found herself giggling, foolish and flustered. Happy. Now next to her father, Ted looked like a sapling, frail and flimsy. He looked like he would be buffeted by the storm, afraid of being snapped in two by the slightest gale.

"Eleanor." Her father smiled but there was no benevolence in the expression; it was the tight smile of company. He was polite and yet grim. It was the expression he showed when he had just shot a gopher out in the orchard. "Young Mr. Anderson came here today with an invitation," he said.

Ted did not meet her gaze. He looked at the chickens, at the watering trough, at the road. She willed him to look at her, to make the request or extend the invitation, or whatever he had come up here to say. Excitement bubbled up inside her.

"This is probably a bad idea. I'm sorry to have bothered you, Mr. Abbott." Ted spared her a glance but didn't speak to her. The smile he passed her didn't reach his eyes.

"I told your friend," her father started. Ted shrank a little at her father's tone. "I told your friend that it wasn't likely that you have time for anything more than chores. Now that we're coming into season."

It was always season for something. Every month of the year, every day, every hour there was always some work that needed attention. Even in the winter, when the ground was frozen hard and inhospitable there was quilting or mending or preparation to be done. Did her father imagine for the rest of her life there would be no parties or dances? No rambling walks home hoping a boy would hold her hand? Ted had held her hand once. Hers was calloused as milking, scrubbing, toting, and weeding had all taken their toll. The thing is, Ted's hands were calloused too. He helped on his father's farm or at his brother's.

"Surely there could be some time for fun," Eleanor stood with her hands at her sides, fingers clenching and unclenching at the futile confrontation.

"I don't think so," John Abbott turned toward her, excluding Ted from the conversation, ignoring him with body language, ignoring him entirely, dismissed. "Without your sister and your mother, you're needed here."

And there it was the sentence, the conclusion, the decision. Her father needed no further inquiry and he requested no further information about the situation. His world was black and white and of course green from his precious fields. The farm required many contributions to be successful; Eleanor's time and sweat and labor was just one of these.

"Yes, Papa," she said. She turned without a word to her father to head back to her place, the kitchen.

"Eleanor!" he bellowed. "Are you daft? Don't go back empty-handed. Bring those milk pails down to wash."

The big galvanized pails clanged together as she walked back to the house. She did nothing to stifle or dampen the noise. She let them clang and clunk and ring--ominous, sonorous, loud. The buckets made the sound she didn't dare.

#

She had grown accustomed to her role as a spinster, unmarried at nearly twenty-nine, but despite her father's vitriol, she found the nights in the old house to be lonely since his passing. With Millie back home Eleanor knew that her gloomy, quiet days were over; it was impossible to feel down in the child's presence. She imagined the nights would still prove to be a challenge, even when most times fatigue claimed her before she was even in her night clothes. She slept in her clothes from time to time. Sometimes when the skies were clear, she wandered the property from one end of the orchard to deep into the sugar wood. Jessup bounded along beside her at the start, but eventually even her trusted companion tired and good sense sent Eleanor off to bed.

Tonight Eleanor left Jessup behind. The dog settled himself, as she had hoped, on the braided rug at the base of the stairs in the front hallway. He raised his head in interest briefly as she left, then flopped back down. From this position he could hear any movement through the whole house and she knew from experience he was vigilant, if for no other reason than the prospect of food. She wouldn't go far this evening but she had to go somewhere. The thoughts, regrets, mourning, and memories would quickly swamp her if she had to stay put.

Eleanor knew the path from the house to the barn better than she knew any other place on earth. There was a depressed gully in the left track that made a fast river down the hill when they had a hard rain.

In that gully lived a dedicated and determined patch of little purple violets that sprang up in the middle every spring, no matter how much traffic they endured. Eleanor could walk this path in the moonlight or on a dark night like this one. There was comfort in the familiarity of knowing where things lead, but also a condemnation. She felt like Sisyphus some weeks, doomed to walk this path, never getting anywhere, never accomplishing anything, never finishing anything, never making things right. She didn't even know what right was anymore.

This evening's rambles took her toward the barn without consciously meaning to. It was as if the pull of her usual path was greater than her instincts to stay as far as possible from the unknown William Hart. There was no light or sound coming from the hired man's quarters as she rounded the building, so perhaps she could consider herself fortunate. She looked to the wood pile; the majority was still massive, useless, reckless, and cruel. She wanted to spit or flee every time she saw it. A portion, a relatively small fraction, had been civilized and tamed. Stacked neatly by the side of the building, the cordwood was reduced once again to mere utility. She knew it absurd to attribute so much meaning to a simple thing, like an uneducated heathen seeing meaning in the oracle of tea leaves. She held her breath and then released it slowly. She had been holding that particular breath for nearly a year. It was time to let things go.

She wished she sent that extra quilt for him up from the house. She had been bitter and untrusting so long that kindness no longer fit easily. Perhaps realizing this change was the first step. "Sleep well, Mr. Hart," she said quietly to herself as she walked by, unseen. She felt the first tentative drops of the storm and prayed that the rain would wash her clean of the past.

#

Millie still had nightmares sometimes, but she had been taught by her parents to keep them to herself. Most of her dreams were of being chased by something terrible. There was a creature she'd seen in a book, a witch with bony fingers and long fingernails. One time she dreamed about leeches. She was alone in a beautiful place on a sunny day. There was a lake and it was hot and she waded in slowly, still wearing her white nightgown. The water felt soft on her skin like dusting powder. She felt supported and loved by that water. Little fish nibbled her feet and legs. When she emerged she saw that they were clinging to her skin. The leeches were fat and black like oil. There were dozens, hundreds, and each one had chomped down on her flesh with teeth she couldn't see. At each point of connection there was a little trickle of blood, her blood, running down her legs and her arms and belly.

She woke shaking from that one, but she never made a fuss. She just kept quiet and counted to one hundred. When she had the dream about Scarecrow, William had been with her and she went right back to sleep.

Tonight's dream featured someone chasing her down darkened streets. She was in a huge and twisting city, no specific details of the place-- metal trash cans, mailboxes, milk trucks. It could have been anywhere but the dark man had found her and she had to run. Every time she entered an alley he was at the far end. He was at the top of every staircase. She knew in the dream that there was no escape, but she kept running and running and running.

When she woke up this evening Jessup was there. When she opened her eyes he was standing up, with his nose inches from hers on the pillow. His eyes were deep brown and he blinked both eyes real slowly while he wagged his fluffy tail. He was fast when he ran, very agile and strong. Most warm nights he stayed outside and watched over the chickens. She was glad that tonight he was watching over her.

#

The next two days Eleanor didn't see William Hart, only the evidence of his presence and Millie's reports on his activities. Eleanor tried, unsuccessfully, to keep Millie close at hand or at least within eyesight. The child was like a wild creature newly freed from captivity. She made journeys throughout the property in expanding circles. She explored the house, then the closest gardens, and finally told Eleanor of a journey to the farthest surveyor post at the end of the back field.

"Have you ever seen a giant snake?" Millie asked over dinner. It was just the two of them at the table. Eleanor had sent some bread and cold chicken up to the hired man's quarters on Millie's excursion that way in late afternoon.

"I've seen large snakes," Eleanor said. "My father killed one with a hoe that was over four feet long."

"William showed me a snake, a huge snake that was living in the rocks of the front wall. He let me touch it! And I thought it would be slimy, but it wasn't. Not at all! William said that snakes like to lie on rocks because their blood is cold and they can't make their own heat. He said the best thing a snake can do is lie on a sunny rock on a cool afternoon. He said it's a snake's favorite thing! He said most snakes don't want to hurt people, they just want to be left alone."

"What was Mr. Hart doing by the front wall?" Eleanor asked, eager to get the discussion away from reptiles.

"He was just looking at it. He was looking at some of the rocks that had fallen down. I guess trying to figure out how to fix it."

Millie paused for breath and a nibble at her dinner. She looked dubiously at the lima beans on her plate, spearing one individually with her fork.

She continued, "He told me not to go near that part of the wall unless somebody was with me. He was afraid I would get hurt. Not afraid of snakes!" She snickered at the thought as she ate another bean. "William lifted one of the stones, the small ones, and he said it was terribly heavy and could crush my toes if I dropped it. That sounds terrible, doesn't it? Crushed toes!"

Eleanor agreed that anything crushed sounded bad and echoed his call for caution. Millie told of how she and William had visited the orchard and the fields and pond and the ice house. Eleanor suspected that his urging Millie to read for the afternoon was an effort to preserve his own sanity. William Hart struck her as a quiet man; Millie Cage was not a quiet child.

In the early evening as Millie rummaged through the rag bag for suitable material for doll clothes, Eleanor sat near her kitchen door and listened to the rhythmic clatter of William at her wood pile. He didn't rush but set a steady, grueling pace. Periodically he paused. She envisioned him gulping water or stretching his back. Eleanor honestly didn't know how she would have managed. Each time she passed on her way to the barn the neat stack of useful wood grew a little bit taller.

That night Eleanor didn't wander, and she didn't dream. She slept. She awoke rested for the first time in months. The sun shone gently on her face through her eastern window. As a farm girl, she knew from the angle of the light that hour was later than her father would have dictated, but the last hour of sleep felt like the best of her life. Millie was already at her duties; Eleanor could hear the chickens chuckling as they emerged from the coop.

Eleanor didn't see William some mornings, but found two full buckets of water waiting for her outside the door. She sent Millie up to his room with a bowl full of hard boiled eggs, some apples, and another of her father's worn shirts. She didn't see him every evening, but found a stack of firewood near the door and her milk pail carefully washed. She delivered, via Millie, an extra blanket for his bed. The temporary, unspoken nature of their arrangement was quickly becoming absurd. On the third day she met him in her kitchen.

"You should stay." Eleanor said it quietly, the words barely making it past her teeth which she was just barely able to unclench. She said it to his back but with the knowledge that fear no longer served her.

He set the metal bin full of kindling down. It clattered and shook with the weight, three trips worth if she had to do it for herself. He pulled the red handled broom from the corner and swept away the remnants of dust and scraps of bark he had left. Two full buckets of water sat near the door. A third one, empty, sat overturned in the courtyard ready to be filled. She knew he would carry it out to the pump without being asked when he returned to his work.

They hadn't had any help with the farm since her brother Johnny died. All through her childhood her father had taken on workers--sometimes in the summer, always in September when the apples came in. The kitchen was loud with laughter and jokes, complaints of sore shoulders, and gratitude when Eleanor delivered another platter of buttermilk pancakes.

"I'd appreciate it if you stayed," she said. It was May and she could see the summer stretching out before her. Some market crops were already past; she missed the spring lettuce almost entirely this year. The sugar house had been idle and cold in February. But the asparagus pushed their lacy green tendrils through the blanket of leaves and mulch as they always did. A row of straight pale spears soaked in vinegar brine on the pantry shelf. The crop was abundant, undeterred by neglect. She had been surprised to see the first sprouts, somehow having forgotten that spring would return. The cyclical motion of the farm would not stop just because the interior of her house had been so quiet.

And now the orchard was already abuzz with bees on the fragrant pink blossoms. Her daffodils came back every year, even multiplied. The sunny place along the edge of the house glowed with the brightness of their cheery trumpets. Millie had cut a little uneven bouquet. The subtle fragrance tickled Eleanor's nose each time she passed by on her way to the staircase.

"All right," William said without really looking at her. He said it as if it was inevitable that he would stay; immutable like a tree or a stone.

Millie let the screen door slam and rattle behind her, barely slowing as she entered. Her feet were bare and she left a dot of mud behind with each step. A jar of murky water sloshed in her left hand.

"No running," William said in a warning tone. When she stopped quick a little puddle trickled down from her arm. He pulled his handkerchief and bent to wipe it away as Millie disappeared into the parlor with exaggerated caution.

Eleanor thought she heard him say thank you, she may have been mistaken. Millie was above them; the door to Johnny's room had always creaked.

In her kitchen Eleanor knew where things were. She knew the proper placement of each canister and cup. Outside, the farm, her father's farm, was waiting, inevitable, unstoppable, and sometimes overwhelming. When William left her kitchen he made no sound, it seemed he never did. His steps were quiet, the screen door didn't squeak, or slam. He bent to retrieve the bucket and shook it to dispel the last drops of water.

"Breakfast in half an hour," she said to his back as he walked away. She removed the striped tea towel from the top of the big bowl and punched down hard into the mound of dough that had risen inside. It gave a satisfying swoosh of release as it deflated. She covered it again and set it aside to rise once more before she baked it. It was enough for two big loaves and one small one. She could send the smaller for William's lunch the next day.

#

When William came back to the farmhouse kitchen, Eleanor had started the cook stove for breakfast preparations. He took the empty bucket from the door and filled it with water to heat for cleaning up after the meal. Next he would restock the wood pile near the kitchen door making sure to chop up some small kindling for her.

Could it be this easy? Was it possible that if he worked hard, and was helpful, a kind woman would cook him breakfast and a sweet little kid would invite him to watch a handstand demonstration or offer to read him a story after school.

The Abbott farm looked like heaven to him; an unlimited supply of back breaking work and someone to be grateful for it. He entered the kitchen to the scent of French toast and bacon. He felt like he had hit the jackpot.

Millie greeted him from the counter. "Did you know that chickens slept with their heads under their wings? Every chicken lays one egg every day, so if you want more eggs you just get more chickens! We're going to hatch some new babies soon so we can have more layers, because Eleanor thinks you probably eat a lot."

"Millie!" Eleanor blushed from her place at the stove. "Finish cleaning those eggs and go brush the hay out of your hair. Your breakfast will be done in five minutes."

Millie set her last eggs, clean from straw, in the basket before racing out.

"That girl wakes up talking," Eleanor said as she set the plate heaped with French toast and bacon in front of him.

"I do eat a lot," William said cheerfully. The slices were good thick bread and the syrup was warm. The bacon was cooked curly and crisp.

"There's no money here," she said quietly. She attended to her skillet and didn't look up.

"I don't need any money," he said. "A bed. Some food."

Eleanor, he suspected, was a woman who didn't like to ask for help, ask for anything, so she retreated to what she could handle right now--eggs, bread, milk, bacon. He ate, savoring, wiping chunks of the golden bread across his plate in attentive circles, sopping up the syrup. Millie entered noisily in another pretty dress, too big, and Eleanor presented her with a plate, grabbed her own off the warmer, and sat down.

"Good news," Eleanor said as she smiled at him then turned to watch Millie's expression. "Mr. Hart is going to be staying on to help us for a while."

Millie's piercing shriek of excitement rattled the china in the cabinet and sent the dog scrambling in terror. She barely remembered to congratulate William on his new position before racing out to announce the news to the cats. He reached across the table with his good hand and plucked the remnants of Millie's forgotten breakfast

165

from her plate. It really was excellent French toast.

## CHAPTER TEN
### William Gets to Work

Out in the Midwest the sky seemed bigger. The Nebraska vistas introduced the sky as a major character. Here in Massachusetts the sky seemed an afterthought, a bit player. This was the terrestrial story, a story of the land, hills, rocks, trees. Every square foot was put to its best purpose, from two goats grazing through the hilly apple orchard, to shade vegetables and healing plants growing along the edge of the sugar wood. Vegetables and fields of hay, alfalfa and white clover, claimed all of the available open space with that vast area always used to maximum capacity with a minimum of wasted space. The farm was elegant in its practicality.

"I really don't know what I'm doing," Eleanor said abruptly as William trailed behind. They were in the middle of the aisle between sparse rows of scrawny green sprouts and struggling knee-high plants he couldn't identify. The ground was still muddy from the rain last night but she seemed beyond caring in her defeat. William observed the rich green leaves and peered closely at them, tore a leaf, and sniffed it to detect its lineage.

"Potatoes," she said. "I got them in late this year. Everything is late this year." And then she started to cry, a slow silent trickle of tears that she pretended to ignore.

William had spent more time with men than women in his life.

He had a few girlfriends back home when he was a kid. Peggy Atwood had captured his attention when he was sixteen, but mostly, if he was honest with himself, because she was among the first of their crowd to grow breasts. In their small town, most of the young people were known to each other from the cradle. Nearby Denver offered a glittering array of diversions, but the breasts he could actually hope to one day touch were limited to just a handful, and all those girls were intimately acquainted with his family and his teachers. No interaction with a pretty girl could escape the gossip machine and his mother always knew before he got home any conversation that might have occurred during the day.

"That youngest Atwood girl is planning on coming to the sleigh ride Saturday night. You should invite her to come early and have some cocoa beforehand," his mother said, knowledgeable beyond all natural possibilities.

William had been interested in sitting next to Peggy, tightly packed next to her in the sleigh with a blanket tucked in cozily up over the both of them. What happened was he got a brief feel of softness against his arm and a quick kiss before the party dispersed for the night. After that, Peggy Atwood was his regular girl, joining him at school sponsored dances or an occasional event. Mostly they spent time in the company of others. It was expected universally that they would marry. Peggy Atwood was just one more person that he had disappointed by joining the Army. When he came back, mangled and maimed, she had sent a formal note expressing her thankfulness at his coming home alive, but she never once came to visit. He guessed she probably married someone else. Hearts heal.

As the expanse of his interactions with females had all but ended when he was eighteen years old, William felt at a loss in dealing with Eleanor's tears. If she were a man he wouldn't worry; he would just proceed with what needed to be done and let the drama, with words or fists, work itself out. He walked away from her, further down the field, to where a wire fenced seemed to delineate the property. This end of the field was in even worse shape. The ground looked like it had been worked in many past seasons, but now was left fallow. It was covered with thick leaved plants covered in yellow flowers. He could see a few struggling stragglers of another variety, but for the most part the field was filled with a waist high plants of yellow flowers. He looked back toward Eleanor. She was up on her feet, spine straight, with a cheerful expression plastered on her face. She marched toward him in a determined manner only to have her stride slow as she was engulfed in yellow.

"The mustard weeds have gotten the best of me," she said. Crying had made her face softer, it was as if she had melted a bit, the sharp edges of a block of ice smoothed by the sun.

"I think you know more than you think, Miss Abbott. For example, you can tell me how to cultivate this," he indicated the swath of yellow around them.

Her face softened further and she actually giggled. "Oh no Mr. Hart, these are weeds. The cows won't even eat them." She bent and brushed the invasive plants aside and directed his attention to a pale and narrow spear-shaped leave straining up to get the light. "This was to be spicy peppers. They're in there somewhere."

William estimated a full acre of little yellow flowers spreading out before him. "Sure are pretty, though," he laughed.

"My father told me about a farmer in Chicopee whose sheep died when they grazed too frequently in a mess like this."

"So let's dig it up," William said.

She looked at him as if he were insane.

William wasn't sure about her hesitation, "Don't we need to take it up? I swear I will catch on to all of this eventually. I'm a quick study," he said. His ignorance scraped. It irritated him like an ill-fitting shoe. He wanted to learn everything. No, he wanted to already possess the knowledge to make things grow. He longed for the comfort that comes with proficiency or mastery. It made his left hand hitch. The sensation of his ghost hand increased until he was sure she could see it vibrating.

"It will take weeks," she said. William imagined Eleanor evaluating all the other things that required her attention. Things, no doubt, that took priority over a back field full of weeds.

"I've got weeks," he said, wanting to say months, or years. "Just show me what to do and it's done."

Eleanor pressed the spade into his hand and showed him the basic motions of the task. The front pointed edge of the tool had to be pressed deep into the earth, pressed down hard with the sole of his boots and given a wiggle with his full weight to submerge it into the soil to loosen the dense pack of the roots. Then moved a few inches over and repeated the action until a good patch was broken up. Then he was to go back at it with a three pronged cultivator, tearing the weeds forcibly from the ground. Roots exposed, each plant was shaken to release the dirt and the naked plants tossed in a wheelbarrow to be carted away. When Eleanor had demonstrated she stepped on the spade with both feet and jumped down to sink it deep, then fell back with her whole body to get that clod loose. When William followed he used one boot and one arm to pull the spade toward him. It probably would have taken her weeks. For him it would likely be a matter of days.

"You need to be careful of the plants we want to keep. We'd

lose a season if we had to re-seed. Otherwise we could just use the plow." She fluttered nervously as he tried to find a rhythm. He was figuring that her big wheelbarrow could hold about ten square feet worth of this mess before it needed to be dumped. He wondered if the weeds could go in the compost since the animals didn't eat it, or if the refuse needed to be gathered and burned.

"I feel foolish that I let it get so bad. A tiny bit of maintenance with a hoe will keep the mustard at bay," she said.

"It looks to me that you did the best a person could do." William stopped the work altogether. Machines didn't need reassurance, people did. Eleanor did. "You survived the storm by treading water. It's smart and strong. Don't let anybody tell you different."

It was true. When he had opened his mouth he only meant to spew platitudes; kind words to make her feel better so he could get back to work. He'd have meant them as a sweetness in a life that was sometimes sour, bitter, and acidic. He had good intentions but beneath that, beneath the superficial pleasantries of his youth and the mechanistic peripheral dealings of his adult life, he felt respect and even admiration for this woman.

"I think you have the hang of it," she said. Her voice was shaky and tight. She made her way down to the end of the field where the weeds were smaller and pulled them by hand from the rich dark earth. It was late spring, just a hint of summer in the air as they worked, together but not, in the big back field. When he next looked up from his work she had gone.

He made slow progress as he worked. He had only managed to clear the weeds from a small portion of the field. His inexperience made him clumsy, but the labor calmed him. The trousers he wore had finally lost their new starched feel and now had a potentially indelible stain on the left knee. Eleanor had stopped by periodically to bring him water or a plate of lunch. Millie had stopped by in the afternoon before she went off to do her chores and books to tell him how the neighbor's goose had chased the cat. Mostly he was on his own with the tools and the yellow mustard flowers and the earth. The tiny pepper plants, now cleared with room to breathe, could flourish and produce.

    The sky started to pinken in the west when he gathered his tools, cleaned them, and put them away in their place. Everything had a place here. He could follow the years of tradition easily. The path of history was clearly set with wooden pegs along the back wall at the exact height of the rake or the spade. It fit and each item begged to be put back where it belonged. Some of the pegs were newer or showed evidence that they had been moved indicating to William that new tools had been obtained and adjustments had been made to accommodate them. This level of precision in every aspect of an operation was both a blessing and a burden. He laughed at himself, this was a phrase his father often used. He was a perfectionist both at work and at home. The blessing was efficiency and profit. The burden came in the form of an unrelenting quest for improvement which led to nit-picking his children and his wife without pause. William wondered what the burden looked like in Eleanor's childhood.

    William went into the hired man's quarters to get cleaned up before he went down to dinner. The space had been transformed. It had been swept and dusted; the bed he had slept on yesterday now sported fresh laundered sheets and a soft clean pillow and a blue quilt. A full pitcher of water, a basin, and a towel sat on the chest near the bed. The whole place smelled fresh and lemony. A little vase of yellow mustard weed flowers adorned the table.

In the kitchen Millie nearly popped with excitement. "Did you like your room? Eleanor and I worked all afternoon to clean it! She picked the flowers but I carried the water. Eleanor said it would build my muscles. Want to check?" She's held her arm up and flexed for inspection.

"Just like Hercules from the stories," he said. "It looks real good. Thank you."

She wrapped her arms around his waist and squeezed. Maybe he had missed something, not hanging around kids. He really liked her easy affection and the trust she placed in him. He wondered what kind of father he would be. Hopefully not an absent, distracted one like his own father. Foolishness of course because for that endeavor he would need a woman, which seemed unlikely with the ugly ruined state his body was in.

#

William began his third day in the back field with the biggest of John Abbott's clean sharp spades in his hand. The one Eleanor had used when demonstrating the technique was the smallest, better suited to simple work around her kitchen gardens than the serious expanse of the tangled weed-filled mess in front of him. The wider blade bit easily into the rich dark earth aided by the additional weight of the thick wooden handle. He took his time, feeling the grit of the loam against metal. He pulled out the occasional stone and heaved it with all his might. The plot was so broad that even with all the force he exerted, sometimes the rock failed to sail beyond the field he had yet to clear.

Some people might seize the repetition of the work and the solitude of the vacant field as an opportunity to day dream or plan for grander aspirations. William did not. Instead he focused all his attention on each nuance and variation of the task in front of him. He varied the amount of pressure he applied to the spade and the angle at which he held the handle. He explored whether the blade bit deeper with a quick stomp of his boot or a slow steady pressure. He tested different depths to dig out the weeds. He tried placement of the wheelbarrow to his left or to his right.

He felt every square foot of the back field in his shoulders, thighs and blistered hands. He felt it in his piece of mind and in his growing understanding of what would be involved in reviving the Abbott farm. He might dare say he was starting to feel the land in his soul if he believed he still had one.

But he needn't think of intangible things like souls when he had soil and weeds and fading sunlight to occupy him. He straightened, stretched his back and drank from the heavy earthen pitcher that had appeared in his room. The sun had warmed the exterior but the water stayed cool in the dark inside of the vessel. He moved to his right and drove the spade in again. The amount of land already cleared was a tiny fraction of what needed to be done. He was smiling when he jerked the spade handle back to his chest.

He barely stopped to wash the dirt and sweat from his body under the cold water of the pump before he went inside his room at the back of the barn and collapsed on the bed. The sandwich Millie had delivered at lunch would have to hold him through the night. He didn't have the strength to walk down to the main house to see what Eleanor had fixed for dinner. It had been nearly a year since he had worked himself to the point of exhaustion. He slept and didn't dream.

Millie chastised him the next morning. The sun was barely up and the dew still glistened on the grass and on the leaves of the stubborn weeds. The cuffs of his pant legs were wet with it. Millie advanced toward him from the house as best she could; she dodged torn up clumps of dirt and the rubbish heap behind him. She swung her egg basket in an agitated syncopation, stopping in front of him. As a big man, a scarred man, he rarely came face to face with heated anger. People generally expressed their displeasure from a safe distance, beyond arms reach. Millie poked her small finger into his abdomen.

"I learned how to bake applesauce cookies," she said. "But you didn't come." She slapped a small bundle wrapped in a yellow napkin into his hand and headed toward the hen house.

He pulled the kerchief from his back pocket and wiped at the dirt on his hands. Unfolding the napkin revealed a stack of four misshapen, golden cookies. He lifted one to his nose--cinnamon and apples. The flavor was rich and sweet, the texture moist and buttery. They were probably even better still warm from the oven. Millie was a good pupil; Eleanor a good teacher. He ate two before he redoubled his efforts. He ate the remainder after he had washed and changed his shirt. The sun was still high with another hour of good light to work through. He declined it and instead made his way down the hill to take his place at Eleanor's table.

Down in the house he felt Eleanor's initial quiet like a heavy, dampening shroud. Her silences were not malicious; she harbored no hostility toward him. The austerity of the Abbott kitchen was born of discomfort and memory rather than disdain. Millie could talk about anything, and did, but her aunt was clearly no role model in this regard. Eleanor meted out words as if the expenditure of each syllable were a burden or a risk. William himself had nothing of importance to add; his grasp of tools or the scent of the dark earth after last night's soaking rain were better experienced than referenced. Millie was the only one who spoke in most interactions, and she did so without restraint. She laid the table with three place settings and neither Eleanor nor William had the inclination to disappoint her.

#

The meal was a hearty stew, some crusty sourdough bread and a salad of bitter spring greens. Millie entertained them with tales of her classmates in Chicago with descriptions so vivid that William thought he could identify any of these children if he saw them on the streets.

"Less talk, more chew," Eleanor said from time to time. She said it cheerfully, pleasantly, with patience. Millie was as filled with enthusiasm and stories as Eleanor had seemed empty of conversation when they arrived. She soaked it in like a sponge, encouraging Millie with jokes of her own and stories of growing up on the farm. Periodically she directed Millie back to the cooling food, more from a parental obligation to nourish the child than from growing weary of the chatter.

A matched pair, he thought again. They fed off each other, each comment leading to a response, each riddle with an answer. Eleanor eased up on her inquiries about Millie's past. He was sure the questions still nibbled on the edge of Eleanor's mind, but this evening they faded into the background in favor of pleasures of the present.

He couldn't remember when he'd last just sat over the dirty dishes and laughed. The sky faded behind him, but he didn't want to leave. His body was done, but his mind was still engaged. For the first time in a long while his thoughts didn't scare him. The relief was palpable.

When he finally gave in to sleep that night he dreamed not of guns and gas and mud, but of ever-expanding fields of yellow flowers. The air in his dream smelled sweet and it was warm and heavy, almost sticky. He felt slow in his movements like he was walking with lead boots through deep water. He was whole, two eyes, two hands, and

Eleanor stood very far from him. She hollered something but he couldn't make it out. He strained to hear her but couldn't. When he awoke he was peaceful, with a heavy delicious feeling that he was welcome here. That he was home.

#

He'd been out in the field for weeks. Three weeks to be exact and in that time he had cleared the entire back field. The entire back field. Eleanor found herself attaching great value to this simple action; it was as if he were erasing her shortcomings and mistakes with a shovel and a rake. Each yard he cleared felt like he gave her back a year of her life.

She spent the first week he worked in the field treating him like a guest, a novelty, temporary and transient. Then he had asked a simple question, "What will we do in that field when the weeds are gone?"

The Tuesday of that first week, after she cleaned up and settled Millie to bed, she took a long walk down North Road. The dog was always happy to have some company; he ran up ahead to sniff at trees, from time to time racing ahead after some unseen creature, returning to her side to check in and to sniff intensely some more. Eleanor walked down the hill slowly, enjoying the sounds of the night, insects, wind and leaves. She came back an hour later; no lights were visible from the farmhouse or the barn. She crept in quietly, the only sound was Jessup settling in his usual place on the porch, where he could hope to see a raccoon or porcupine picking its way along the property.

It was a trip to nowhere, it accomplished nothing but to clear her head a bit. It could not, however, clear the nibble of that question of William's in her head. The farm on the hill was her legacy, her responsibility, her burden, but she had never received preparation or education for its care. She had her own role, a woman's role, which she had learned, and learned well, at her mother's side. But even as her contribution to the farm had grown, her voice in its operation had not. Her father had never once asked or invited her opinion on anything of consequence.

The second week William spent in the field digging weeds, Eleanor found herself unreasonably restless. It was like she had a fever. She was unable to focus on anything for longer than a minute or two, flitting from task to task without finishing anything. She felt hot and glazed. Dinner that night was bland as she'd forgotten both salt and chives in the mashed potatoes. Neither Williams nor Millie had any complaints. They didn't even seem to notice anything was amiss. They ate with their customary abandon, Millie's patter an ever-present background music to the meal.

The third week William dug weeds, tall invasive yellow mustard weeds that choked the life from everything else, she was starting to feel settled and secure with the arrangement. She started to feel possibilities. He came to dinner each night, breakfast each morning. In the evenings he chopped wood before retiring to his room. Millie floated, noisy and joyful, through both their days.

During that third week she remembered things. She remembered how to knit a Celtic princess braid and how to sew a Dutchman's puzzle quilt. She remembered how to make lye soap and how to blend tea for headaches and make a poultice for poison ivy. It was as if a dam had broken in her mind. She knew things again-- how to care for a broken bone, how to cure bacon, which flowers grew it best in sun and which in shade, the capitals of every state. She could once again recite the Gettysburg Address or sing five verses of

Amazing Grace.

One night she had a dream. She was at the near end of the back field, filled with yellow flowers, and she was trying to make herself heard to William in the distance. She was shocked to find that she was speaking another language. She opened her mouth but what came out she didn't understand. She didn't even know what she meant to say. Her thoughts were tangled, jumbled even to her. She only operated in impressions, the smell of sweet vanilla, the sun was warm on her face, the sound was a slow cello in a minor key, the mood was peaceful. As she awoke she thought, could it be this easy?

#

When William came down to the house late one morning, Eleanor was working in a small greenhouse built against the sunny side of the kitchen. She inspected wooden trays on a sturdy waist-high shelf. Hundreds of little plants were nurtured and protected in the spring.

"Tomatoes," she said. "I can't help but see the future when I come out here." She laughed as she ran the palm of her hand over the softness of the seedlings. She knocked them around with her touch, but they sprang immediately back up. Resilience. "These should have gone in a few weeks ago, but hopefully they'll have the heart to produce for us. Come the late summer, if we're lucky, these tender babies will produce hundreds of bushels of fruit."

She identified each variety without hesitation even though to William they all looked the same. "Roma, beefsteak, yellow pear, those are especially delicious, Cherokee black, Amish paste tomato. This variety is called 'moneymaker' isn't that a hoot. This one is called brandywine, that's a nice one, big," she cupped her hands in a six inch globe to suggest the size when it was ready.

Eleanor was showing him her kingdom, her subjects, her

children. "We start them from seed behind glass to give them a head start. Keep them from the cold, give them some sunshine without stressing them too much out there on their own."

She hoisted one of the trays with a hand on either side. At her nod, William came behind her grabbed one tray in each hand and balanced it on his forearm. She marched up the hill to the back field he had just cleared.

"I don't figure the peppers will mind sharing the space." William was right behind her, right on her tail with the two trays. He set them on the ground next to the one she carried.

"I'll just get you started," Eleanor said, as if by surprise, "then you should be able to continue. And I'll do," she paused, "something else."

She smiled then and he began to think of how soft her hand felt when she brushed a clump of hay from his hair. He thought how soft Eleanor looked as she dozed through Millie's rambling story about hibernating bears. These thoughts were not the ones that woke him in a cold sweat of terror and remorse. When Eleanor smiled, he could taste one of her big tomatoes, still warm from the vine, sliced on a white plate, the moisture beading up in places where the salt was sprinkled. He could imagine the feel of the soft pad of her thumb if she were to wipe the juice off the corner of his lip.

"Listen to me, racing ahead and talking a mile a minute like Millie," she said.

William could listen to Millie talk all day. "Lead on," he said.

Eleanor knelt at the edge of the row of rich soil, made a tiny hole, and gently separated one of the little plants from its neighbor in the tray. She placed it in the hole, not too deep, not too shallow, and patted the soiled gently around it. She started on the next plant, which she placed about fourteen inches away. "They like to have a little drink of water once they go in. And again later tonight, then tomorrow morning. This will firm them up and they should get on all right if we don't have too dry a summer."

He knelt beside Eleanor and mimicked her actions. When she left to join Millie on a trip to the mercantile, he continued alone. His hands were too big for this precision work. The plants seemed so fragile and vulnerable; spindly stems, branching roots like fine hairs. He felt seven times too big, but he kept on. He planted the seedlings as she had shown him and then went down the hill to get some water and bring up another couple of trays.

His tendency was to move fast, but with this delicate work he took his time. For once the pace didn't frighten him. He still had another couple of cords of wood to placate him if needed. The day was warm, the air was heavy but the rain would likely stay away until late in the night. He had hours of daylight, hundreds of tomato plants, acres of rich soil, and no boss leaning over his shoulder or coworkers chewing his ear off. He could exhaust himself or take his time as he felt was right. No one was scared of his looks; the bees, birds, and cows didn't care one way or the other.

## CHAPTER ELEVEN
## The Barn

The sky spit a light drizzle the morning William walked Millie down the hill. She had renewed some friendships with a few of the local girls and he had planned a trip to the hardware store to see about getting supplies to repair the barn roof. He didn't expect to leave with anything; he just wanted to suss out what was available nearby and what would necessitate a trip down toward Springfield or one of the larger surrounding towns. He also needed to make an estimate of how much the repairs would be. He didn't know what Eleanor could afford, but he knew for sure that Miss Abbott's pride wouldn't set well with any assistance from him. Maybe in time she would soften to the idea, but for right now he resigned himself to playing poor and hoped that some of the Yankee ingenuity would rub off. He had never repaired a roof before.

A good hardware store has certain universal characteristics: the scent of mineral spirits, the ever present layer of dust, metal shavings piled up in corners, the sustained mystery of useful objects aching for purpose. This one had been here a while; the floorboards were scuffed and settled, creaking in places under his steps. Here the rows were only partially filled, one bottle of lubricating oil on a shelf that could've held a dozen. The depression had diminished Harris Hardware. Items that should be necessities had become optional.

People made do without.

As he approached the counter, the three men huddled over a newspaper rose to attention. He heard the hum of their appraisal. He was a stranger in a small town, and a big ugly stranger at that. His clothes and motion showed him to be a working man, their customary patron, and therefore not much of a threat. Once they assessed him as a potential customer, the air in the room changed.

"Good morning!" The greeting was a little too bright and the forced optimism had the opposite of the desired effect. It made William slightly suspicious. He would thoroughly inspect anything he purchased here, for fear of being short-changed.

The man who offered the greeting was in his early forties, neat and trim with an ambitious mustache that made his face look weak. Across the counter was an older man with the same thin face, his father. Toward the back was a man in his early thirties, with the same looks, but packaged like a rugged man with the boxer's nose. He puffed his chest out like a bulldog. The younger man smiled too, but it was only temporary. The wrinkles and lines on his face showed his usual expression to be something less gracious.

"Morning." William nodded at each in turn. "I need some roofing supplies and maybe some advice if you have any knowledge on that."

William didn't know why, but the place gave him a bad feeling like something important left behind. He felt a reaction rising in him, a reaction without stimulus. The pinky finger on his left hand began to twitch.

"We'd have to order the shingles, but I've got some tar paper in the back if that'll do you. Is this just a patch job or are you replacing the whole thing?" the man with the mustache tapped his fingers on the counter as he spoke. "It's always best to do it right," he said.

William could smell the proprietor's eagerness to make a big sale whether the customer in front of him actually needed the supplies or not. He understood it. Things were hard all over, but it still didn't sit easy with him. William professed his ignorance as a test to see what he would get in response. From the moment he had walked in here he was perfectly willing to go right back out. It would be more convenient to get what he needed here, but he was sure with a little time he could figure out the logistics of getting goods elsewhere.

"I'm not really sure. I'm going to have to get up there with the ladder and see what's what. I just wanted to get a feel for what was available locally," William said.

Curiosity got the better of the stocky man. He came forward a few steps, just shy of aggressive. He breathed through his nose in short, noisy gasps. "Which property is this for? Maybe I can tell you what you need," he said.

"I'm helping out up at the Abbott place," William said. William didn't lie. Ever. He didn't say much, he remained silent more often than not, but every word he said was the truth as he knew it. In this instance he wished he could have fabricated something. He'd said Abbott and the atmosphere changed. The temperature in the store dropped dramatically. The proprietor remained neutral but the old man looked embarrassed, and the younger man seemed excited at the prospect of devouring some weaker creature.

William wasn't afraid. He was never afraid but this conversation went against his basic inclination to try and avoid conflict whenever possible. He wondered what had happened up on North Road to elicit such a reaction.

The younger man came out from behind the counter. He

moved fast, but with small tight steps like he was holding something between his knees. He came right up to William, his chest a mere ten inches away. He didn't appear to be hostile, but rather had a lascivious leering grin as if he and William were old friends preparing to share conquest stories of women past. He rocked on the balls of his feet. "Are you enjoying Eleanor?" he said. William expelled a breath as the bulldog gyrated his hips suggestively.

William wondered at this man's intelligence at engaging a stranger, a much bigger, battled-scarred man, with such a blatantly disrespectful remark while in a hardware store. Within five feet of him William saw at least a dozen items that could cause harm to this idiot. There was a galvanized pail containing Phillips head screwdrivers of various sizes by his left elbow. The wall behind him displayed hatchets and hammers. A wooden barrel near his knee was stocked with sturdy hickory axe handles. He could also just use his hands, left or right, to make the point, although Eleanor would likely fuss if he came home bruised.

William turned and walked out without comment. He was nearly down the street when the older man caught up with him.

"My youngest son is a right moron," he said decisively. "I'll come up on Tuesday to have a look. John Abbott was a good man; his hogs shouldn't have to pay for the foolishness that went on before." The older man nodded hello and goodbye and the conversation was settled before William could say a word.

Were people in this small town stupid solely because they got to live somewhere beautiful and always had plenty to eat? Did their isolation breed an ill-placed bravado? William would have to think on this some more. Maybe even approach Eleanor for some facts. But probably not. It hardly seemed worth it, like stirring up trouble where it wasn't needed. He had the problems he could handle already laid out; the wood, weeds, hogs, cows, the truck in the barn, the holes in the roof, how to plow, how to plant, how to heal, how to be calm, how to sleep, how to dream, how to live. He ascended North Road feeling more at ease with every step.

#

"William, I want you to walk me to church this Sunday," Millie said over the dinner table. "Annabel doesn't believe a person can have only one eye." She scoffed at this, like she couldn't believe a sensible person would doubt her stories. "She thinks you're like a Cyclops. I tried to explain that you used to have two eyes, but she couldn't get it."

Eleanor sucked in her breath sharply. She didn't mean to. She didn't intend to express any opinion, good or bad, regarding Millie's interactions with her friends. She wanted to paint with a neutral palette where Millie was concerned, so that the little girl might have a chance to make her own way, to be accepted or rejected on her own merits, rather than being judged based on actions that had taken place before she was even born.

However, Millie didn't understand that a small town operated on gossip, innuendo, and prejudice. She didn't know that William's presence in town would raise questions about his place here, about Eleanor's character being alone with a man so far from civilization. Millie didn't understand that William might be ridiculed and vilified for his appearance and his past. She thought of Frankenstein's monster being chased through the streets by villagers with pitchforks.

"Problem with taking her to church?" he asked as Millie kept talking about her friend's doubts. His voice was calm and smooth and quiet. Eleanor worried she was being foolish and petty. Was she destined to always be afraid of what other people thought? William didn't look away; it was as if he were studying her face, looking for words that she didn't say.

"Sorry Millie," he said quickly. "I've got things here that need doing. Maybe next week," William said. He didn't stop looking at Eleanor. She turned away first.

"I could take you," Eleanor said.

"That's okay," Millie said, still cheerful even though she was disappointed. "Everybody's already seen two eyes."

Then she launched right back into a lengthy description about how surprised and excited everyone would be to have William finally make an appearance. He seemed to accept his role as a novelty and even seemed to revel in it a bit as he manipulated several items-spoons, coins, keys, with his damaged hand at Millie's command. He took no affront at being treated like a circus act for the benefit of some ten-year-olds. He was willing to play the clown if it pleased Millie.

Millie walked to town on her own with the dog trailing behind her. She sang as she went and Eleanor could hear her sweet voice as she faded out behind the trees.

"Is there a problem with me going?" William asked directly. He had come up right beside her without her noticing. For a big man he was quiet, like he never wanted to draw attention to himself. Of course this was impossible; you had to look at him. Looking at his right profile, one sees a rivetingly handsome man, with thick light brown hair that would lighten in the sun to a warm golden color. He had high cheekbones and a straight nose. He was tall, at least six feet, and had powerful arms that came from hard work. His hands were big and calloused, but clean with nails neatly trimmed. The left profile showed a body ravaged by war. Where his left eye should be there was a large savage scar. It was as if whoever had stitched him back together had chosen the most grotesque configuration to reassemble a face. She knew sewing and she had practice stitching up her father's various wounds. She knew that there must have been a way to mend his face so he could still look like a man. From the left profile he looked like a monster, like something designed to frighten children. Combined with his claw-like hand the picture was both horrific and worthy of pity.

Put together, looking him full on, he was intriguing. His face was a story and it was compelling to hear it all. The tale would be cathartic and full of suspense. William, she was sure, always chose to keep the details to himself.

She knew, when she was thinking clearly, that the war was long over. He had been scarred like this for a long time and he'd gotten on just fine without a mother hen watching over him. The hesitation at him going into town fell solely to her. She worried, always worried, what the judgment would be. Always, always her head circled around and around any topic like water down the drain.

"There's no problem really. No problem at all." She had felt the worry build in her gut like she had eaten too much of something fatty and slightly off. She thought of all the ways her life could be worse when William's presence here was known. She got vague flashes, Maud Hawkins' snide remarks at the library, Ron Thompson refusing to buy maple syrup next spring. The truth was that as a woman alone, a spinster, she had already basically hit rock bottom when it came to social standing, so one more slap would make little difference. This thought was soothing to her. Joyous even. Hitting the bottom had its own kind of relief. She didn't have to fret anymore about how to make things better. That struggle was over. Just like William's scars, she imagined some things you got used to. If she could, she would be a recluse, never leaving the little farm on North Road.

William's gaze was beyond direct. It was as if he could see the truth of her behind her social lies and subtle obfuscations. But there was no judgment on his face. He knew her, all her faults and foibles and still found her worthy of respect and compassion. By his size and battle scars she knew he would be a formidable foe. It humbled her that he might count her as an ally.

"It's all silliness in my own head," Eleanor said. Her voice was smooth and strong and quiet. "You go wherever you like," she said. "You can't know how much I appreciate all your hard work."

#

The following Tuesday, Mitchell Harris arrived at the farm promptly at eight in the morning. His automobile sputtered and coughed as it came to a halt at the edge of the driveway. The car was new in 1926 and Mr. Harris's pride and joy. The finish was spotless and all the metal gleamed, but clearly Mr. Harris was over his head and behind his pocketbook in terms of keeping it in good repair. Still, the older man was here, as he had promised at his son's hardware store last week.

His clothes were cleaned and pressed as if he were making a social call. His top button was fastened and he tugged at it restlessly as he came out of the car. William stood up to shake the man's hand, but Mr. Harris looked past him nervously, toward the kitchen door. Millie burst out first, followed by Eleanor and the old man with the thin face straightened up and approached her. His bearing was contrite and apologetic, as if Eleanor had the power to bless or condemn him.

"Mr. Harris!" Eleanor exclaimed, clearly surprised to see him. The older man softened, melted, blossomed, whatever words William could come up with wouldn't be enough. Mitchell Harris drank in

Eleanor's welcome like a cool drink of water on a hot day.

"I'm so sorry I didn't come up for your father's service. And I'm sorry about. I was....And.." His excuse was so flat he didn't even bother to finish it. He was clearly a proud man and his failings had been eating at him. The relief at its expression was palpable.

"You were a good friend to him while he was with us," she said, grasping his hands between hers. "That's all that really matters."

"Ahemm," Millie cleared her throat dramatically for attention.

"Forgive my manners," Eleanor said firmly, reminding the little girl to mind hers as well. "Mr. Harris, allow me to introduce my niece, Millie. Caroline's daughter." She placed her hands protectively on Millie's shoulders. From William's position he saw her glare at Mr. Harris. Richard Cage's name or exploits were not to be mentioned.

Mr. Harris was no fool. "Nice to meet you, Millie," he said and shook the little girl's proferred hand. "Pretty as a picture just like your mama when she was a girl."

Millie executed a delicate and graceful curtsy. "My mother is with the angels now, but thank you for remembering her." She looked up to Eleanor for approval and received a smile in response.

"Off to your errands with you," Eleanor said gently, effectively ending the conversation or at least Millie's part of it. She stood there making polite chit chat as Millie scampered off down the road.

"What brings you up our hill today, Mr. Harris?" she asked. She had cooled some from her initial greeting. William could see her anxiety, chewing at the edges of her polite smile and warm surprised welcome. Eleanor was waiting, no she was bracing herself with cautious dread for some burden to be heaped on her. She would take it if she had to, to keep things hale and whole for Millie, but the guarded edge to her made William nervous. His left hand twitched.

"Your man asked me to come up and take a look at your barn," Mitchell Harris said in a hurry. He gestured at William in case she was unclear at which of her men she meant. Mr. Harris was nervous too. Interesting.

"I never fixed a roof before," William said. "I thought I could benefit from an experienced eye."

"The barn," she exhaled the word like it was a wish on the breeze. William wondered what she expected the topic of conversation to be. The story of Eleanor Abbott would unfold slowly. He guessed that there were parts of her he would never know. She closed the question down, forgotten it would seem, except for the tightness around her eyes. "Today is the luckiest day. I've just put in a batch of that gingerbread you have always liked. I'll be sure to bring some up to you as soon as it comes out of the oven. Thank you so much for coming, Mr. Harris," she said as she disappeared back into the kitchen without leaving a ripple in her wake.

The men knew they had been dismissed and were happy of it. Hammers, nails, shingles, ladders-these were concrete things to latch onto. Mr. Harris stood in the doorway to the barn and looked up at the holes above him.

"John Abbott should be ashamed of himself," he said without preamble. "I know he was sick, and I know he was mourning his losses, but I can't believe how bad this has got. Whole thing needs to come off, my boy. Get that ladder. My daughter don't like me to climb anymore; I got the shakes.'

The older man extended his hand and demonstrated the tremor. William held his left hand up for comparison.

"They did a crap job stitching your hand," Mitchell Harris

said. "Not to mention that ugly mug. Sheesh. Back in the day, a wound like that you didn't come home. You seem to get along all right, though." The older man assessed him thoroughly, but in a silent, easy way, as if William were his responsibility, as if he had contributed to the damage to William's body and was sorry for it.

"Get up on that big ladder. Bring a sturdy pole or something, so you can poke around and feel how far the rot has gone. You're going to want to mark where the wood is good. You need to cut away the rest. Once it's scoped out you can put some tarps up there to cover things and work on it bit by bit if you need to."

Mitchell Harris stood in the barnyard and watched as William climbed the ladder and poked the roof with his stick. He got the hang of the task long before Mr. Harris stopped instructing him on the practice. It was all right in this circumstance; William knew the value of being useful and he liked the old guy's company. This last piece was foreign to him,. He enjoyed companionship this morning, it felt easy to him, natural, as he knocked down chunks of rotten boards and marked what was good.

The end looked worse than it started. Just a lattice remained that would have been beautiful, but it was skeletal and sparse. Hay, animals, tools lay exposed and helpless to the changes of the sky.

"The good news is....," Mr. Harris started.

"Dear Lord, tell me the good news!" Eleanor stood just outside the debris radius he had knocked down. She looked up at the roof with dismay.

From up on the roof William could see a long way, all the way to the sugar wood, to the plowed field, to Eleanor's pretty gardens near the kitchen, to the apple orchards. He could see down into his room, that section would need to be done soon if he wanted to stay dry. He saw the sunny place where Millie sat and read her books from the library. He could see the neighbor's spread and realized he wondered who they were. In the distance, down North Road, he saw the glimpse of the town, small and tired.

What he saw was his town, his farm, his place. He knew he would stay as long she would have him.

"The good news is that we can reuse plenty of the shingles. Needs time for doing, but not so much. Come on down and I'll show you," Mr. Harris said.

When William came down, Eleanor had succeeded in working her way deeper into Mitchell Harris's heart with her gingerbread and iced tea. The tension had faded, and she laughed at tales of his eldest son, Clarence, riding one of her father's goats. They reminisced about pageants Millie's mother had organized and how her deceased brother Johnny had helped birth a cow when he was eleven years old.  Johnny was dead at fourteen, same year as Mrs. Harris; they remembered this too, Eleanor holding the older man's hand when he got choked up.

"I put a little bit of wintergreen in the tea," Eleanor said like she was confessing a misdeed. "You see, the leaves are still green and the berries are bright red even when we get some snow. I think you can taste the essence of winter in this tea and I felt like it would help things along to get that new roof on easy and quick. So drink up, gentleman."

William and Mitchell Harris drank as instructed, thanked her for the refreshments, and went back to work.

"Don't recall that a woman ever made me roof tea before," cracked Mr. Harris, but both he and William felt a renewed enthusiasm for the work as the day wore on. Despite his shakes, maybe because he could no longer effectively do for himself, he was an excellent teacher, patient and precise. He showed William how to remove the nails from the salvaged shingles and how to lay them correctly on the new structure so it wouldn't leak.

The new lumber for the frame would be a significant investment, upfront and necessary before the project could progress. Those cans of money in that Chattanooga cemetery gnawed at him as he said goodbye to Mitchell Harris and went back to the rooftop to lay the tarps; a temporary measure at best.

The irony of this moment in time was not lost on him. Right now, there were a thousand board feet of strong, straight, pine waiting in a lumberyard somewhere, desperate for someone with a little money to buy them and take them home and put them to use. There was a chance, a very strong possibility, that some of this wood was imprinted with his own name as they had come from the Hart Mills of Golden Ridge, Colorado. One telegram from him, maybe two telegrams so he could explain his absence, and it would be delivered next week. One short trip to Tennessee to get his money would yield the same result.

He found himself at the mercy of his own urge to altruism. No not altruism, it was selfishness that drove his thinking. He put away the big ladder, picked up a few residual roofing nails and the tar paper from the work area. He made a sweep that had become second nature; he inspected the fields, the barn, the orchard for anything left behind from the day's activities. Millie's shoes were under the bench, a trowel was left among the onion sets. He didn't think he had the burden of perfectionism driving him, rather he coasted on a layer of comfort and order. It just felt good to circle around and gather things up. He had begun to feel protective, like he had a stake here, like he was working toward something that might last.

He entered the kitchen. The windows were steamed up from dinner boiling on the stove. The aroma of whatever she was cooking was warm, soft, intriguing, but undefined. He would eat it, learn something he didn't know, maybe try something he never tried. As Eleanor had gotten used to him at her kitchen table, the dishes had gotten richer and more distinctive in their flavors. When he had first gotten there, Eleanor was constrained by the simplicity of the ingredients. Now she drew inspiration from her limited palette, which would only expand as the varied crops began to come in.

He approached her at the stove. Both of her hands handled the pots, shifting them gently over the heat as the water simmered at the back. "I need to talk to you after dinner," he said.

She didn't look away from her pots, she couldn't, the flame was too high and her vegetables were close to done. "Problem?" she asked, seemingly of her frying pan.

"No problem. Just something to discuss." The steam had stuck a strand of hair to the side of her face. They formed a perfect question mark against her pale skin.

"Do you need to talk to me, William?" Millie said squeezing in between them.

"Always," he said. "How are the barn cats doing today?"

"Terrible. They've been displaced and disturbed by all your...," she poked him in the chest, "Racket. Lucky I made them a cozy nest with some apple crates and an old blanket. I encouraged them away from the barn with some food to keep them safe."

"You need to stay safe too," Eleanor said over her shoulder. "You stay out of the barn while they're working up there."

William leaned down conspiratorially as Millie drew him out of the hot kitchen to the parlor where it was cooler. "Don't worry. It won't be too much longer."

#

After dinner they sat in the little courtyard her father had paved outside the kitchen door. If anyone else had asked him to carry those heavy slate slabs up from the quarry, John Abbott would have declared it a monumental waste of time. For his wife Sarah, he would have done anything. He would have paved the whole yard if she had asked it of him. John Abbott was a hard man, but Sarah had softened him, making him kinder, easier to get along with, socially smoother. Eleanor always felt that conversations that took place in her mother's courtyard were better than elsewhere. Thoughts and conversations here were buoyed by her father's largess, her mother's smooth stones, her sister's red roses, Johnny's pear tree, and Eleanor's herb garden. William sat down next to her on a bench under the pear tree. He left a couple of feet between them and pressed himself to the end furthest from the house.

"Does it hurts? The scars?" This change of conversation surprised even her. She'd been wondering this since he arrived, but the itch to do some good had been buried beneath the heap of decorum, uncertainty, indecision, apathy, and despair.

"Some," he said. He said it so slow and he looked at her with such sadness and fatigue. It was the last thing he wanted to discuss. He had long ago resigned himself to his disfigurement and pain but wanted to pretend it didn't exist. She understood this instinct; not all scars were visible.

"I don't mean to pry. It's just that I have some experience with healing scars, nothing so extensive or so settled, but I've been told I've helped people." She suspected she could help him and she wanted to, needed to, try. "Can I touch it?" she asked and waited for his invitation.

He scooted closer to her on the old wooden bench. It gave a little under his weight and she could feel his nearing as much see as his approach. She closed her eyes and ran her fingers gently over the ruined and wrinkled skin. It was warm to the touch, rough in places, and tautly tugging at his undamaged face. The whole thing radiated anger and hurt, psychic or physical she couldn't be sure. She began formulating in her head: the reddish glow of St. John's wort oil, the cool comfort of chamomile extract, comfrey root in a slithery poultice. She could feed the healthy skin so it would relieve some tension around the scar. Nettles, horsetail, pot marigolds, corn silk. In her mind's eye she saw the tools she would need, mortar and pestle, double boiler, beeswax, honey. Teas, infusions, scented oils would make this better. Not healed, never whole, but better. She could make this better. He turned his head so her palm lay flat on his cheek. She could feel the smoothness of this morning's shave. She imagined if he moved just a little further he could lay a kiss against the palm of her hand. She didn't take her hand away. She was frozen, couldn't move, couldn't think, temporarily addlepated by proximity.

"You're the first person to offer to help me," he said. His voice seemed small and far away like he was a child in a deep cave. "I appreciate anything you can do."

He didn't realize he'd already done more than she'd ever expected. They sat there, just that way, for good long time.

#

Eleanor spent the afternoon making an apple pie with a fancy crust, scalloped potatoes with chunks of salty ham, and helping Millie practice her long division. She also found the time to mix some herbal potion that she would smear on the scars on his face.

"Guaranteed to make me better looking, Doc?" He joked as she coated him with the oily stuff after dinner. She blushed and looked embarrassed as she quickly wiped her hands on a towel and prepared a hasty exit. "Hey, I didn't mean anything by that," he reached out, his whole hand, to grab her arm but her need to evade him made her unreasonably quick.

"Millie, you were watching, right? You can do this for him other nights, can't you?"

"Yes ma'am." Millie answered, tentatively touching the oil on his face. "I'll be just like a nurse!"

"I could also do it myself," William said and quickly added, "but nurse Millie could certainly fuss over me if she wants to." And he pulled the little girl quickly into his arms and flipped her over his shoulder to squeals of delight. "I appreciate all the mending I can get." He set her down on her feet and she put on a comic scene of being dizzy, or sea sick, or drunk, stumbling all over the kitchen.

He kissed her on the head and thanked Eleanor in the formal manner which she seemed to appreciate, before heading back to the wood pile to burn off some of the thoughts that weighed on his mind. Mallet, wedge, metal on metal, metal on wood, ash, maple, rip, fall, toss. The action of the thing could happen with no words, no nuances; a perfect replacement for human interaction. Cord wood was without subtext or intention. Without hurting someone's feelings. Without making someone uncomfortable and not understanding why.

When he stopped to breathe, to think, he knew that Millie's fingers rubbing his face with medicinal oils could never feel like Eleanor's caress. Or rather a caress was his distant hope, clearly not hers. She was doing him a service, a great kindness, like a goodhearted person would do for a wounded dog.

*Foolish. Foolish. Foolish,* he thought as he let the ax rise and fall again and again and again. He worked until the day faded. Down at the house, a light shone in the front bedroom, Eleanor's room he knew and the first floor was dark. In his own room, in the hired man's quarters, the water pitcher had been refilled and the basin wiped clean. On the table the little vase of yellow flowers, mustard weeds, was gone, replaced with star shaped flowers the color of the summer sky. He touched the wild meandering stems and leaves covered with soft fuzzy hairs and thought, *Maybe she thinks more of me than a dog.*

#

The next Sunday, Millie made him promise to hang behind as they approached the church. She wanted a grand unveiling worthy of PT Barnum. She would have had musical accompaniment if she could have figured out how. She wasn't cruel, never unkind, but she had learned somewhere how to make an effective entrance. The day was warm and most of the congregation lingered in the churchyard before going in to the service.

Once he had gotten past the congregants' expressions of ill-concealed horror barely hidden by social pretense, he found himself surrounded by a dozen eager, inquisitive children. The adults stayed back, respectful and cordial, but wary. He had met some of them as he ran errands, but most he had not. They nodded, but didn't speak.

The children flocked around him like Eleanor's chickens. They touched him, every one of them, his eye, his hand, the scars on his back when he lifted his shirt. They asked him questions. How did it happen? What does it feel like? Will you get better? Did you cry?

One little boy, smaller than Millie, hung back at the rear of the crowd. He held a crooked angular stick shaped like a gun. "Did you ever kill anybody?" he asked in a loud firm voice like a challenge.

"Yes," William answered without hesitation. "I don't recommend it." Just then the bell in the tall steeple rang and the children filed reluctantly in. Millie held William's hand and the two of them stood to the side of the heavy door until everyone else had entered. They took a seat on the far back pew. From there he observed kids craning their necks to see him.

Several surreptitiously waved throughout the sermon. It had definitely been a mistake to avoid kids so long.

#

The morning was fair and dry, and with Millie and William in town at the church, she found herself feeling a bit stifled and musty. The air in the house was thick with things past.

She beat the rugs and dusted picture frames and damp mopped the floor. She opened the doors, all of them at once, upstairs and down. She rubbed the window sashes with soap where there was a sticky place or a creak, washed the glass with white vinegar and water until it shone, and then opened them for the breeze to come through.

She took all the quilts from the beds and the closets and spread them on the line in the sun. Most of them her mother had sewn, some were her grandmother's, some from a maiden aunt. Eleanor had never finished a quilt of her own, just bits and starts of one or another. They were all different colors. The soft greens her father favored, yellows her mother loved, bright primaries from Johnny's room, soft blues and pinks from Caroline's trousseau and Millie's favorite soft ones. Eleanor liked the crazy quilts, rich tones and mixed shapes. All hung like this they sang a song, a symphony, but Eleanor could not follow the tune. She stopped trying and just looked at the prints and remembered where each scrap had come from. She let the fresh air do its work.

She had been unwilling to go to church this week and claimed a headache like a schoolgirl who hadn't studied. Truthfully, she'd made this excuse before, even when there was no one here to hear it.

Truthfully, she hadn't stepped foot in the church for six months. Still, Millie's arrival had spurred her sense of obligation to attend services. William's continued presence on the farm quashed it. Her problem wasn't with God. She was sure she would find peace and respite in the end. Her problem lay with the judgments and failings of the human population.

Her self-imposed exile from the church started right after her father died last fall. She'd always taken comfort, although not fervor, from the dark wood of the long straight benches in the austere sanctuary. As a child she came here with her family and she knew, from her mother's insistence that they sit quietly and not fidget or fuss, that God must expect an orderly existence. Nobody made much noise, not even babies, and Eleanor didn't even want to. The wavy glass in the tall windows, the somber tones from the upright piano in the front corner, and the smell and the weight of the cloth-covered hymnals calmed her and made her think of peaceful things.

John Abbott died on a Wednesday in November. It was a cold day and windy. The fire in the stove did nothing to warm the interior of the house. It was like she had forgotten to light it. Although the metal sizzled and hissed when she heated the water to wash the body, nothing radiated. A foot away the room was like ice. When their mother had passed the whole house was filled with mourners, helpful women who brought casseroles and did laundry and cried. When Johnny died it was the same, more so because he was so young and held such potential. When Johnny died it wasn't just the adults who were upset, his school friends also came to pay their respects.

By the time John Abbott died, her father was a broken and bitter man who had turned away many of his old friends. She could lay some of the blame on Richard and his misdeeds, but John bore the brunt of it himself. She suspected he blamed himself for not chasing Richard off with a shotgun when the man first came sniffing around and not preventing the other deaths in their house. It was regrets of this inaction that finally killed him, the pride and ambition and protective instincts of his youth hardened with time to something black and cancerous growing inside him.

When she undressed and washed the body she saw how small he'd shrunk. He'd shriveled to nearly nothing.

By the time John Abbott died, Eleanor was glad of it. Caroline had not come home, not even responded to her letters and the sole burden of nursing him had fallen to Eleanor. In his last days he had taken to a day and night moan punctuated by words in no order-- Sarah, Angel, kerosene, Sycamore, Sarah, and mother, mother, mother. But his last hours were spent without words, his breathing became increasingly wretched until it stopped.

When her father died a single set of tire tracks disturbed the snow that Wednesday. Doc Fuller stayed fifteen minutes, confirmed that John was dead, made arrangements for the burial, and delivered two hard, cold loaves of black bread with condolences from his wife.

Eleanor didn't sleep that night, just sat in the rocker near the stove and tried to get warm. It was impossible. The cold ached in her bones for days.

When Eleanor emerged from isolation, down the hill and into town, it was just before Christmas. On the surface of things nothing had changed, time had continued on. There was a creche set up in front of the church, a little pine tree on the town square draped in red ribbon. People were different though as no one lifted their heads or extended any greeting as she entered the shops, the library, the church. She worried she might be a ghost herself and had fought the urge to race from house to house, pounding on windows and doors, forcing someone to acknowledge her presence. Maybe she had died too, maybe she was frail and shriveled as well, tiny, helpless, worthless. It was as if when the last breath left John Abbott, the story of the family was complete.

Eleanor was just a girl, sixteen, when Caroline made that bad decision and set her fate with Richard. She was never quite sure what had gone wrong that day the world changed. She had no head for business and no knowledge beyond her little town. Almost everything Eleanor knew about the world then existed in the three square miles around her house. She knew the ways of plants and animals, she knew how to keep house, she knew the kitchen and the hen house and the creek behind the barn. She had been to Springfield two or three times every year for an afternoon. She knew of a broader world, the teachers college in Amherst for example, or the shoe mills in Lowell where some of her schoolmates had gone. Places like Chicago, the Grand Canyon, or the moon were just pictures in a book or dots in the sky.

She questioned whether she knew anything more now that she was grown.

"Probably not," she said to herself as she laughed and went back and beat the rugs some more. It was ten years ago since Caroline met Richard, actually thirteen. Long enough to mourn for something that never was. Long enough to yearn and dream, to fail and forget. Thirteen years was long enough to be punished for something you didn't create or even comprehend.

She beat the rugs some more, far beyond the needs of any dust. She swung the broom in a wide arc, feeling the pull of it in her shoulders, then the weak thud as it connected with the heavy woolen braids of the coiled rug she had taken out of the dining room. It was a big oval, at least ten feet at its longest axis. She could only carry it if she rolled it up and flopped it over her shoulders like a fireman.

Of course, William could carry it with one finger probably, so she'd just let him take it up to the hired man's quarters himself. She planned to put it there anyway. She thought it would be nice in there as it was a big room, and likely to be chilly in the winter. She imagined him here in the winter, and if she were honest, she imagined him here this winter, next spring, next year, five years, ten, twenty, forever.

When he asked her the previous week if her oils could make him better looking, her first thought was unkind. She felt ashamed that her gut response had been a selfish one. At that moment she thought, *I hope not.* She thought, *If you get any more handsome you won't even talk to me.*

Her first thought was petty and small and she ran from it. She ran from him, which was the opposite of what she really wanted. He had been nothing but kind and helpful to her and she was acting like a spoiled child. Maybe in her heart she would always be the plain little sister of Caroline Abbott. Second best.

"I think that rug is dead," William joked as he came up behind her.

She had to laugh as she turned around. "Dangerous stuff, daydreaming while holding a weapon."

"Anyone in particular?" he asked quietly.

"Just myself and old ghosts. Oh, and your rug."

"Mine?" He fingered the wool, appreciating it with his touch.

"For your room. If you like it." Tongue-tied, foolish, a little breathless, she fought to form a complete declarative sentence. "I thought you might like to have a rug for your floor. It can get drafty in the barn and I want you to be comfortable."

"I'm already comfortable; this will make it close to luxurious. Thank you."

She had experienced old men, sharp men, cruel men, small men, weak men, scared man and on and on and on. Her wish for William was that she could transcend the labels and see him as a peer, a partner, two adults working side-by-side.

As she cooked dinner on Tuesday, she could feel William come into the kitchen. Not just the rush of cool air coming from outside, it was him, like a magnet and she with no more self-will than some iron filings dancing around as if by magic. What if they were both magnets, twice the power in the joining?

So when he leaned in close and said we need to talk after dinner, it made her head swim in all directions like a startled fish. It made no difference what he actually said, her mind jumped from topic to topic without reason or pattern. All through dinner and through the tucking Millie into bed she postulated and manipulated that conversation without evidence to guide her. When he finally revealed that he wanted to talk about the roof on the barn, she was relieved beyond all common sense to have something concrete on which to focus her attention.

"The barn," she breathed placidly.

Her sigh had not escaped his notice. "Something else that wants discussion?" he asked, amused but not derisive.

"Seems like that's the most impressive of the immediate pressing problems here at Abbott farms, doesn't it? Worthy of at least a few conversations. Before you tell me the whole bad news let me ask you a question. How does your face feel? Did that oil make any difference? I can tinker with the recipe if I need to."

He clearly wasn't expecting this change in the conversation. He touched his scar as if he had forgotten he had been injured, like he had forgotten he had ever been in pain. "I think it helped actually. Thanks. I didn't imagine anything would," he said as he touched the margins of the scar with the fingers of his damaged hand. Again, if she looked fast with her peripheral vision it was all there, whole.

"So the barn? Will it cost a fortune? It needs to be done, I understand that, but perhaps it can be put off until the harvest. Ha! Maybe it could be put off until the country and the banks come around." She felt herself racing like Millie, grasping for any possibility, jumping through options; fairies could fix it. A magic potion. A wish.

"It'll cost some," he paused. "But I've got it. I've got the money."

"Oh," the syllable hung in the air between them. It floated over her mother's yellow place mats, hovered over her teacup and saucer.

"I just have to go away for a few days and get it." And then the syllable dropped on the tabletop with a splat.

"I see," was all she could say. The phrase squeaked out of her ever-tightening throat. She had heard this before, almost word for word, from Richard. She always thought Caroline the fool to accept it. She remembered Caroline, when she was pregnant two or three months, sitting up for hours sobbing. When Richard came back finally, he had been gone five months and looked pale and thin like he had been locked in a very small room for all that time. He never did say where he had been.

"Seriously, a couple of days." He moved to touch her in reassurance, but her hands were already under the table hidden from view.

"Make sure you say goodbye to Millie before you leave."

Eleanor could barely say that much. She trolled through her brain to think of what advantage could possibly come to him from her farm. William had done more work in one summer than most people did in a whole life, so she figured they were square on that front. She wished he hadn't torn up the barn. She might have gotten another few months without any intervention, but according to Mr. Harris it would need to come off sooner or later.

"Really no more than a week. Three days maybe."

The strange thing is that she wanted him to come back. She wondered if this cold feeling in the pit of her stomach was what Caroline felt when she was crying over Richard all those times. If it was, Eleanor could see how that it was something her sister would want to avoid. Caroline never liked to be uncomfortable. When they were kids if it was a little too warm upstairs Caroline was in Eleanor's room, in the middle of the night sometimes, opening the windows to get a cross breeze. A splinter would disrupt things for days. Caroline wasn't necessarily delicate. She was just more sensitive; things bothered her more than other folks.

On the other hand, if the cold ache was regret and remorse and missing someone as the result of something as simple as love and longing, Eleanor was equipped to press that down in favor of doing what needed to be done. Millie had the same ability, she would be her cheerful self in no time. No time at all. But it would hurt no matter how it went, and it would be hard for the little girl for a while, and for that Eleanor was sorry.

Eleanor Abbott was sitting in her kitchen with a man she didn't even know a few months ago. Her back field was weeded and planted, most of the wood for the winter was chopped, the animals were healthy, her house was sturdy and whole, Millie slept peacefully upstairs, with friends to play with, the hired man's quarters were ready for whoever slept there next, and her house and rugs were aired and cleaned. She was much better off since William Hart had arrived on her farm.

She pulled her hands back up on the tabletop, both hands, and she grasped his, half and whole, across the expanse of the smooth white enamel. "Thank you so much Mr. Hart. You have done this house a great service, sir. Thank you." She gave a squeeze.

"Eleanor, I'm coming back," he said.

She said again, "Thank you." And she meant it.

CHAPTER TWELVE

The Shape of the Summer

William hopped a couple of freight trains on the way down to Chattanooga, Tennessee; the noise, the smell, the smoke as he passed through tunnels, all unpleasant. He resolved that the moment he didn't have to travel that way, he wouldn't. That moment came at 7:15 the next morning.

He had rolled into town in the middle of the night. He was freezing cold, dirty, hungry, and about as low as he could be, except for the thought of Eleanor and Millie sleeping safe back on the farm. It was funny how just a couple of months had changed things. His attitude was the first big difference; he now felt peaceful most of the time, the way he did after a long day's work; nothing left to him, nothing to think about, nothing to nag him. This peace felt subtly different; it had a sweet taste and a velvety texture. He must be tired because that sounded ridiculous even to him.

Chattanooga was dark when he arrived, nobody on the streets, no drunks, no deliverymen-- nothing. He hunkered down outside the Sunday school room in a brownstone church, slept and tried to get warm, tucked away from the wind in a pretty church portico. As the dawn broke, he saw his good luck had put him next to a big clay pot of frilly pink flowers. He picked it up and arrived at the cemetery just as the caretaker was opening the gates at seven. With a borrowed shovel, he redecorated his chosen grave with pink flowers and left with three rusty cans of cash. He didn't know how much was in there, but it was a decade's worth of earnings. He had spent very little aside from food and shelter. He had accumulated no possessions beyond the clothes on his back. William hadn't cared enough to put down any roots; he cared now. Whatever happened beyond the next growing season this money would stay at the farm on North Road. He wouldn't be back to Chattanooga again.

He went to a diner in town, ordered steak and eggs, and a cup of coffee. In the bathroom he emptied the cans of cash into a large plain handkerchief and tucked it into his belt, leaving a few small bills in his pocket to spend. He didn't count it, but the parcel had weight. Years of his life and all he had to show for it was a pile of cash. He hoped the next decade would be more productive and fulfilling. He was eager to get home.

He went out to the front of the diner to eat his eggs, drink his coffee, simple things, regular life. The depression had changed the world. The little restaurant was practically empty even though the food was good and reasonably priced. Of the businesses up and down the street, two thirds of them were boarded up and the rest of them had a sign in the window advertising a sale. He thought of the hard-working people who had watched their businesses implode through no mismanagement or failings of their own and for the first time he wondered how his family had fared through the rough times. He always pictured his father's mill exactly as it had been when he was seventeen, bustling with machines and workers, shipments leaving continuously. But he realized that this wasn't necessarily accurate; the building jobs had dried up, so their orders from suppliers had likely faltered too.

He left a ten dollar bill under his mug and stopped at the next shop he came to and bought a couple of shirts, a warm jacket, a new pair of pants, and the satchel to carry everything in. Nothing fancy, the clothes of the working man, which he was.

The train to New York left at 9:30 and he was on it at 9:15. He settled into the seat, let the porter bring him another cup of coffee and fell into a deep sleep with the sound of the tracks soothing him and the comforting weight of the money pressing against his belly.

It was too late to do much by the time he arrived in Springfield. He got a room in a clean little boardinghouse near the train station and in the morning made his way to the nearest lumberyard and ordered supplies for the barn. Despite Mr. Harris's assistance, he didn't yet feel convinced that the businesses in town had earned any of his money, based on what he surmised about their dealings with Eleanor. He felt better doing business as an anonymous stranger in a bigger city. They were happy to take his order and his money with no memory of anything. They only knew it would keep them afloat, and the guys employed, a little while longer. Delivery was set for two days. He was satisfied to see the Hart name pressed into the lumber as he inspected it.

He sent a telegram to his mother that morning. He knew she had been worried; she always worried. His message was full of apologies about not having written, but no return address. Not this time. He started out the front in the direction of Hemford and stuck out his thumb. He got a ride right to the town hall.

Walking up North Road after a couple of days away, he started seeing the world in color again. He figured he could be pretty happy if he never left again. As he neared the top of the hill, Jessup came racing out to greet him. He ran in mad circles, up and back, frantically, foolishly excited at nothing at all, but some company to greet to break the monotony of his life sleeping in the sun. He barked joyously just to hear his own voice.

"Hush!" Eleanor called to him, wiping her hands on a towel as she came out to see what he was about. William guessed that once in a while the dog actually had something interesting alert him, a visitor to report or a predator, which made it worthwhile to check on his frenzies. Eleanor clearly wasn't expecting anything as she came out to tell him to be quiet.

Slow motion filled his head, time sank slowly in measured steps: the dog leaping, bees at the base of the pear tree, Eleanor approaching, her dress pink dress flapping in the breeze, her hand against his face like it was something dear, her arms around his neck, his hands spanning her waist, the lift of her feet from the ground. When it was over, back to real-time, Miss Abbott and Mr. Hart again, except for the way her hand stayed pressed on the center of his chest like it was something she had forgotten.

"I hope you had a good trip. Are you hungry? I'll go fix you something."

"I already ate," he said. "Just sit with me a minute." He could see her thinking, practically smell the thoughts heating with friction as they raced around and around. "Just sit with me inside," he said.

She led him to the formal front parlor overlooking North Road. He never came in this way. This was the entrance that company used, the door of bad news, of bill collectors, of late-night doctor visits. None of the furniture in this room was especially comfortable; the centerpiece was a horsehair covered two-seat sofa, stuffed in such a way to send the victim sliding one way or the other to be pressed up against the carved wooden arm. All the side chairs were stiffly angular, rigidly enforcing good posture. The tables were delicate and too small, likely to be instantly ruined if used without a proper coaster. His parents had a room just like this in their house. Nobody went in there either.

Eleanor sat primly on one of the uncomfortable chairs. She perched on the edge of it, with her hands in her lap and her ankles crossed. She longed, itched, to fix him something to eat to coat the bad news she was expecting.

William thought that probably Eleanor's father and his weren't too different. People who lost big time in a depression for those who had overextended themselves or spent money that they didn't have on things they didn't need. The wealth represented in this room was old, at least a couple of generations worth, but the family never had to touch it to keep the cows fed or the kids in shoes.

"The place looks good. Grass needs to be cut." It was a faulty first statement. He regretted it almost immediately. She sat even straighter in the chair.

"It grows fast this time of year. I'll have Millie convince the goats to trim the yard rather than dine on my lilacs," she said. Eleanor could stay still as a statue when she was upset or nervous. She did so now. She didn't even seem to breathe.

William wasn't exactly sure how he had wanted this conversation to go, but he felt he had not gotten the results he wanted from it. He pulled the wrapped bills from beneath his belt and tossed the bundle on the table in the center of the room.

"I'm going to go outside for a bit. It's good to be back. I just want to make a life somewhere. I'd like it to be here, but it can be elsewhere if necessary. I hope it's here."

Outside felt better to him. He filled the buckets near the door, brought the slop up to the hogs. He'd begun to think of them as compatriots as soon as they stopped trying to kill him when he repaired the fence around the pen. The big ones were massive, the biggest four hundred pounds easy. They were generally docile, content to eat until the day they would be eaten. Once he figured out how to lure them into a holding pen for the promise of apples until he was done it all went smooth as silk. He was still dangerously green at the ins and outs of farming, but he'd get it eventually, hopefully not before fracturing anything important.

She caught up with him as he was checking on the tomatoes. "Did you just leave hundreds of dollars in my front parlor?" She said it quietly even though there was nobody to hear her for miles.

"More or less," he answered. It was probably closer to a thousand. The tomatoes looked good, just like she said they would. "Did it rain here yesterday?" he asked. They already looked a little taller, but that was probably just his imagination.

"You shouldn't have done that. Who's going to come looking for this?" She tried to press it into his hands.

He gave it back. "Nobody's looking for this. It's mine. I earned it. I stashed it away."

She looked down at the bills. It was a wad of non-sequential, twenties, tens, fives, and singles. Some were crumpled, some wrinkled, some marked with greasy thumbprints. "How long did that take?" She didn't take her eyes off the money.

"Couple of years."

"You left a couple of years worth of savings on my parlor table?" Now she didn't take her eyes off him.

The assessment was complex and indecipherable. He had to fight to be still and let her look. He didn't think anyone had ever observed him so carefully. He could feel Eleanor examining his three-day stubble, new shirt, and familiar scars. He found the silence uncomfortable. "And I'll have to use some of that money to pay the balance when they bring the wood for the roof."

"You paid for the roof." It was a statement.

"Not quite yet. And I also have to hire a few guys from the lumberyard to help me for a few days. So you'll have less left when all is said and done."

"It's still a lot of money!" her voice became shrill. "For what?"she asked coolly. Control regained, spine straight; Eleanor Abbott was small, but not fragile or afraid today.

"I'm sure there's something that needs to be bought, or fixed, or replaced that I can't even pretend to predict. For you, for the farm, for Millie."

She thought about this for a while and then said, "These men you hired, are they big like you?"

"Not quite," he smiled.

"Still guess I'm going to have to cook one of the smaller pigs to feed them." And then she wandered off toward the kitchen to plan the menu.

So began the summer upon North Road. The roof went on, the crops grew, Millie learned to swim, William learned to fish, something he had never had the patience with before. Eleanor finished a quilt, a log cabin pattern in shades of blue. In the evenings they sat on the porch and talked while Millie chased fireflies. When the little girl went to bed they talked some more. The yard was noisy with crickets and cicadas and peepers around the pond out back. The summer was hot, with plenty of rain at regular intervals. William learned to work the plow finally. He followed Mr. Harris to learn techniques passed down through the years. There was a rhythm he would never finish learning; infinite in variations, but forgiving of improvisation.

She kissed him on July 31. It was a rainy night, hard driving rain that had them both worried about the state of the fields. Would they wash out? Would the crop be damaged? They sat on the screen porch in the front, he in the ladder back chair with the legs worn from decades of being tipped back, she in a rush-seated rocker that needed repair. The woven seat was almost more holes than substance and held her weight but wouldn't support him. The air was cool after a sultry hot day with portents of a bad storm. The temperature had dropped fifteen degrees in a matter of an hour about 7:30 and the winds picked up to a frantic pace. By 9:30 it had settled a bit but the rain still felt ominous in its potential.

Sitting in the dark, veiled from the world by a wall of water, sounds muffled by the roar of the rain, sharing a common crate of worries – the intimacy of the moment was set like props on the stage. When a crack of thunder startled him, reminiscent of artillery and grenades, he jerked too abruptly, unseated himself, and sent the chair clattering to the floor and himself flat on his back with his head hitting the floor in a resounding thud.

William wasn't surprised but he was pleased when Eleanor was instantly at his side, nursing him, running her hands over his hair, checking to find him whole. She pressed her body against him, alone, in the dark, against a backdrop of rain, and she kissed him as if her lips were just another sensory organ to ascertain his state of well-being. It was a chaste kiss, a thing of kindness.

Of course William admitted to himself what he had known all along, kindness was not the only thing he wanted from Eleanor Abbott. He kissed her back. He wanted, needed, to express emotions for which he, in his limited experience, had no abstractions available, only concrete nouns: raindrops, hemline, razor stubble, tongues. With

Eleanor it didn't matter which hand he used to touch her, he was whole when he was in her orbit.

"Oh, thank God," she said against his neck.

The first time they made love it was in the hired man's quarters on another day of rain.

Millie had left the house early, dwarfed by John Abbott's big black umbrella. Her promise to stay out of puddles was broken before she was out of sight. She hopped deliberately in the first big one she came to, sending the cool water spreading over her calves and speckling the hem of her skirt with mud. Millie walked alone down to the Hamilton's place as no amount of cajoling could lure the dog from his dry space on the porch.

Eleanor entered the hired man's quarters at the back of the barn soaked through. The rain slicker she wore was useless. She miscalculated the weight of the storm. What had been a slow persistent drizzle when she had left the house had become a deluge as she walked up the hill. Eleanor had come here to straighten up and take the laundry down. She was surprised to see William sitting at the little table poring over a seed catalog.

Eleanor entered the hired man's quarters in a rush, a huff of breath, frustrated. She removed her rain coat and gave it a decisive snap, spreading beads of water swirling around her. She stood near the door and tried to contain the water dripping off her.

"I hadn't expected to find you here," she sounded surprised and yet pleased.

"It's raining," he said, satisfied just to watch her search for dryness.

"I'd noticed," she laughed as if his statement of the obvious was just what she'd been waiting to hear. The room seemed too big then and her position near the door too far for comfort. He grabbed a towel from the nail by his bunk and dried her hair from behind. Today she smelled of lemon oil and soap. Yesterday, baking day, she smelled of cinnamon and yeast.

"I could lay a fire," he said. He continued to run the towel over her hair, down her neck and over the contours of her shoulders. There had been moments like this before-- quiet fleeting instances of familiarity. Two adults who worked together had these from time to time, ordinary and casual. Then she kissed him, but had applied no meaning beyond that and hadn't spoken of it. She smiled at him, laughed with him, worked by his side, fed and nurtured him, shared her favorite books, her knowledge, and their mutual love of Millie.

He continued to rub the towel over her hair and she continued to let him. "A fire would be nice," she said quietly. "The weather brought a chill with it and it doesn't want to move along." She leaned back toward him ever so slightly, just a hint of a tilt, content and comfortable like a satisfied cat.

He stepped back and took a deep breath. His body responded to her and raced ahead beyond all common sense. His mother would likely not approve of the direction his thoughts took. He hoped the action of kindling, matches, and flues would re-civilize him.

Eleanor sat on the bed, his bed. The squeak of the springs filled the room. "Millie's staying over tonight with Gretchen Hamilton," she said as she bent down to remove her soggy shoes and socks.

The kindling was dry and the conflagration inside the black pot-bellied stove was almost instantaneous. A single match set the blaze. He watched it burn just to be sure. He wasn't really sure of anything except for the dryness in his throat, the tightness in his gut and Eleanor's bare feet dangling over the edge of his bed. He grabbed a few larger logs from the stack near the hearth and packed them into the stove. It would be hours before they burned to embers and needed adjustment.

She said, "I'm always surprised when the seed catalogs arrive. Another year flown by so quick."

"They're what farmers read when it's rainy or cold, right?"

"Are you a farmer now?" she teased. He knew her words were incomplete. She posed just a sliver of a bigger question.

He had been a soldier, a logger, a miner, a carpenter, a longshoreman, a mechanic and a dozen other jobs, more than most could claim in a lifetime. She was asking him if he planned to stick. He didn't answer right away; how could he? His heart and throat were clogged with her--her shoes aligned neatly by the door, the damp of the dress clinging to her thighs, a wisp of hair blonder than the rest, curling as it dried. The little stove pumped out heat and the room was almost too warm for comfort.

"I'm just being silly," she backtracked. Her words were heavy with chagrined pride. She sounded like a woman who had made a misstep, a faux pas.

"I like silly," he said. He looked at his hands, both hands, and showed them to her. They were permanently dirty, calloused, raw from work--a farmer's hands. Inadequate to prevent it, he pulled her in, enveloped her in a bear hug, the swell of her breasts against his torso, her back against the wall.

"Millie's at the Hamilton's tonight," he repeated. When he would have stepped back to let her think or refuse, she dug her fingers into his arms, pulling tighter. The rain persisted until well past dark.

Their courtship had to be fit gently in around the whims of the farm, of Millie, of the town, of the sky. He would have been just as happy to marry her to simplify and solidify their relationship. He'd have been just as happy to wake up in her bed before setting to work, rather than waking up alone and pretending he'd spent the whole night in isolation. Millie already treated them as a unit, substituting permission from one as the blessing of the pair. The folks in town knew that if they saw him on the street he was there at her behest or on some errand for the farm. He was part of the community already, asked for advice about a neighbor's car after he had gotten the farm truck back on the road, inviting him over casually only to ask for help with something heavy.

Eleanor kept to herself mostly, never leaving the hill if she didn't have to. When asked about her solitary ways, her reply was always the same. "That bell can't be unrung," she would say and continue on with whatever needed to be done. The story of Eleanor Abbott would unfold slowly, or not. Some things would never be voiced.

Still, he was content, in her arms or out, naked or clothed, secrets shared or not. He'd had a telegraph from Colorado and hoped she and Millie would travel with him as family, even if here William would remain the hired man. It had been a long time since he'd been out west and he found he missed the mountains and the folks. But when he said home he thought about the farm.

## CHAPTER THIRTEEN
### Richard Returns

The dog didn't bark the day Richard Cage walked up the hill to the Abbott farm at the top of North Road. Jessup was on his best behavior all day, sitting patiently by the door until Eleanor let him out, then walking quietly by her side from the kitchen to the barn and back. Once in the house he laid respectfully on his blanket by the stove, never once nosing along the counter as Eleanor sliced cold ham for William's lunch.

He was the well behaved dog she had always hoped he could be. She said, "I think there's something wrong with the dog. Millie you didn't feed him any of those cookies you brought home from Miranda's party, did you?"

"No, ma'am," Millie said as she bent down on her hands and knees to examine the dog. "I ate those cookies myself since I didn't think Jessup had the discerning taste to appreciate them. I saw him eat a squirrel head once, you know."

Eleanor shuddered to think of all the horrifying thing she had seen that dog eat; carrion, wildlife, fish heads, frogs, insects. Generally he would be panting and heaving before he relieved himself of his stomach contents. "Millie, take him outside so he doesn't make a mess."

The dog was in no rush to exit. He patiently sat to the side of the door, leaving plenty of room for Millie to open it and escort him out to the courtyard. His improved nature was welcome but she couldn't help but wonder at its cause.

William would tease Eleanor about her tendency toward suspicion, even if the occurrence was exactly what she had so vociferously desired. She shooed both child and dog out of the kitchen. She pulled down her big bowl covered with a green dishtowel, removed the round ball of dough, placed it on the floured surface, and gave a final knead to the bread she would bake for dinner later.

They had the first hint of cold last week, just a promise of the change that would come. She would make carrot bisque today, cinnamon and thyme subtle in the background and a brush of fresh rosemary at the finish. The early apples had already started to come in. In the next few months they would be up to their ears in apples, though not as much as in her childhood. The trees had been neglected some in previous years. William, Mitchell Harris, and Arthur Wilkinson had been up in the orchard several times in the past few weeks. Mr. Wilkinson was a quiet old man who probably hadn't said more than a dozen words to her in her whole life, but he and her father were friendly and he had always been respectful to her. His eyesight was going, nearly gone by now probably, but he still had forty years of farming in his back pocket

William had sought out these experts from all over the county; Mr. Wilkinson, Mr. Simms whose arthritis was so bad he couldn't tie his own shoes anymore but he knew every intricacy of fine finish carpentry, Mr. Kent with a bad back couldn't lift anything heavier than a book, but could fit a stone wall so tight you couldn't feel the wind through it, that would stand for a hundred years. The farm had been visited by orchard men, cattle experts, well diggers, roofers, farmers and one man who specialized in sugar maple trees. None of these experts was under the age of fifty. William collected wisdom from these men, who had nothing else to offer, and they gave it gladly, happy to have an eager pupil with a strong body to do the work they couldn't.

And at every visitor's arrival, Jessup had erupted into a joyous fit of hysterics.

Eleanor had tasked Millie with cleaning some of the glass jars that had been in the root cellar for several years. The boxes of heavy glass jars that William carried up were covered with dust and had been colonized by ambitious spiders. When her mother was still alive, every jar was used every season. Several years they had to find new by the middle of September to keep up with the bounty the farm had produced.

It was always a great blessing to have fresh vegetables to eat or sell, but the vast majority of the harvest was put by to last the winter. With tomatoes they could be dried then packed in oil, stewed with various spices, or made into sauces. Cabbage and cucumbers could be pickled, apples could be made into sauce or jelly or filling for pies. Every fruit or vegetable that came out of the fields needed an extra step to preserve it, harnessing the sunshine and nutrients, keeping it safe to eat for the future. And this process required a jar to put it in.

Her mother's death, then Johnny's, had slowed her father bit by bit. The first few years, the pantry was as full as it had ever been, shelves sagging under the weight of these jars lined up, colored and rich like jewels. Each season that passed the harvest was less. The change was slow; ten bushels came in, then eight, then six. Eleanor still seasoned and salted and stored as she always had, but year by year, the number of jars used was less and less. What wasn't needed stayed downstairs, out of sight. Last year she had ended the winter with only twenty jars in an otherwise empty pantry.

This year they had used two hundred jars for just the tomatoes. The imminent apple harvest necessitated the reemergence of containers that hadn't seen the light of day for nearly a decade.

Millie griped at first at the quantity of work before her, then resigned herself to it and did a good job with washing each in a bath of water with a sprinkle of vinegar. She arranged them in a spiral on the grass to sparkle in the sun as they dried.

That day Eleanor had to repeatedly banish Jessup from the house. Any time either Millie or William would enter for any reason, the dog would come in with them, stealthily and without fluster, he was back at her side, five or ten feet away at all times. He didn't appear to be scared or sick, but his vigilance was noteworthy. By mid-afternoon he had settled at Eleanor's side as she sat at her kitchen garden pulling tiny weeds from among her plants. He emitted a low and persistent snarl.

"Oh, hush," she said as she caressed one velvety ear.

"Hello, Eleanor," Richard said.

It was as if he had appeared from nowhere. Eleanor had been lost in her own thoughts more than usual recently, tangled in memory and conjecture to the exclusion of caution and perception. One moment she was alone in the garden; the next a ghost was speaking her name. The hair on her neck stood straight up just like the hackles on the dog. "It's okay," she said to Jessup, even though it wasn't. William and Millie had gone out to the orchard with a big willow basket and weren't likely to return until supper. Her nearest neighbor was some distance away.

Eleanor had loved Richard Cage the moment she first saw him; in the only way a sheltered sixteen-year-old can, Full of dreams, she painted him with a corona no flesh and blood man could ever deserve. He was tall, handsome, refined, and flirtatious. He looked just like a picture in one of Caroline's magazines.

Mrs. Jensen had broken her arm and she asked Eleanor to come and help with some things around her house: the washing, fixing dinner for Mr. Jenkins and the children. For this labor Eleanor received five cents a week, which she had planned to save to see a picture show in Springfield when she got the chance. Her father didn't want her to attend the picture show alone, and Caroline had no money of her own, but Eleanor's desire for the experience led her to the decision that paying her sister's way was worth it if it meant that she could finally attend. Eleanor stood outside the theater after the program, impressed by the spectacle she had just witnessed. Caroline lingered in the ladies room, no doubt primping.

"Quite amusing, that Mr. Chaplin," Richard said as he puffed on a cigar next to her, blowing smoke politely off to one side.

"It was wonderful!" Eleanor beamed, captivated by the film, the thrill of being away from home, by the lushness of the seats in the moviehouse, by the bustle of the city streets as she waited for Mr. Jenkins to drive her home, and the handsome stranger was smiling in her direction. It was officially the best day of her life.

Caroline's emergence from the dark interior created the same ripple as it always did; all eyes turned her way. Eleanor was eclipsed by her sister, but not completely dismissed by Mr. Cage. Throughout his courtship with Caroline, Eleanor retained her role as companion and confidante, the little sister with whom one could pal around, while actively pursuing the superior prospect.

From her position as an adult, she knew he had led her along far longer than was appropriate, hedging his bets that he would snag at least one sister if his primary objective failed. He kept her on tenterhooks until he and Caroline eloped. The night before their wedding, Richard had kissed Eleanor in the hallway while her sister slept on the other side of the door.

"You're the only one who really understands me," he had whispered seductively as he pressed himself against her and grasped her breast.

Now, on her own farm, as she stroked her agitated dog, he looked much smaller than she remembered. He was still handsome, still perfectly groomed, and dressed in what she was sure were the latest fashions, but the gleam in his eye was less intoxicating than when she was a girl. His mischief here in town, news of Caroline's passing, and his disposal of Millie a thousand miles from her family added to Eleanor's distance from the daydreams of her youth.

"What are you doing here Richard?" she asked. Her stomach clenched and roiled, burbling like oatmeal on the stove.

"I'm home," he said as he dropped his valise and crossed the distance between them in three long strides and tugged her into his embrace. "I've come home at last."

At her side the dog bared his teeth and increased the volume of his snarl. Eleanor said, "good dog" as she untangled herself and backed away.

"Thank God, I'm finally home," he said and then he sat on the bench under the pear tree, buried his face in his hands and wept.

#

When Caroline returned to the farm on North Road three years ago she came alone, with just Millie and an over-sized suitcase. It was morning and she arrived in a vehicle Eleanor didn't recognize. Caroline looked fresh as a daisy, as if she had just come downstairs for breakfast instead of from Timbuktu or wherever she had been. It was days before she stood still long enough to make mention of her absent husband or her two-year absence. Caroline was instantly back in her role as a social butterfly; inviting church ladies for tea, organizing a dance in the barn, visiting shut-in neighbors. She dragged Millie behind, picking at the girl, making sure each bow was aligned and spotless.

"Where have you been? Why didn't you write?" Eleanor pleaded, physically holding Caroline's arm to keep her in place.

"Here and there," she said. "Everything's fine. Richard is fine. Aren't you glad to see us?" She smiled but it was false, like it was painted on, like she was a doll with a pretty porcelain head.

The world had changed just months before--banks closed, businessmen jumping from windows, people sleeping on the streets. Eleanor imagined it all suddenly desperate and destitute. Here on the farm nothing much had changed; they were still no poorer today than they had been yesterday.

"You could stay, you know. You and Millie. We have enough," Eleanor said.

Caroline had actually laughed in her face, still smiling like she had just come from the ballroom at the palace, "You think this is enough?" And then she was off to find guests and frivolity.

Richard arrived two months later, dusty and tired, with no explanation. He packed up Caroline and the two of them left the next day. Millie spent the summer at the farm, becoming brown as a bean in the sun, with brier scratches on her legs from playing in the woods with her friends. Eleanor was captivated with her seven-year-old niece. She loved how Millie sat tucked up next to her on the porch as they read together. Millie was a bright child, sounding out the words as she followed along with her finger. By the end of the summer she wanted books of her own, and the two of them sat quietly side by side most afternoons. Then Richard came and picked Millie up in late August. Caroline stayed in the car, engine running. She didn't say more than hello. There were no niceties, no goodbyes. It was the last time Eleanor had seen her sister.

#

As Richard sat crying under the pear tree, Eleanor felt no need to comfort him. She dismissed him from her consciousness as a nuisance like a biting gnat. Instead she thought, 'I've got to get that bread in the oven.' She marveled at how little Richard's presence affected her. She thought about the rosemary for the soup and to remember to bring the clay pot inside before the frost hit. She'd had that plant for years and wanted to protect it. In January it would bloom soft blue-gray flowers if it were happy with the sun where she had placed it. Sometimes it blossomed splendidly, sometimes not, and she hadn't yet cracked the code of where it did best.

She thought of bread, soup, and of course chicken to be prepared. Maybe William could catch a few fish. To Richard she said, "We'll put you in Caroline's room. Dinner at 5:30." And she attempted to go about her business, still reeling from the idea that he could be so easily ignored. She could be gracious but no more, and life would continue as it had, day by day, season by season. She thought of apple cider, pumpkin pie, then maple sugar, then the first sprouts of spring greens, then back to summer tomatoes, interrupted by a long soft winter. She would need to move William down to the main house for everyone's comfort. The separation had become absurd; she could no more stay out of his bed than stop breathing at this point.

Richard rose quickly, "Oh Eleanor, Caroline's not coming. I need to..." He attempted to detain her but she dodged him without a thought, simply moved to the side.

"I know that Caroline passed. I'm sorry for your loss." She said it and she meant it. The two of them were, sadly, a matched pair. She realized she had stopped grieving for her sister long ago.

"How did you...?" He looked entirely puzzled. She could see the calculations in his head. He had tried to leave no paper trail leading to his past as evidenced by Cage, Gage, Cagney, Gagnon, and she was sure a hundred more than Millie didn't know. There could have been no official notification. Caroline would've died an anonymous death under an alias on the other side of the world. Eleanor hadn't considered this before and it made her cold inside. She wondered what life would have looked like if her pretty sister had married one of the "doltish farm boys" she'd had always despised. Would the two Abbott girls be baking bread together this evening?

She didn't answer him or her own musings. She just went into the kitchen to live her life.

#

When Caroline, Richard, and Millie were in town five years prior the farm was a different place. John Abbott was quietly bitter without his wife and Johnny, but still a vibrant hulk of a man. His hair had a shock of white, a trait of the men in his family, but he had an air of competent vitality. He was respected in the community for his good sense and many evenings a neighbor would stop by to discuss an unknown pest or chickens that had stopped laying. John Abbott could be counted on to help with the installation of a new stove or the repair of a farm wagon.

That visit they arrived in the night. Richard and Caroline drove up in an automobile that looked new, but had an ugly scrape down the side and mud caked on the tires. Richard had a fading bruise on his left eye that he pretended to ignore with his impeccable suit and shiny shoes. He removed his big, unnecessary overcoat with a flourish and handed it to Eleanor in the kitchen like she was a housemaid. He gave her a broad wink and a grin before he dismissed her and turned his attention back to John. Richard was welcomed, not as a prodigal son, but as Caroline's husband and the father of a precious grandchild. John shook Richard's hand but kept his distance as if approaching a spider or a snake.

Caroline looked tired with puffy eyes, as if she hadn't slept for days and had been crying. Millie collapsed into Grandma Abbott's old rocker by the stove where she cuddled up into a helpless cocoon of arms and legs. Eleanor picked the little girl up; she didn't weigh more than a down pillow, and carried her upstairs. Eleanor put Millie into her own bed, still warm from Eleanor's interrupted sleep, and went to make Caroline's room up.

Caroline had always had a big bed. When they were little, the girls had often slept together, though Caroline had stopped this practice, barring the doors sometimes, when she was thirteen and Eleanor was ten. Caroline was grown up the moment she could be and had never once exhibited that she would revert or question this path. Eleanor had moments, when her mother was still alive, when she needed to climb into bed with someone and just be held.

Caroline's room and Eleanor's were mirror images each on opposite sides of the front of the house. Caroline looking west and Eleanor to the east, to the dawn. Millie's room was tucked between the two and Johnny had slept in a little sloping room at the back over the kitchen addition. Her parents had always slept in a small dark room at the back downstairs, so her father would be available to see to the farm in the night if any problems arose.

Five years ago their mother was dead, Johnny was dead, Caroline was moved away, and only John Abbott remained. He was without softness, worn down to bare metal by his sorrows. That visit had only lasted a week. It was late August, a busy time on a farm, and Eleanor was in the kitchen from morning to night, preparing and preserving the harvest as quick as John could bring it in. On the Tuesday of that week, Eleanor was canning green beans. The kitchen was full of steam from the parboiling of the beans and the sealing. She watched them go from dull to bright green, then they were packed in clean containers, salted, and the jars filled with water to the top. Then they were capped and set in a bath of boiling water to seal. Beans prepared correctly will last a year or more. Prepared incorrectly, they would rot, leaving a jar of poison and mold on the pantry shelves. It was precise work, and the glass jars were heavy, and the kitchen was filled with an inferno of bubbling water in massive pots.

Caroline was there, but not really. She was concerned, as was Eleanor, about Millie getting hurt in all the activity, but Mrs. Wilkinson, their nearest neighbor, had offered to watch the girl for the afternoon.

Caroline wouldn't hear of it. She insisted that Millie be always within eyesight, but she didn't really mind the child, instead peering endlessly out the window or standing near the road, looking eagerly for Richard's return from wherever he had gone to that morning.

Eleanor tried to make conversation from time to time. When the jars were sitting waiting to cool before being put on the shelf she went out in the yard. Even with all the windows and doors open, the interior of the kitchen was blindingly, oppressively hot. Eleanor sat on the bench near the pear tree her father had planted when Johnny was born. In the spring it was covered with delicate white flowers and surrounded by happy bees. Now it was covered with pears not yet grown, smooth teenagers of fruit, yet unmarred by insects or storm damage. They were plump and green now, and would deepen to a warm gold, like honey, as they matured.

"You must have seen some grand sights on your travels," Eleanor said with a sigh. It was cool out here and a pretty day. Millie came over and cozied up at Eleanor's side, swinging her legs off the edge of the bench.

"Oh we've seen some things." Caroline laughed but not joyously. She laughed in a way that would have been bitter in another woman, but Caroline seemed genetically incapable of presenting unpleasant emotions. It was impossible for her to be anything but beautiful and charming, even if on the inside she felt ugly and cold.

"What time is it?" Caroline asked for the fifth time that hour. Eleanor knew that she wouldn't be able to compete with whatever Caroline thought she was missing as she looked anxiously down the road toward town.

"I guess it's time to get back to those beans," Eleanor said and she rose to return to the hellish interior of the family kitchen.

To this day Eleanor didn't know exactly which batch of beans had gone wrong. Was it the one where Millie burned her hand on the hot tongs that had just come out of the big pots? Was it the batch where her father roared into the kitchen demanding lunch with recriminations about her lack of attention? Eleanor silently guessed that it was the batch that she was just finishing as Richard came up the hill and Caroline ran into his arms, sobbing with relief, as he swung her around and around. They immediately retreated to her bedroom upstairs, leaving Millie and Eleanor in the kitchen, unacknowledged.

In January, when the world was cold and covered with deep

snow, Eleanor looked at those ruined beans, a full third of them toxic and inedible, metal tops bursting and distended with germs. Eleanor willed herself to box them up for disposal without crying.

#

"What's this one called?" Millie asked William after she took a big bite of a tart green apple.

"That's an easy one, it's called Granny Smith. You shouldn't talk with your mouth full," William said.

"Sorry. I forget."

"Me too," he said. William was carrying a big basket of ripe apples from the orchard to the house. Millie had a smaller basket in which she had tried to collect one of each variety they grew, whether it was ripe or not. William stuck to one variety, Macintosh, and was bringing the very beginning of the crop to see if Eleanor might make a pie or two. Working in the orchards, tending the trees and smelling the ripening fruit had given him a hankering to taste some of his labors.

The house was silent as they approached, not exactly still, smoke climbed from the chimney in weak intermittent gasps, but the place seemed subdued from the usual pace of a Saturday afternoon. It was like the way a thick blanket of snow made everything quiet and anticipatory when it fell at midnight. It felt like a start of something, or the end.

"Millie, did you check on those kittens today? I wonder if that yellow one is feeling any better this afternoon?"

He answered her dilemma of carrying her apples down to the house or going to the cats by extending his right pinky so he could loop it around the handle of her basket. She scampered toward the barn to see her patient.

Eleanor saw him through the window as he approached and rushed over to open the door and take Millie's portion of his burden. "You want pie, so you brought half the orchard." She laughed, happy to see him, happy to see the round red apples, but there was something else in her that he couldn't read.

"Not half the orchard, only a tiny fraction of the orchard. The trees have produced better than we'd anticipated. We're going to need some extra help for the picking in a couple weeks." He was excited. It felt like a small triumph to him. A good part of farming, he discovered, was patience; there was always something to do, which suited him-- chopping, repairing, caring for the animals-- but if something took one hundred and eighteen days from seed to harvest then that's what it took. It might be one hundred and fifteen days or it might be one hundred and twenty five days, but there was no way to rush or fool with the schedule. The process was in mother nature's hands and he was just a servant. This knowledge both humbled him and soothed him.

The other part of farming was being a good steward to the crops, nurturing, protecting, encouraging. Sometimes the plant could be modified, bent to the will of the farmer, but only so far. At their essence plants were wild things and could be only be expected to follow their own nature and tendencies.

"We have a house guest," Eleanor said in a low formal tones. Here was the tension he had seen – polite smile, spine of steel.

"OK, but I brought you apples," he reminded, hoping to soften her before he became once again Mr. Hart.

"Yes, you did," she exhaled the words, just let them drift toward him like a kiss.

From the parlor he heard the creak of the front door and the measured steps of smooth soled leather shoes. His brother, Tom, had purchased shoes just like that when he received his first executive paycheck. Tom was about twenty-one at the time, trying to impress some girl from Denver, and the shoes had been completely destroyed by slush the second time he wore them. William and his brother Robert had mocked Tom mercilessly over that.

From the parlor to the kitchen, those shoes brought a man eerily like the one his family had hoped to groom before he ran off and join the Army; dark flannel pants, crisp white shirt, handsome face, new haircut, gold cufflinks. On closer inspection the suit was poorly tailored, as if it had been custom made but for a much larger man and the thread on one of the buttons was starting to fray. He was a man who dressed to impress, but on the cheap. His appearance was a fabrication, sheep's clothing for this big bad wolf.

"Richard Cage," he extended his hand in greeting. "Welcome."

William wasn't a man for words. To him they seemed elusive and evasive, never quite expressing what he meant to say. He preferred to communicate with actions: ten pounds of apples for Eleanor, a thousand mile journey with Millie, a punch in the face for Richard. Civility won out on that conversation, but his left hand itched to make its point.

Eleanor touched his left arm as if she could read his thoughts and congratulated him on his restraint. "Richard is Millie's father," she said in even tones of warning. Tread lightly.

Richard did not catch this interaction between them, perhaps he was too caught up in his own version of events to acknowledge anyone else's role. "Poor Millie, she was with her mother when it happened." He resumed his seated position to continue the grieving process. He covered his face with his hands and moaned.

Eleanor gasped and flew past him to the oven where she

removed the loaves of bread, a good deal darker than usual. She pulled them quickly and she pulled the chicken out as well and gave it a stir in her cast iron Dutch oven. William liked the way she stuffed the cavity with herbs and tart apples surrounded with carrots and onions.

"Millie's in the barn, Mr. Cage," William said. He shouldn't have smiled, but he did.

The kitchen door opened. "The yellow kitten is perfectly fine!" Millie exclaimed as she wiped her feet on the mat as instructed countless times. "I've got to think of a name for him. Something that means he's yellow, but all the names I can think of sound like girl's names."

William felt the air change as Millie saw her father sitting there. If she could conjure thunder they would all be in trouble. The frustration, regret, anger, and resentment she felt radiated off her for a split second but she tamped it down, barely. Clearly, she thought her association with Richard Cage had ended when he dropped her off in Chicago. William thought, *Both my girls are stronger than I've ever been.*

"Hello Papa," Millie said. "I trust you had a pleasant journey." She matched Eleanor's enunciation measure for measure, note for note. She sat at the table across from him like it was a business meeting; good posture, steepled fingers. She was tiny sitting across from him, but she was running the show. Lazarus raised from the dead was too impressive a miracle to be ignored.

"How...?" Richard swallowed hard. "How did you get here?" He wanted to hide or run or accuse or deflect, but he could find no traction to get him back on his usual road.

William stepped to the table, set one hand on Eleanor's shoulder, the other on Millie's, and said, "Millie will tell you the whole story after dinner." To which Millie nodded vigorously. William said, "Let's go out back and wash up, Millipede."

"That's not my real name either," she giggled and followed him out.

William was restless and indecisive like the dog as he opened the kitchen door to exit. On the one hand, he didn't want to leave Eleanor alone inside with the past; on the other hand he had to get out of there and breathe some fresh air and talk to Millie in private for a minute. He needed to gauge her reaction to the situation and see how she wanted to proceed. Personally, William thought of Richard Cage as something he would scrape off his boots, but he needed to consider Millie's feelings in the matter.

She hugged him, hard and desperate. She said, "I don't want to leave here. I don't want to go."

"Then you stay," he said. William didn't lie, he didn't argue, he didn't retreat, he just kept doggedly on toward what he thought was right or necessary. And if he didn't know or wasn't sure which direction 'right' lay then he waited until the answer became clear. This perhaps is why he never took to business; he saw no shades of gray. Ambiguity didn't frighten him; it was just that uncertainty, second-guessing, and things left open to interpretation seemed less efficient than just seeing your path and moving on. Questions of whether Millie belonged with her biological father had become moot the moment Richard dropped her off in an orphanage and then lied about it. Millie would stay.

At Millie's urging he lay down on the grass with her and named the shapes in the clouds. "That's a rabbit," she said. "And over there is a bicycle."

William could only see ugly shapes on the horizon. He saw snakes, spiders, and stinging insects. He saw guns, bombs, and bayonets. He saw baseball bats, barbed wire, mud, graveyards. He kept this to himself saying only, "I think you're better at this game than me." He picked up her jars and put them back in the crate. "You did a good job cleaning these," he said. He carried them toward the kitchen just to move, just feel like he was of use, just to check on Eleanor, just to turn off the thoughts in his head – baseball bats, cemeteries, snakes, mud.

The kitchen was empty when he got there. He set the crates in the corner. Even with his heavy boots on, he was light on his feet and made no creak or clatter as he traversed the first floor: empty kitchen, empty parlor, empty back bedroom. He ascended the stairs, not trying to be silent, but still making no noise. It was as if his feet didn't touch the floor, he might have been without substance; a film of smoke or a ghost.

He heard a conversation from upstairs, Richard's full and rich voice carried. He appeared to have recovered from his shock and now made a pitch like a carnival barker or a snake oil salesman; he was utterly confident in his speech. William heard the fringes of it, but he knew every syllable as bull, a litany designed to captivate and entice. Richard threw around big words-- fiduciary, amalgam, remediation-- but he used the words incorrectly, true to the dictionary definition, as if he had done some research, but it was choppy and awkward, just missing the true meaning.

Eleanor wasn't buying what he sold; her voice was steady and subdued. William couldn't make out her words but she seemed to be offering a thousand variations of *no thank you* over and over. William thought about that pie, warm bread with butter, chicken with sage.

William wondered what it felt like to be jealous. He had seen men pushed toward irrationality, blind to reason, blundering, running on the pure heat of the uncontrolled combustion of possession, suspicion, something that called itself love but was not. When he heard Richard's voice upstairs with Eleanor, all he thought of was how to extricate her from a situation likely to be uncomfortable. With Eleanor the temperature of his life was warm like a spring day after a long winter, comfortable like a pair of boots well-broken, durable like a tool that would last a hundred years if you cared for it correctly. He had the urge to give her finery, but he couldn't even think of what that would be; all he could give her was his back, and his legs, and his hands, mangled or not. Upstairs, Richard offered her the world and her answer remained the same; no thank you, no thank you, no thank you.

"Eleanor!" Millie called from downstairs. "There's smoke coming out of the stove!"

"Oh, good heavens!" Eleanor exclaimed as she sailed past William. Her face was flushed. "If that dinner is burned, I will kill him," she snarled as she disappeared from view.

Richard emerged then, cock of the walk. He adjusted his clothes as if they had been mussed and actually winked at William as he followed leisurely behind Eleanor's path of departure. William didn't wink but he saw, through his dead eye, the day that Richard Cage would no longer darken his door.

Millie sat quietly through dinner. She used her napkin. She cleared the table without being asked. She didn't have seconds. When she finished, she excused herself and went up to her room to read, promising to tell the story of her journey tomorrow.

The only one who really spoke was Richard. He talked about opportunities out West around the building of the Hoover Dam. Opportunities in Chicago, opportunities in Texas. William had been to most of these places Richard was talking about. Some people there were making money. There were always a few favorably positioned people around, but for the most part all of these places had to offer were long lines, dirty faces, and guys undercutting each other to work a twelve-hour day for fifteen cents. The bootleggers and the mobsters got on okay, but you needed to be connected, needed to know somebody, needed to be on 'the in' before anyone would even open the door. William had worked as a bouncer in a speakeasy in Cincinnati, but left because it was both brutal and boring. A guy like Richard might last a day or he might end up immediately in an alley somewhere. He struck William as just slippery enough to get on for a little while, but not quite smart enough to make it out alive.

Killing people like Richard Cage was the kind of work William had been offered when he was in Cincinnati. He could have had money, girls, booze, whatever he wanted. He preferred to feed Eleanor Abbott's hogs; it was easier to sleep at night.

"You need anything?" William asked Eleanor. He put his hand on her shoulder and squeezed. "I'm going to go make sure everything's gathered up and then I'm heading to bed." The sky was fading to purple, the daylight nearly gone. She'd had to light the lamp already and stifled a yawn.

"I'll be fine. It's fine. It'll be all right." She soothed him like she did the dog. "I'll be fine," rubbing her palm over the wrinkled skin on his hand.

William found that how people reacted to his scars told him a lot about what kind of person they were. Millie had expressed curiosity and compassion, and Eleanor worked to make it better. Some people noticed and thanked him for his service, some turned away in horror, some tried to ignore as a means of being polite. William observed Richard's impression when he first walked in. Richard appraised him like he was at a horse auction or slave auction. He wanted to assess his carrying capacity and check his teeth. Richard took an inventory of his measure as a man, found him lacking, and dismissed him as no threat and no benefit. William was the damaged hired man and nothing more.

William checked the enclosures around the animals, then walked through the fields and the orchard. He found one of Millie's books in the near field, a single canvas glove dropped on a path, and gathered them up for safekeeping. It wouldn't rain tonight. In the inky sky a million stars shone, free to beam loud as the moon had waned to nearly nothing. Not as cool tonight as it was last night, but still promising frost soon enough. Tomorrow he'd go through the vines again and pick the stragglers before they popped from cold. Even what was green would need to be taken soon and left to ripen on the window sills. He thought about the seeds he had saved for the next year.

It was nearly dark by the time he entered the barn. Richard was waiting for him in the shadows. William was done with the conversation before it began. He was tired, behind his usual schedule, and weary of dealing with this fool. Richard Cage had been on the farm for less than twenty-four hours and it already seemed a lifetime too long.

Richard propelled himself sinuously from the wall he had been leaning against. William saw the faint orange glow of the cigarette and smelled the acrid smoke. "You know we're standing in a tinderbox of dry hay, right?" he said, aware of the placement of two buckets of water by the door. Richard saw it too and dropped his butt into the clean fresh water to be extinguished.

"Good call," Richard said. He straightened up and in two long firm steps he was within arm's length of William. "You strike me as a hard-working chap." He looked as if he were ready to offer a congratulatory squeeze of Williams bicep, but at the last moment he thought better of it. "We could use a big man such as yourself around here. How long do you plan on staying with us?"

William thought, *a hundred years*, but he said nothing. He thought, *long enough for the farm to be profitable, long enough to hold Millie's babies on his knee, long enough to sleep in Eleanor Hart's bedroom.*

His silence made Richard answer for him. "I understand. A man doesn't want to tie himself down if he doesn't have to."

William thought that Richard was handling both sides of the conversation so well he might as well go off to bed. He crossed the barn, checked the cows, the old horse, the hogs. He wondered what Eleanor did with them in the snow. Did the hogs mind the cold? He'd to have ask her tomorrow.

His movement made Richard agitated. He rushed over, treading carefully to avoid stepping in anything unpleasant. He said, "I don't guess you are as stupid as you seem."

"Thanks." William bent to pet one of Millie's kittens then exited, preparing to shut the big barn door behind him. "After you," he said, urging Richard to proceed him outside.

Mr. Cage was reluctant to take direction. He hovered, still within arm's reach, as if he had something important to say, which William knew to be impossible. There was nothing Richard Cage could say that William Hart needed to hear.

"Listen." Richard said, man-to-man earnest. "I know Eleanor is a soft touch, and a goodhearted woman, but she's off limits. I know the appeal; her sister was incredible."

Richard droned on and on and William thought, *mallet, sharpened ax, splitting wedge, fifty-pound chunk of seasoned hickory wood.* He said, "Morning chores come early around here. Have a good night, sir," and he began to close the barn door. Richard had to scramble to keep from being crushed.

Eleanor didn't come to him that night, nor did an easy sleep. He didn't bother to light the lamp; there was nothing to be done and he was too jangled to read. He just lay there, looking at the stars for a long long time.

## CHAPTER FOURTEEN
### Richard's Departure

Eleanor slept in Millie's bed. She supposed they both could use a little extra comfort this night. When Eleanor entered the little girl was sleeping, soft breath and warm body. One foot had emerged from the covers; Eleanor covered it with the quilt as she climbed in. At her on weight the bedsprings, Millie shifted, throwing her arm across Eleanor's belly. They were entangled that way until morning.

The chickens and the cows didn't realize anything was different on the farm; they still expected to be tended as they always were. This thought soothed her; some things don't change. Millie went to the hen house and Eleanor heard the usual ruckus as they greeted the day, rushing and clucking to see the usual delights. Oh, to be a blissful hen!

She was lost in the rhythm of the stream of milk hitting the bottom of the pail. The simple actions both buoyed her and anchored her. She had thought she wanted to see the world, but the farm on North Road felt like home, now more than ever. William's affinity to the place had rekindled her love for it.

William came up to her, silent as always, and spoke over her shoulder. "He tried to warn me off you last night." He leaned close and whispered it into her ear, warm and sensual. Blossom twitched her tail nervously and then settled right back to her feed.

"I sincerely hope he was unsuccessful," she joked, easy and focused on her task.

"I'll take my chances," he said as he ran his damaged hand through her hair. "I figure I'll put him to work today, if that's all right with you. He can muck the stalls. I figure even Richard can't mess that up too badly."

"Probably not," she smiled at him over her shoulder. She couldn't remember Richard ever doing any work around the farm. Caroline thought it was because he was busy with other important duties, John Abbott thought it was because he was frail and delicate and likely to make some crucial errors.

"How long do you think he plans to stay?" William asked. There was some tension in his voice, just a little note of irritation, like a shoe too tight, a finger's brush of stinging nettles, salt mistakenly in one's tea. William's tension was nothing disastrous, but it was real.

"He probably won't stay past the first stall. You can assign him to do the hogs too, if it makes you feel better," she said.

It was around 11 o'clock before Richard came downstairs, sluggish and out of sorts. She was in the kitchen, up to her neck in the late crop of kale and spinach.

The leaves needed to be washed, then chopped, then parboiled, then canned. Eleanor had already felt two steps behind those greens. They were forgiving of her tardiness, but only so far. They would need to be finished, completely, before the apples came in and took over. She wished Millie were just a little bit bigger and she could lend more of a hand. As it was she had to assign more chores to the little girl. Millie was now responsible for feeding the animals, taking out the trash, and making the beds. It would be all that Eleanor could do to keep up in the kitchen from now until the snow came. It was an embarrassment of riches and she wasn't complaining, but next season maybe they would need to hire a girl to lend a hand. Prosperity suited her, Eleanor decided.

"Don't you have any coffee?" Richard said as he pawed through her cabinets for what he wouldn't find. Eleanor hadn't purchased coffee in two years. She had enough trouble affording flour, and if she could make that herself as well, she would. Coffee had been a luxury too dear to scrimp and save for, although now with William's money, perhaps she should ask if he'd like to have some.

But she would definitely not be buying coffee for Richard Cage. "Sorry, there's chicory tea if you'd like. That's got a nice bite."

"Yeah, okay," he said and sat down as if he had expected her to bring it to him. She filled the kettle.

"Cups are on the shelf near the window; tea is in a tin in the pantry." She decided to jump right into the topic on her mind before he could start talking. "William needs you to help with something up at the barn."

"Does he now," Richard laughed and lit a cigarette from a silver case. He leaned back in his chair and watched her work. He took long leisurely puffs, blowing the smoke out in clever rings, puff, puff, puff. "Do you think your father would appreciate the hired man giving orders?"

The kettle jangled and danced at the back of the stove. When she saw he wasn't going to get it himself, she moved the kettle off the heat. She could use that water for her own tea when she took a break later. The water was perfectly good and needn't be wasted. "Go on up to the barn when you're done. He's either there or checking the orchard," and she went back to chopping greens.

\#

When Caroline and Richard were here nine years ago, Millie was just a baby. She had been a colicky infant, and cried for hours straight. They had been at the farm when Millie came and for a few months after. The crying had started almost immediately after she was born, high screeching sounds of pain. Although she had a fairly typical delivery, Caroline stayed in bed for two weeks, muffling the sounds of Millie's misery under her quilt while Eleanor stuffed cotton in her ears and rocked the baby, offering her a steady supply of healing tea: fennel, ginger, dill, and honey. The crying lasted for weeks, leaving everyone but Richard exhausted. He had taken to spending his nights in town.

A few months later, the colic had long passed, but the fussiness that preceded teeth had put them into a panic. "Eleanor, you have to help me," her sister said, thrusting the squirming baby into her arms. Millie was clearly frustrated and uncomfortable, but she smiled through her tears in recognition. She lay her head on Eleanor's shoulder and whimpered. "It's starting again," Caroline said to the mirror. "Look at the bags under my eyes. I can't go without sleep again. Richard has something important in the works and he needs me to look my best so I can help him."

Eleanor wasn't aware that Caroline had missed any sleep the first time. But she didn't say so; she was enthralled with her niece in her arms. Millie had a brown corkscrew curl that grew out of the back of her head and other less impressive curls formed a halo around her face. Her apple cheeks were still damp with tears. "She's probably just teething," Eleanor pulled a firm cool carrot from the basket and offered it to Millie. The baby grabbed it with her chubby fingers and happily gummed it.

It must've been around that same time of year, kale and spinach then too, but back then Eleanor let them sit. She sat in the rocker and held the baby all day, just smelling her, holding her close, trying to soothe her. When Millie fell asleep, Eleanor didn't get up right away. The kitchen was warm; the chair creaked gently as she rocked. She thought about her own babies she would have some day. She thought about who her husband would be and wondered when she was going to meet him or if maybe she would end up with one of the boys she already knew. Of course, none of these boys could measure up to Richard Cage. So, if truth be told, as she sat in her mother's kitchen, holding her sister's baby, she fantasized about what it would be like if he were her man instead of Caroline's. She dreamed about what it would be like to share his bed instead of being upstairs alone in hers.

Richard kissed Eleanor behind the barn one afternoon. She wasn't expecting it and she didn't initiate it. But neither did she protest greatly. She turned the corner as she returned from gathering some staghorn sumac from the marshy place near the pond and bumped right into him. She carried a big basket of the fuzzy berry clusters in front of her. The tart taste and bright red color made a wonderful addition to tea. The day was unseasonably cool and she wore a blue sweater she kept forgetting to mend. It was missing two buttons.

"What's your rush, sweetheart?" He always called her that. He laughed at her blushing reaction, but he didn't release his steadying grip on her arms. In fact, he moved his hands slowly up and down in a gentle way. No one had been gentle with Eleanor since her mother died. She reveled in the attention.

From where she stood as an adult, in her own kitchen chopping spinach, that first kiss and all subsequent interactions between them had been engineered by Richard, then twenty-four and worldly. Eleanor had been a dreamer and envious of her sister. Alone in her room she was frantically romantic and foolish. Richard created countless coincidences when they could be alone. Eleanor chose not to see through his subterfuge.

Eleanor had never kissed a boy. She was shy and bookish. She sometimes blamed Caroline for casting such a deep shadow on her little sister, but in truth Eleanor behaved nervously and preferred the safe company of adults. She and Teresa Jensen talked incessantly about boys, but neither of them went much further than an unfocused daydream.

When Caroline and Richard left, Eleanor was deep in the sugar word gathering mushrooms. She had a big basket, half full, when she heard the slam of a car door and the rumble of the engine. She had to fight the urge to run and check. Caroline had decided to keep Millie that day, which should have been her first clue. If she had been thinking clearly that action alone would have told her all she needed to know. She told herself that it was all okay, even though she knew it probably wasn't. The inside of her felt empty and sore, impossible to ignore and yet impossible to address. No one on earth wanted to hear what a fool she had been. The tears, if she were to cry them, would be only a testament to her own stupidity and nobody else's business

#

"It's for the best," Eleanor said, quietly, to no one in particular. It was true then, as it was now. That spinach wasn't going to chop itself. She lifted the buckets that William had filled and topped off the big pot at the back of the stove. "You just go on up to the barn when you're ready," is all she said to Richard Cage.

The rest of the day rushed by in a haze of green. She was vaguely aware that Richard had left, his dirty cup and saucer of cigarette butts the only evidence that he had been there. Millie came in, had a snack, and was quickly off to rush through her chores so she could return to the story that she had only gotten halfway through before the teacher had confiscated the book for the day. From now on her library selections were to stay at home. Eleanor got through the spinach, and the kale, and part of the chard before dinner was due. The best she could do for dinner was a spinach pie with eggs, the last of yesterday's tomato soup, and a loaf of poppyseed bread.

Richard didn't come to dinner that night. Eleanor heard him enter in the middle of the night. It was as if he wanted to alert them all to his return with slamming doors and clomping footsteps. Eleanor slept in Millie's room again, with the little girl tucked in against the wall and the snarling dog on the rug by the door.

"Good boy," Eleanor whispered as Richard made his noisy way up the stairs. His steps were uneven, maybe he was drunk. She felt the dread grow as he approached nearer and nearer. She thought it was ridiculous to be cowering to avoid an unwelcome guest in her home, protecting a child who was more hers than anybody's from a man who saw Millie as an inconvenience, to have William sleeping behind the barn that he'd paid for, all for the sake of a social convention. The final straw fell when she heard the door to the east, her door, open with no attempt at silence or stealth.

"Eleanor," Richard slurred at street volume, "I..."

She didn't give him the opportunity to complete whatever absurdities were going to come out of his mouth next. "Hush!" she said out in the hallway. Jessup was at her side, a low growl in the back of his throat. "Just go to bed, Richard."

"But Eleanor, I need you. It's always been you." She could smell the liquor pouring off him. She wondered where he'd got it, but then she stopped. Eleanor was done caring about anything where Richard Cage was concerned.

"You just need to get to bed," she said, slipping past him to open the door to Caroline's room.

If she were asked to remember that moment it would be like she wasn't even there, far removed, like an old folk tale passed down through several generations, a tale translated from another language with a different alphabet. If the night that Richard Cage came home drunk was written, it would be unpronounceable, Cyrillic, guttural, just missing the mark of her understanding. When Richard grabbed at her, all groping lips and hands, wrapped in the stench of cigarettes, moonshine, vomit, and perfume, Eleanor forgot how to be civilized.

She pushed him not once, but many times, slapping his roaming hands and devilish intentions. In a half acknowledged effort to not wake Millie, she tried to be silent in her assault. The only sound was the reserved percussion of her soft hands against his soft flesh. She barely hurt him, no broken bones or ruptured skin. The closet door echoed sedately as she pushed him against it. None of her blows were enough to unsettle the sturdy design of John Abbott's house. Her attack was a result of frustration and sadness, of self-respect and self preservation, of the protection of a sleeping child, of annoyance and hurt over a thin layer of rage.

Richard fell as drunks often do, into a soft puddle, protected from consequence by his own selfishness. All muscle tone or tension had been dissolved by drink. She heard the rattle of his head as it hit the last step, the creak of the worn middle tread overwhelmed by percussion of bone on wood. He landed on a big braided rug she helped her mother make one winter. A blossom of blood spread across his eyebrow and into his eye. She expected the back of his head had also taken some lumps as he had tumbled end over end to the bottom. The stain of blood spread across her beautiful rug. His left leg was out at an ungodly angle, dislocated maybe, or broken. He didn't scream, though she imagined he was in pain. She couldn't make sense of his silence. In her experience, when Ralph Henderson fell down at the quarry for example, he carried on in at an ear-piercing level. Even as Eleanor had clambered down to bring the medicine and the men prepared to bring him up, Ralph had continued to holler loud enough to wake the dead.

As Richard Cage lay broken and crumpled at the base of her staircase, not screaming, making no sound at all, he looked at her with confident expectation that she would help him. He assumed that she would take action as she always did, to ease his suffering, to heal the broken body before her. He looked at her with hope. The blood spread across his face in a slow but steady trickle. Already Eleanor could see the bruising and swelling rise across his cheek bone. A little trickle of crimson blood exited his pale lips.

She saw the moment when optimism faded from his eyes. He met her gaze, standing high above him, but making no movement toward aid. He tried to make a sound then, but he had forgotten how. As the lifeblood pooled and flowed, congealed around his brain inside his broken skull, he released a low complaint of pain and despair but it fell on deaf ears.

Eleanor rubbed her belly protectively as she turned to go back and close Millie's door. "It's just a dream, sweetheart," she said to no one. Millie was nestled cozy and safe in her little pink room.

Eleanor wasn't sure why she took a seat at the top of the stairs to watch Richard die. She had seen death before, people she loved. She sat at her father's bedside as he took his last breath and had witnessed the still, tragic corpses of her mother and brother. She hoped that they all made their peace with things in the afterlife.

At the base of the stairs Richard stopped even the pretense that he could eventually get up and walk away. He lay on the floor and focused on Eleanor, hoping perhaps to charm her once more, convince her one last time, that he was lovable and sincere and worthy of her assistance. When Eleanor closed her eyes, she could hear him begin to weep as he acknowledged he was lost.

She had lost something too in that instant, but to her it felt like a burden she could finally shed. She was finished with the heavy, grave weight of obligation without reciprocation. How much had she given up over the years and gotten so very little in return?

Eleanor sat at the top of the stairs for the last hours of the slow night, looking at the grain and the knots in the wood paneling next to the step where she sat. She tried to create a pattern in the floorboards and paneling, in the movement of the clouds, or the timing of the cricket's chirps as dawn approached. She searched for some kind of augury to follow but found none.

William arrived just after dawn. "I didn't see the smoke from the stove," he said. "I came to see if everything was all right here." He said this as he stood over the body at the base of the stairs. He bent to check for signs of life. There were none. "Are you all right? Did he hurt you?"

Eleanor could only shake her head. She wondered if she would ever speak again. Her mouth felt stuffed with sawdust. Tears threatened but did not come. She was dry as a bone.

"Millie up yet?" His voice was calm and slow and smooth.

"Soon," she hissed. Panic would certainly be an appropriate response but she couldn't muster it. Her legs were stiff from sitting all night and her bladder was full. She had no emotions though, no regrets, no desire, no ideas of how to proceed. When William asked her if he could take care of 'this' she nodded mutely and watched as William rolled what remained of Richard Cage in her big rug, heaved it over his shoulder, and retreated to parts unknown.

That morning the breakfast table was not set. Eleanor's kitchen table was an uninterrupted field of white enamel.  Millie stumbled into the kitchen a solemn, groggy mess. Her sleep had been fitful and plagued by dreams that she didn't reveal. She pulled dishes for three from the cabinet like she did most days.

"Jessup is supposed to comfort me. He usually does, but last night he was remiss in his duties. Can I take one of the barn cats to sleep in my room instead?"

Eleanor said, "That will be fine. If you can find one to volunteer for the job."

"I'm sure I can," Millie said, plotting which one of her charges would be the best suited for duty. She went out to the hen house with a dedicated purpose and a spring in her step.

It was midmorning when William came slowly into Eleanor's kitchen. She had never seen him tired before. On an ordinary day he worked himself at a maniacal pace, dawn to dusk of hard, physical labor most days, but aside from sore muscles or dirty hands, showed no ill effects. Today he came in, took a long drink of water, and nothing else. He was a lump of a polite stranger sitting at the table.

Eleanor knew certain things about the world. She knew by the way the aspen leaves tipped upside down in the breeze that it would rain before afternoon. She knew that the chard needed another two minutes to be done, she knew that Millie would need new shoes before winter. She didn't know what it meant that William didn't look at her, or speak to her, or move from his chair. He looked out the window to the road, to the town, to the rest of the world.

#

Eleanor's mother died when Eleanor was fourteen years old. Johnny was just thirteen, Caroline sixteen and already dreaming big of a greater life. Sarah Abbott had shining waves of blond hair that nobody ever saw because she kept it wrapped up tight in a bun at the back of her neck. Seeing her mother's hair was a treat that only family got to witness, like the secret decadence in an otherwise sensible life. In the evening she would pull out the pins, shake her head, and send those beautiful bouncing locks down around her shoulders. Eleanor loved to brush her mother's hair, ones hundred strokes every night before it was tamed and hidden in a tight braid down her back for sleep. While she brushed, Eleanor asked her mother questions about the world. Was the ocean really so big that all you could see on the other side was sky? Are there really mountains that are covered in snow all year long? How many people can fit in a skyscraper? Her mother knew some of the answers, but not all, and she never made Eleanor ashamed of the asking. Together mother and daughter would search for the answer the next day, through a book or a picture, until a satisfactory answer was found.

The day before her mother died, Eleanor had learned about the Titanic disaster and she had some questions about icebergs, their formation and prevalence. They had planned an investigation for the next day. Her mother was fine when the children left for school that day. She had fried sunnyside eggs for Eleanor's breakfast at 7:45.

Eleanor wasn't home the day her mother died. She should have been. Her father reminded her of this fact most nights across the dinner table until the day he died. When he stayed silent the omission was enough to drive her from the kitchen after some forgotten task-- sweeping the patio, administering tea to the ailing Mrs. Reynolds, chickens, hogs, laundry, mending. Her father's admonitions were a familiar song that she hummed to herself most nights. Her father's silences felt ominous, like the quiet that precedes a terrible storm.

Johnny said nothing but his missing comments were a futile attempt to keep the peace; their father found fault in any word. He held Eleanor's hand under the table while she picked at her food with her left hand. She was unwilling to release the warmth of her brother's palm.

The day their mother died Johnny was at the back end of the sugar wood gathering deadfall, clearing brush, and checking taps on the trees. The weather had been both damp and cold and their father had predicted a heavy dump of snow before the end of the week. It was Thursday and the ground was still bare. He felt this was a lucky day as they had more time to prepare for the quiet months to come.

Eleanor had stayed after school that day to help her teacher prepare the lessons for the younger children. Her mother had always encouraged this in both her daughters. Johnny was destined to stay on the farm, this had been evident since he was a small boy.

"Never waste an opportunity to be helpful or to learn something, girls," Sarah Abbott said. "Young women need every advantage they can get. Education and kindness will open many doors for both of you."

Caroline had left school that day before the last reverberation of the bell. Eleanor stayed, filling the blackboard in the elementary classroom with her neat, curving script. She liked the feel of the chalk between her fingers and the dusty white powder on the side of her hand as she brushed away and corrected any letter that veered off course.

The sun was nearly down when Eleanor walked home from school. The air had turned a few degrees warmer and the atmosphere was thick with moisture. The sky had faded to a pale sickly white. She could taste snow in the air.

Eleanor loved the anticipation of a winter squall. Trapped in the house, prohibited by nature from any outside work, she and her mother would bake cookies and drink tea in the warmth of the kitchen. Eleanor had hidden a small jar of pale amber syrup in the pantry. It was the first run of last year's sap and it was delicate as lilacs. After the first big storm they would dribble it on big bowls of virgin white snow and eat it like ice cream.

The day her mother died the smoke from the kitchen chimney rose in weak puny gasps. When Eleanor entered the house it was chilled and still. She didn't smell the sage and thyme simmering in the chicken soup as she'd been expecting. There was no clatter of crockery or forks. The kitchen was empty. A drop of blood, perfectly symmetrical, disgraced her mother's spotless hickory floor.

"Mama?" Eleanor called but there was no answer. Her shoes made a sound like a startled horse as she raced to the front parlor. Her father sat in the high back chair his father had built with his own two hands. His shirt was covered with blood.

He said, "Where were you?" but in a tone that indicated he didn't really care what the answer was. His face informed her that whatever she said would not be good enough.

Her throat was layered with gravel. "What happened?"

Caroline sat on the settee near the window. The white sky behind her grew darker by increments. Caroline's shirt was perfectly clean. Neither of them answered her question.

"Where's Johnny?" Eleanor asked.

Behind her sister the spindly lights of an automobile pulled up to the house. The lights illuminated the first tentative, floundering flakes of snow. As the engine sputtered off her father rose and left the room.

"What happened?" Eleanor asked again.

From the front hall she heard Dr. Benson, brusque and matter of fact. Her father was barely audible, as if he had been punched in the throat. Johnny's sniffles turned to sobs as the door to her parents' bedroom opened then closed with a solemn thud.

"Mama got kicked by one of the cows while she was doing your chores," Caroline said. Her posture was impeccable. Her shirt was clean. Tears dripped down her face in a slow, straight line. She didn't tremble or flinch. Eleanor sat next to her sister on the settee near the window. They sat, just this way, for a good long time.

For weeks the house was filled with people. Their house was cleaned and always had of some kind of treat on the sideboard as if baked goods could fill a hole in your life, but it helped. Brown sugar and butter made them mourn with a smile. Soon enough, things returned to normal--that's not true. Soon enough only four people sat in the parlor, then three, then two, and finally eventually people just stopped the Abbott children in passing to pay their condolences. After that nobody went into the parlor unless they had to. Eleanor never did find out what made an iceberg.

John Abbott didn't ever stop his work and he only took one morning off for the service. He rarely sat at all that first year; he was up and working until he slept. After Johnny died, all he did was sit for a month, the start of the downward spiral she realized now.

#

She carried the big pot of chard to the colander on the counter. She dumped the contents and was momentarily hidden by the rising cloud of steam and sounds of rushing water. She moved the colander to a pot of cooler water to stop the cooking, no steam, no sizzle, just the end of the process in good time. She jarred the bright green leaves with red stems, added salt, added water, put the tops on and set them in the big pressure cooker to seal.

William sat like a statue. His glass was empty but he didn't refill it. He held it in his hand, his dead hand, and twirled it around in counterclockwise motion.

"Come outside with me," she said. "It's hot in here." He looked at her as if he was surprised that she could talk, like he imagined they could go the whole rest of their lives without speaking another word.

"Yeah" was all he said, before finding his voice from somewhere deep down. "I could use some air."

As still as he had been in the kitchen, now he was the opposite; he paced, then checked the joints on the bench he had repaired, then checked the stones around her garden, then checked the glazing around her kitchen window. She had wanted him to sit, to talk to her, to soothe something between them on this terrible morning, without and yet now haunted by Richard Cage. She quickly remembered sitting was not William's way.

She said, "You should go chop some wood."

Eleanor could barely breathe with the force of the embrace enfolded around her. "Thank you," he said against her neck.

"Thank you," she replied.

CHAPTER FIFTEEN

North Road

A tenacious patch of poison ivy grew over the place where William had buried Richard Cage's body. It was the only soft place in a rocky section of the property. It was to the north of some dense shrub and scrawny pine, and it was the last place the snow melted in the spring. It was hard to get to, as one edge was bordered by a granite protrusion, and other side was bordered by the swamp where the skunk cabbage grew. William had to walk a long time to get there that morning he removed Richard's body from Eleanor's house. Someone would have to work very hard to find that place, and for what? The poison ivy only served to make it less attractive; the farm, apparently, took care of its own.

Millie accepted the explanation that Richard was just 'gone' as it had been a recurring theme in her life. The legacy that her father left her was that Millie would be adaptable in any situation. No hardship ever set her back for more than an afternoon, but she mostly used her talents to the advantage of others, plotting to overcome bullies or arranging parties to paint Mrs. Wilkinson's house. Caroline gifted her daughter with the love of music; most winter afternoons their house was filled with sound as she played the fiddle and practiced with library sheet music of popular songs.

The week after Eleanor gave birth to their daughter, William planted a single, small cane of wild rambling rose along the front stone wall. When he dug the deep hole Millie looked over his shoulder and questioned his capabilities; it was just a stick with a few leaves and the hole seemed overly large. William was more forward thinking. Over time, years, the spindly little plant grew to form a meandering thicket blanketed with soft, sweet, pink blossoms all summer long. The baby, Rose, was a sweetness neither of them expected.

Eleanor and William never talked about that day with Richard. There was no need. Eleanor didn't want to know where the body was. William didn't care to know how a man happened to be reduced to blood and skin and bones. The absence of this conversation cemented the bond between them more than words ever could.

Acknowledgements

Creativity can't flourish in a vacuum. Isolation is a dream killer. We all need friends.

I am endlessly grateful to have a community of writers. They've read revisions, made suggestions, listened to me gripe, and gifted me with the trust to critique their own vulnerable, fledgling drafts. Special shout out to Susan Riva Earl, Helen Pitts Bradley, Beverly Willett, Joyce Ann Underwood, Charlotte Botsford Getz, members of the Van Toblerones, and many others. I really do use a lot of paper and it's all been gloriously marked up with comments about questionable punctuation, redundant word choice, and verb tenses. Thank you.

Thank you to my loved ones and live-ins who listened to me talk about Millie like she was a real person. (She is!)Thank you to my family who taught me to respect the history of place and vegetables. Many thanks to my grandfather Woody Barry, an early and vocal supporter; he's a big man—gentle, hard-working, and calm.

This book was produced entirely in the coffee shops of Savannah, Georgia especially at the Sentient Bean located at the south end of Forsyth Park. Black coffee and spinach baked potatoes resolved many episodes of despair and writer's block. Cover image courtesy of the esteemed and gracious Margaret Moore.

I lead a charmed life and am truly, truly blessed.

For historical context and some interesting and lovely pictures please visit:
www.thebellunrung.com or email me at thebellunrung@gmail.com

Author's Bio

Kimberly Evans grew up among the artifacts of earlier decades, spending summers in the cool dark rooms of her grandmother's 1863 farmhouse. As a child her diversions there were solid and simple—wooden blocks, corn husk dolls, and thirty-year-old fashion magazines. She made candles, dyed eggs with onion skins, and fed hay to the neighbor's horse through the rectangular holes in a wire fence.

As an adult she studied history and economics at Smith College to better understand "why." As an ongoing occupation she is a nosy, eavesdropping, buttinski compelled to look inside the human heart and write some stories. Ms. Evans currently lives in Savannah, GA.

Made in the USA
Thornton, CO
12/07/24 02:47:55

9d1e906b-ac3e-4044-8be5-1a7e8d6342ffR01